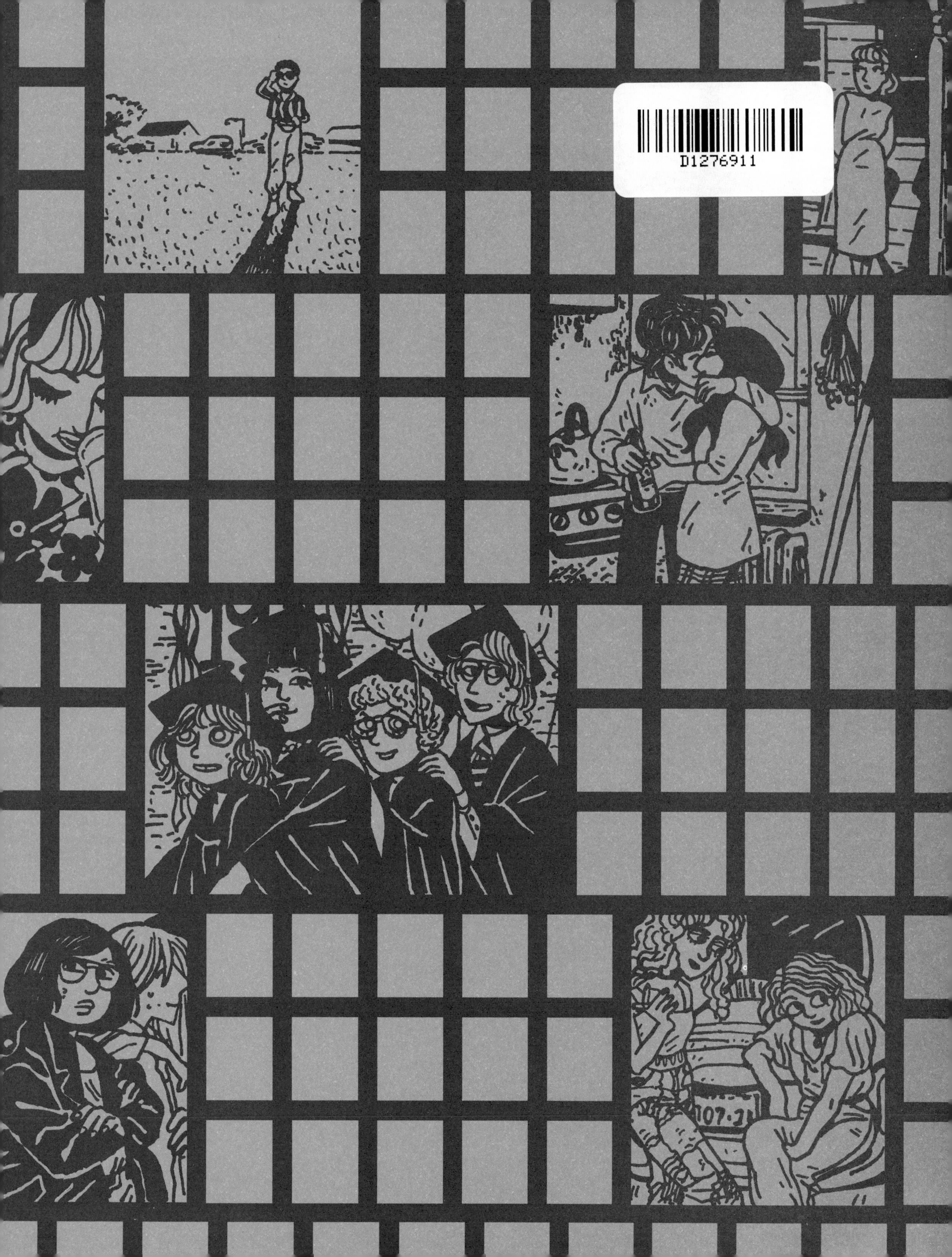

i am young

m. dean

FANTAGRAPHICS BOOKS INC.
7563 Lake City Way NE
Seattle, Washington, 98115
www.fantagraphics.com

Editor and Associate Publisher: Eric Reynolds
Book Design: M. Dean and Keeli McCarthy
Production: Paul Baresh
Publisher: Gary Groth

I Am Young is copyright © 2018 M. Dean.
This edition is copyright © 2018 Fantagraphics
Books Inc. Permission to reproduce content must
be obtained from the author or publisher.

ISBN 978-1-68396-139-0
Library of Congress Control Number 2018936465
First printing: October 2018
Printed in China

*I would like to thank my friends and mentors
of the Creators for Creators Grant for helping
me in creating this book.* — M. Dean

*To Dad and to everything we shared and
everything we never got to.*

I Am Young

M. Dean

FANTAGRAPHICS BOOKS

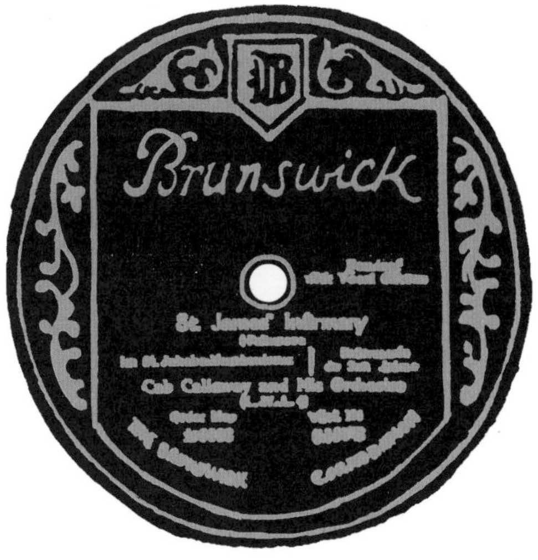
Brunswick
St. James' Infirmary
Cab Calloway and His Orchestra

"Joanie"

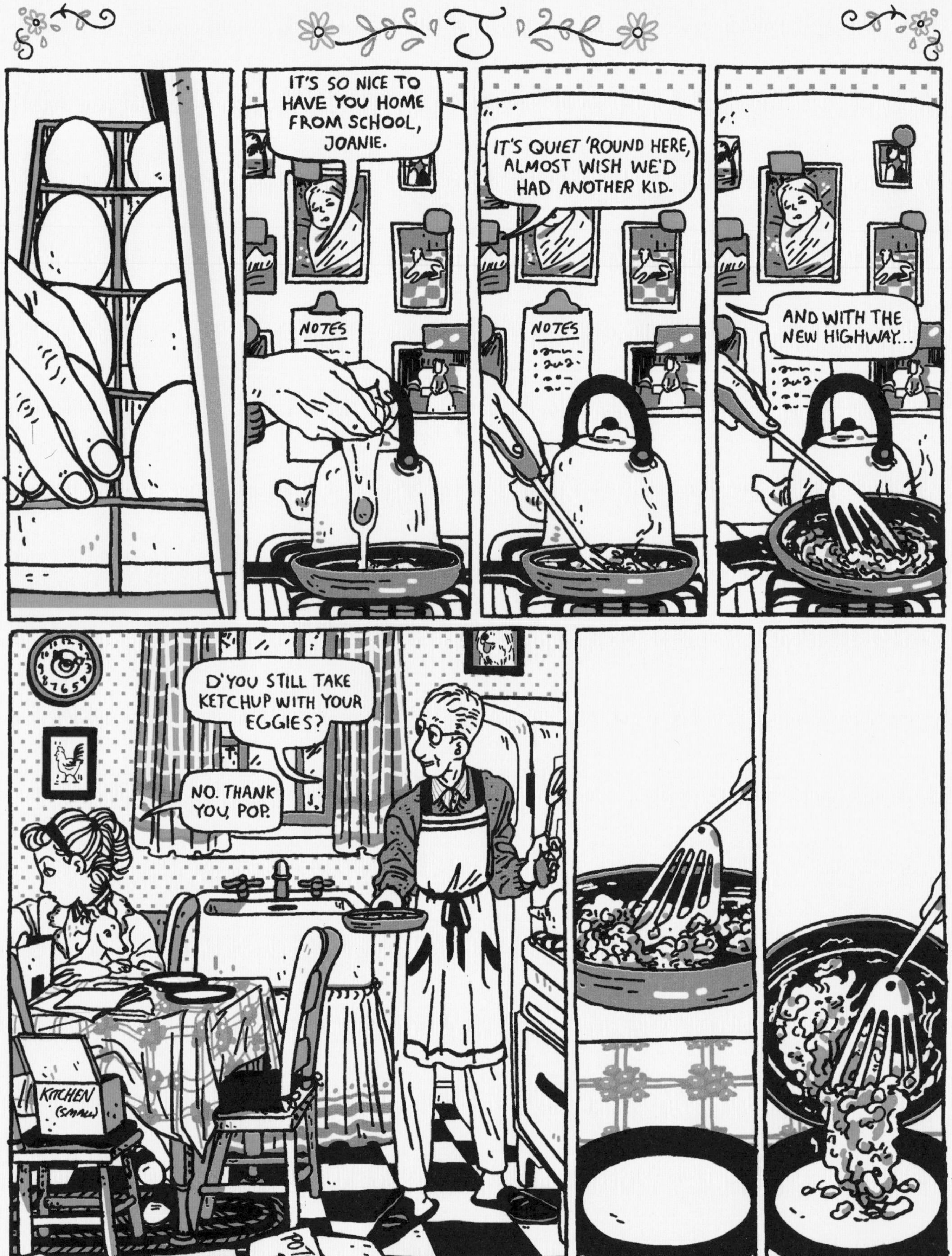
IT'S SO NICE TO HAVE YOU HOME FROM SCHOOL, JOANIE.
NOTES
IT'S QUIET 'ROUND HERE, ALMOST WISH WE'D HAD ANOTHER KID.
NOTES
AND WITH THE NEW HIGHWAY...
D'YOU STILL TAKE KETCHUP WITH YOUR EGGIES?
NO. THANK YOU, POP.
KITCHEN (SMALL)
POTS/PANS
KITCHEN

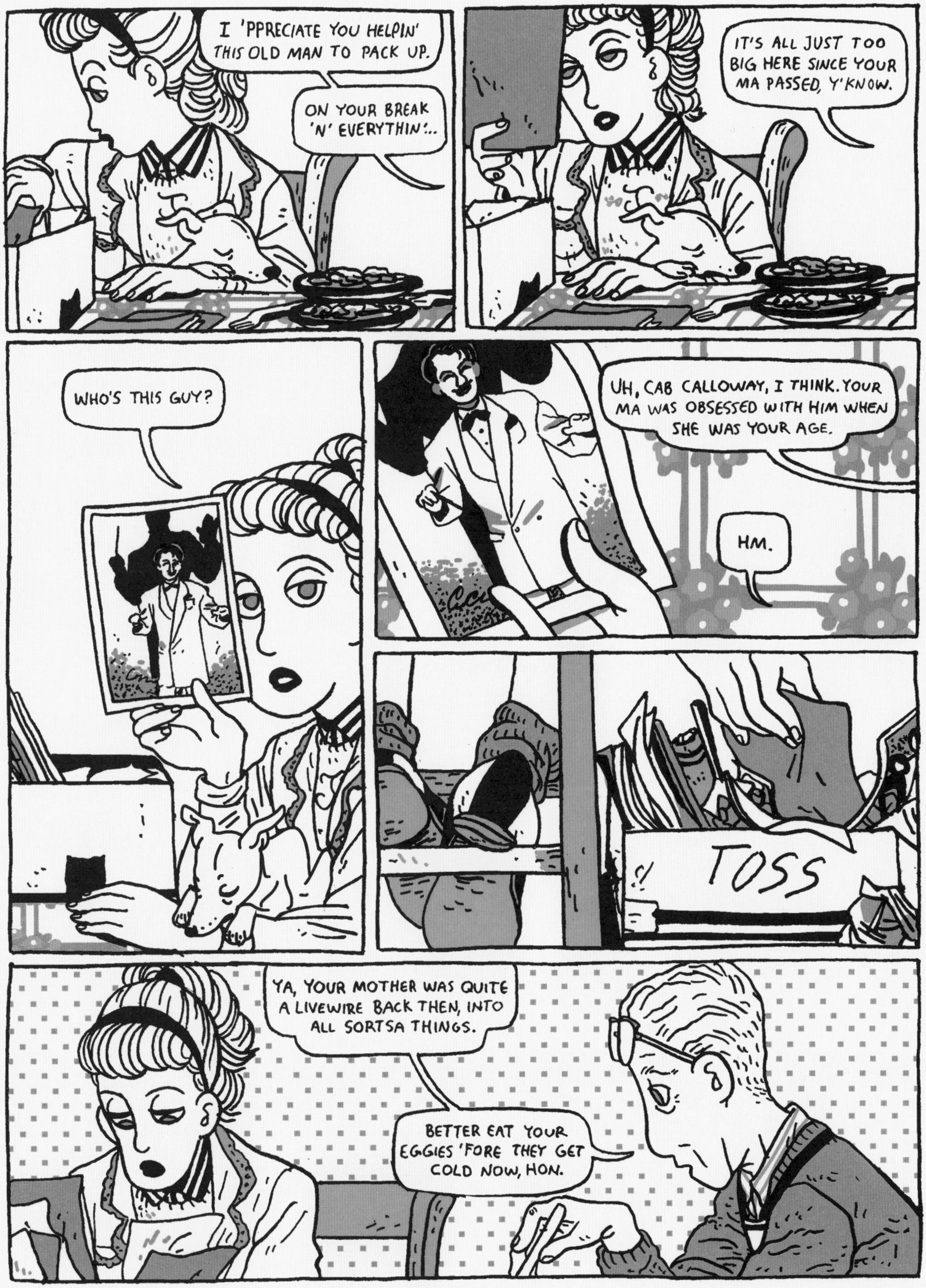
I 'PPRECIATE YOU HELPIN' THIS OLD MAN TO PACK UP.
ON YOUR BREAK 'N' EVERYTHIN'...
IT'S ALL JUST TOO BIG HERE SINCE YOUR MA PASSED, Y'KNOW.
WHO'S THIS GUY?
UH, CAB CALLOWAY, I THINK. YOUR MA WAS OBSESSED WITH HIM WHEN SHE WAS YOUR AGE.
HM.
TOSS
YA, YOUR MOTHER WAS QUITE A LIVEWIRE BACK THEN, INTO ALL SORTSA THINGS.
BETTER EAT YOUR EGGIES 'FORE THEY GET COLD NOW, HON.

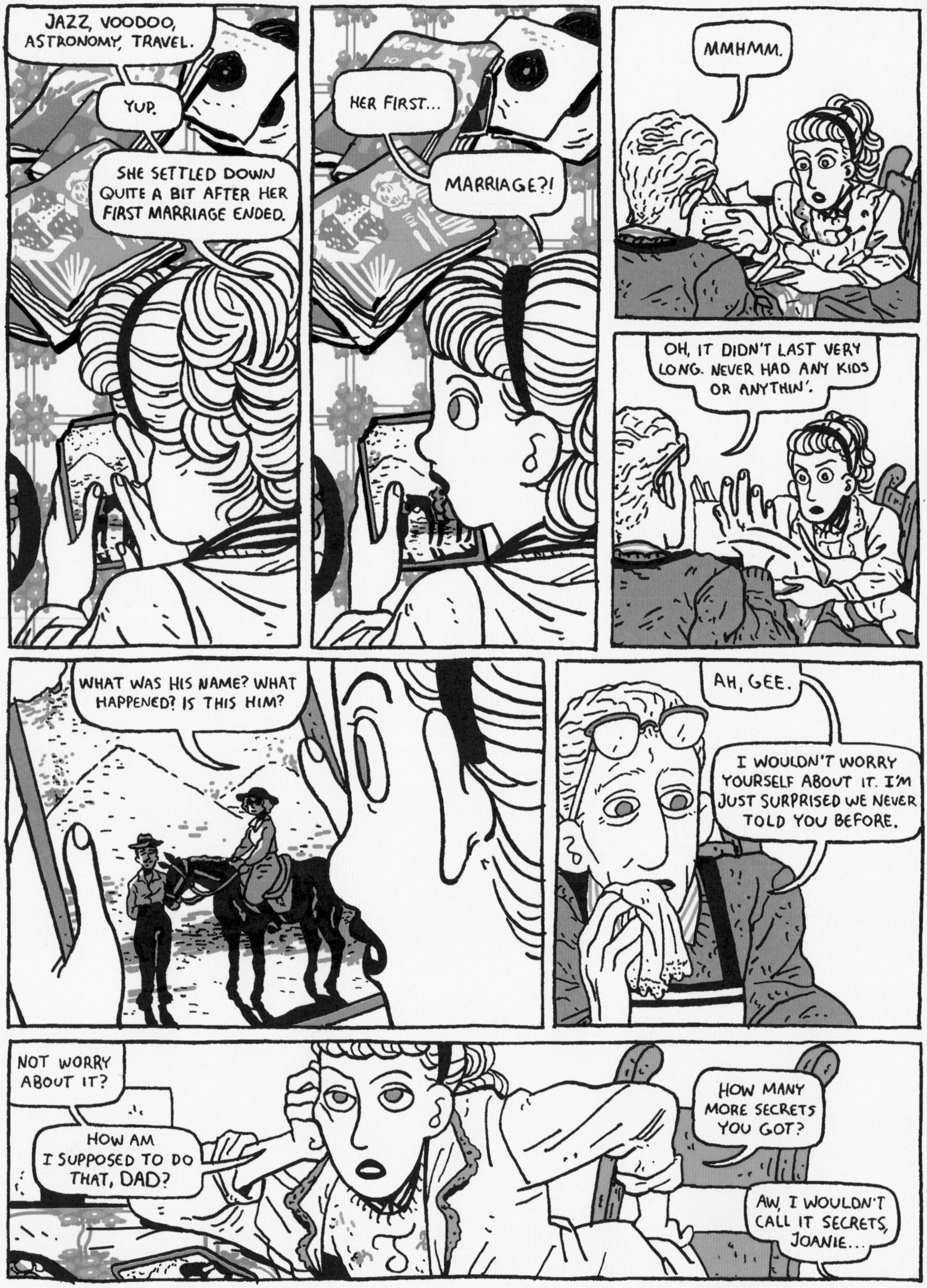

JAZZ, VOODOO, ASTRONOMY, TRAVEL.
YUP.
SHE SETTLED DOWN QUITE A BIT AFTER HER FIRST MARRIAGE ENDED.
HER FIRST...
MARRIAGE?!
MMHMM.
OH, IT DIDN'T LAST VERY LONG. NEVER HAD ANY KIDS OR ANYTHIN'.
WHAT WAS HIS NAME? WHAT HAPPENED? IS THIS HIM?
AH, GEE.
I WOULDN'T WORRY YOURSELF ABOUT IT. I'M JUST SURPRISED WE NEVER TOLD YOU BEFORE.
NOT WORRY ABOUT IT?
HOW AM I SUPPOSED TO DO THAT, DAD?
HOW MANY MORE SECRETS YOU GOT?
AW, I WOULDN'T CALL IT SECRETS, JOANIE...

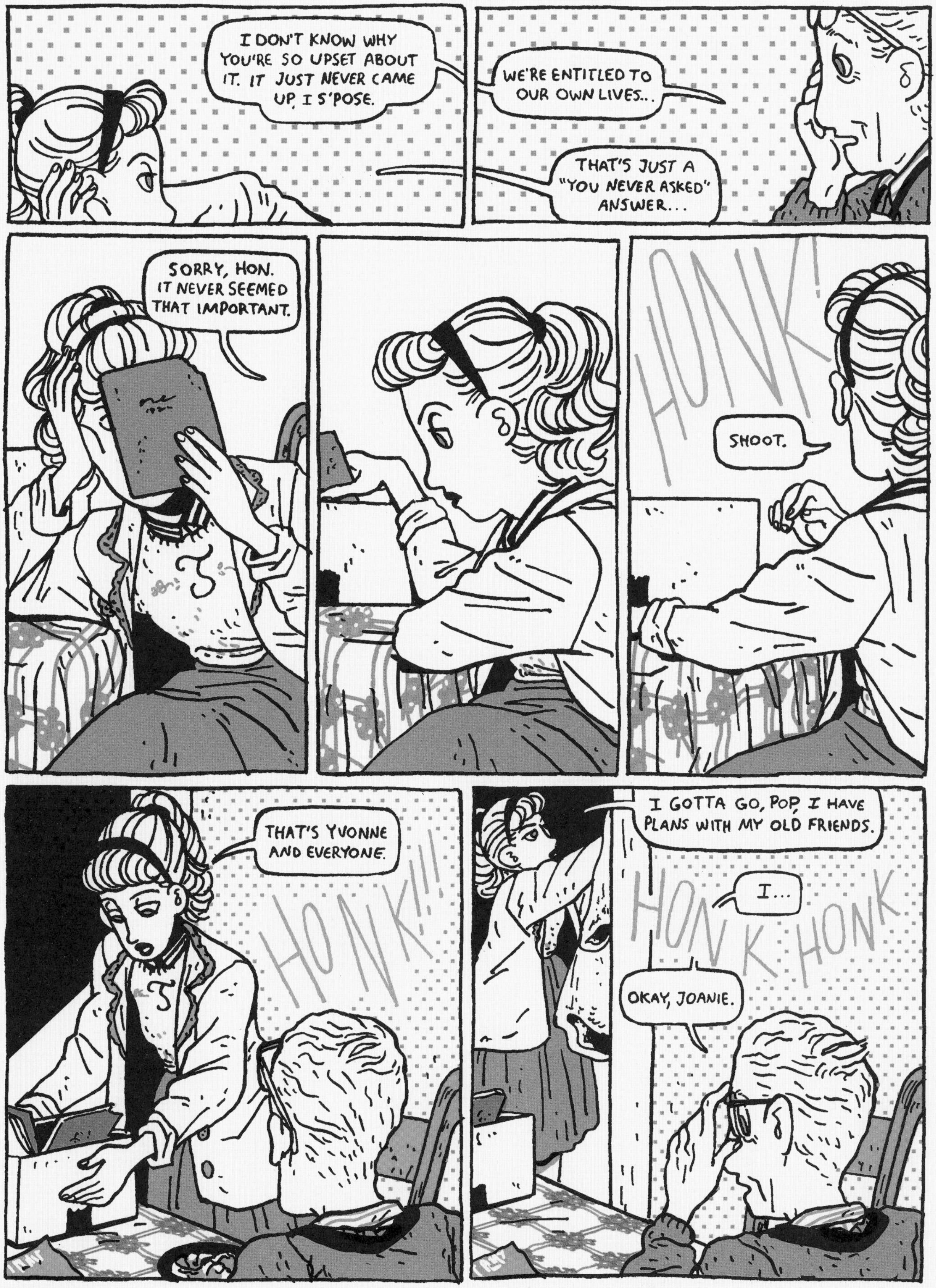
I DON'T KNOW WHY YOU'RE SO UPSET ABOUT IT. IT JUST NEVER CAME UP, I S'POSE.
WE'RE ENTITLED TO OUR OWN LIVES...
THAT'S JUST A "YOU NEVER ASKED" ANSWER...
SORRY, HON. IT NEVER SEEMED THAT IMPORTANT.
HONK!
SHOOT.
THAT'S YVONNE AND EVERYONE.
HONK!!!
I GOTTA GO, POP, I HAVE PLANS WITH MY OLD FRIENDS.
HONK HONK
I...
OKAY, JOANIE.

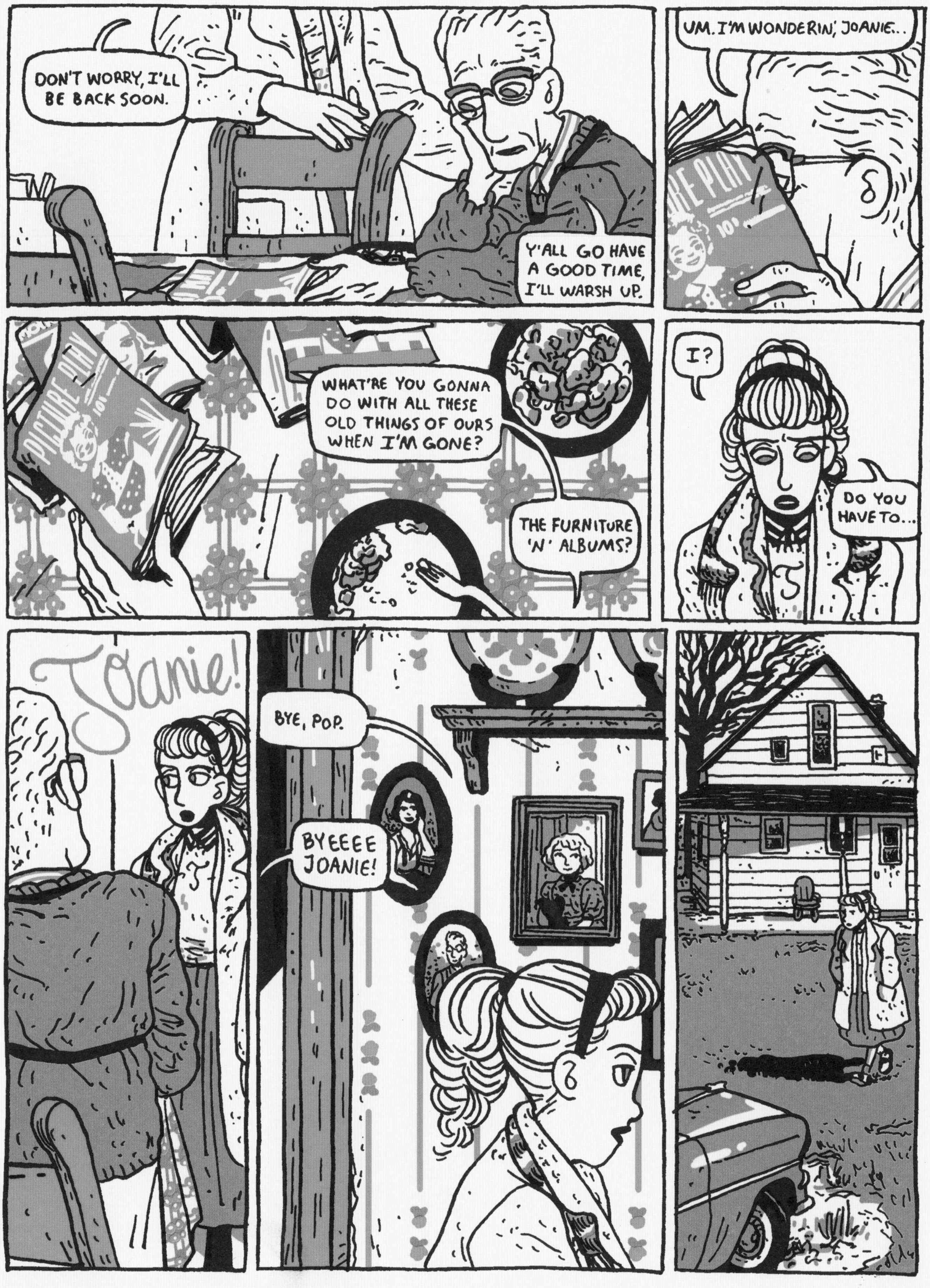
DON'T WORRY, I'LL BE BACK SOON.
Y'ALL GO HAVE A GOOD TIME, I'LL WARSH UP.
UM. I'M WONDERIN', JOANIE...
WHAT'RE YOU GONNA DO WITH ALL THESE OLD THINGS OF OURS WHEN I'M GONE?
THE FURNITURE 'N' ALBUMS?
I?
DO YOU HAVE TO...
Joanie!
BYE, POP.
BYEEEE JOANIE!

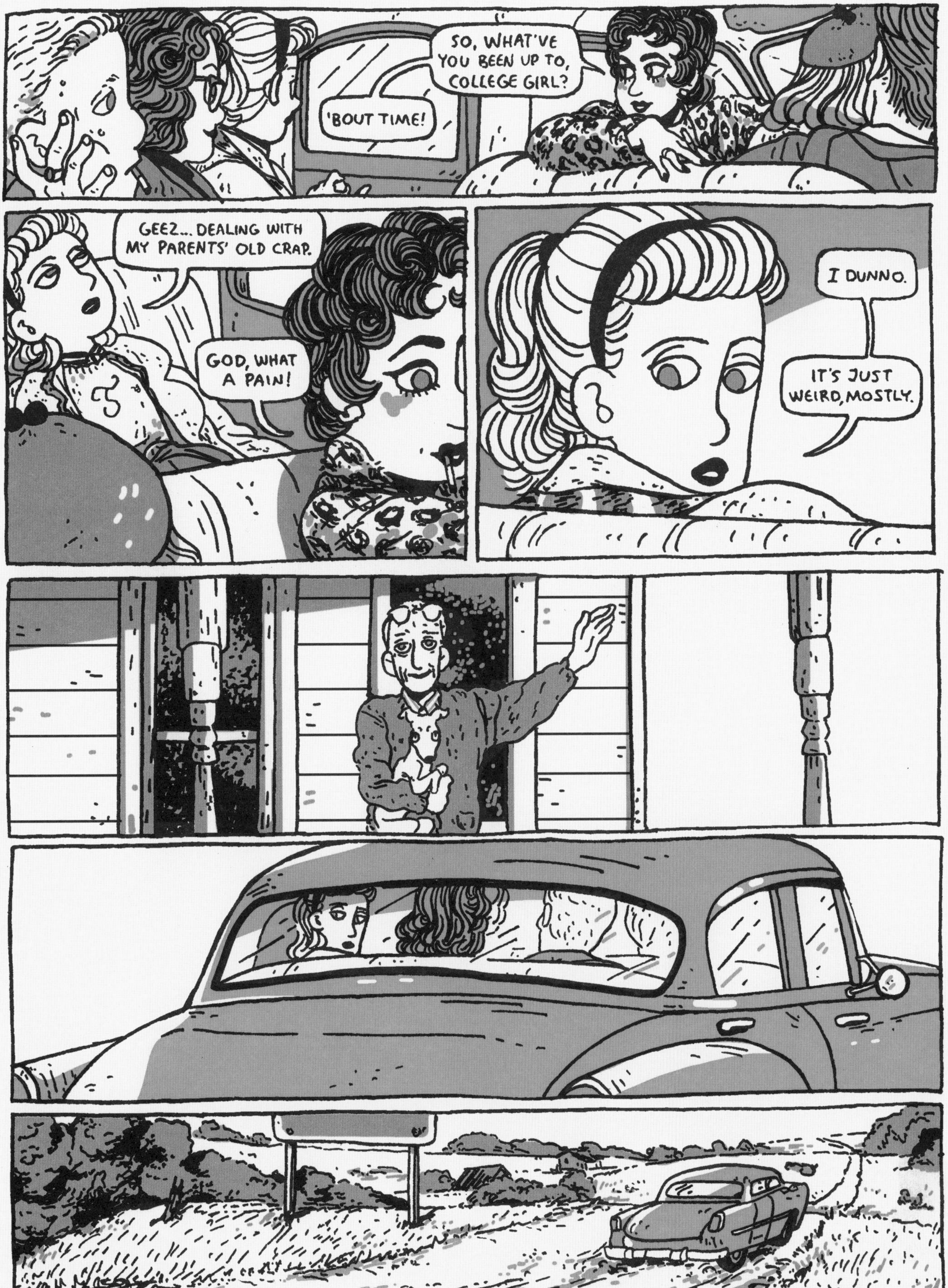
SO, WHAT'VE YOU BEEN UP TO, COLLEGE GIRL?
'BOUT TIME!
GEEZ... DEALING WITH MY PARENTS' OLD CRAP.
GOD, WHAT A PAIN!
I DUNNO.
IT'S JUST WEIRD, MOSTLY.

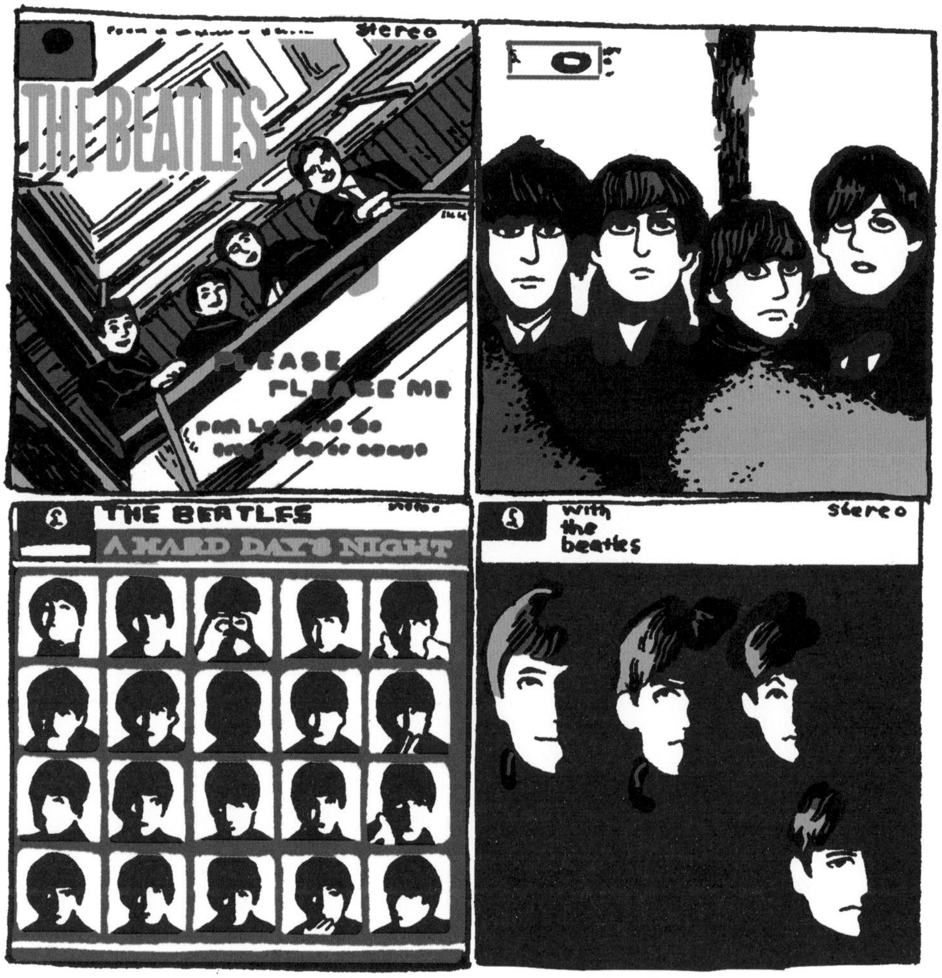
Stereo
THE BEATLES
PLEASE
PLEASE ME
THE BEATLES
A HARD DAY'S NIGHT
with
the
beatles
Stereo

"Greyfriar's Bobby"

When I saw you, it was
love at first sight.

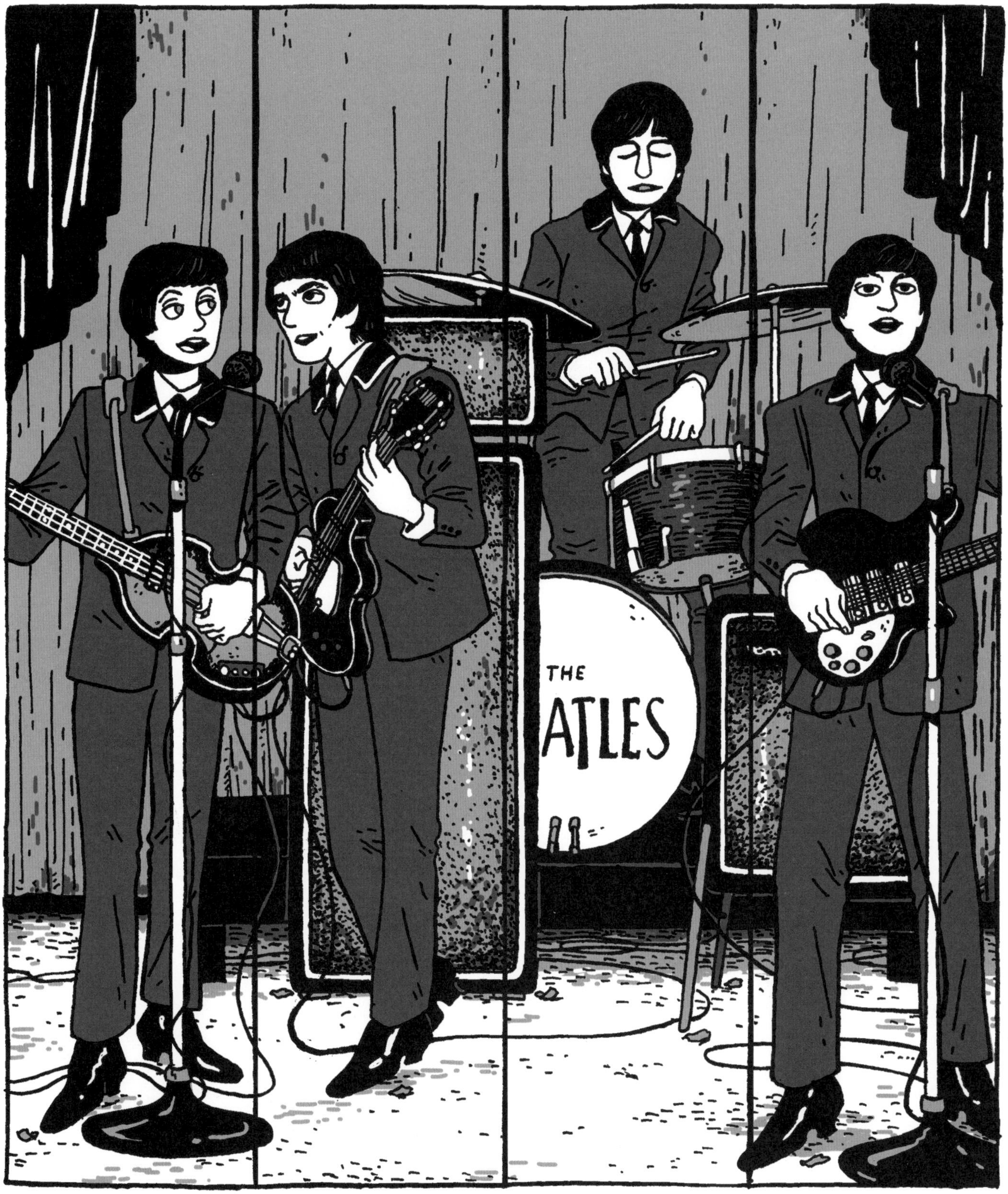
THE
ATLES

when I first saw you, it
was love at first site.

It feels like you could change my world!

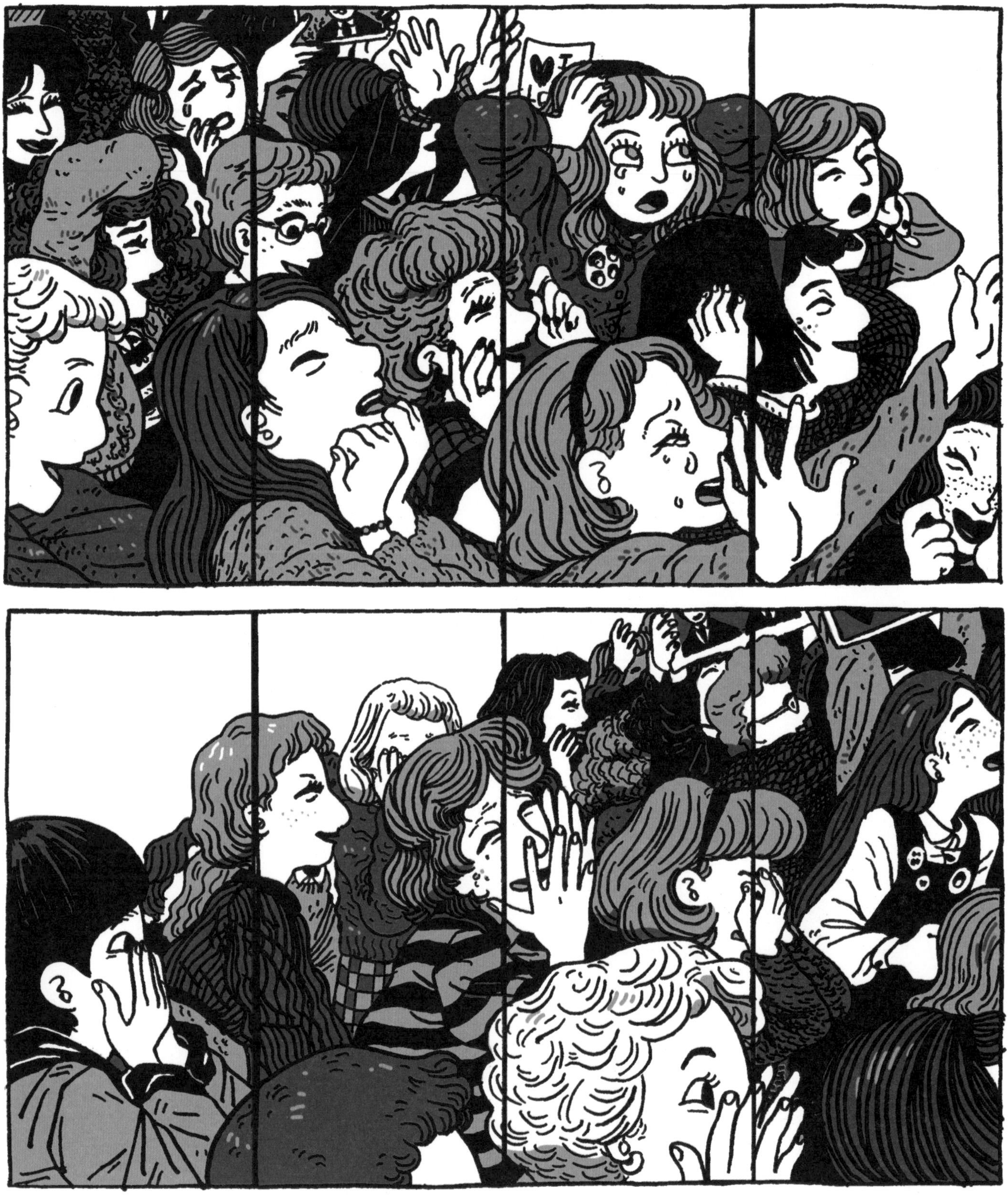

It feels like my hole life has changed,

Sometimes I feel so much I can't even think!

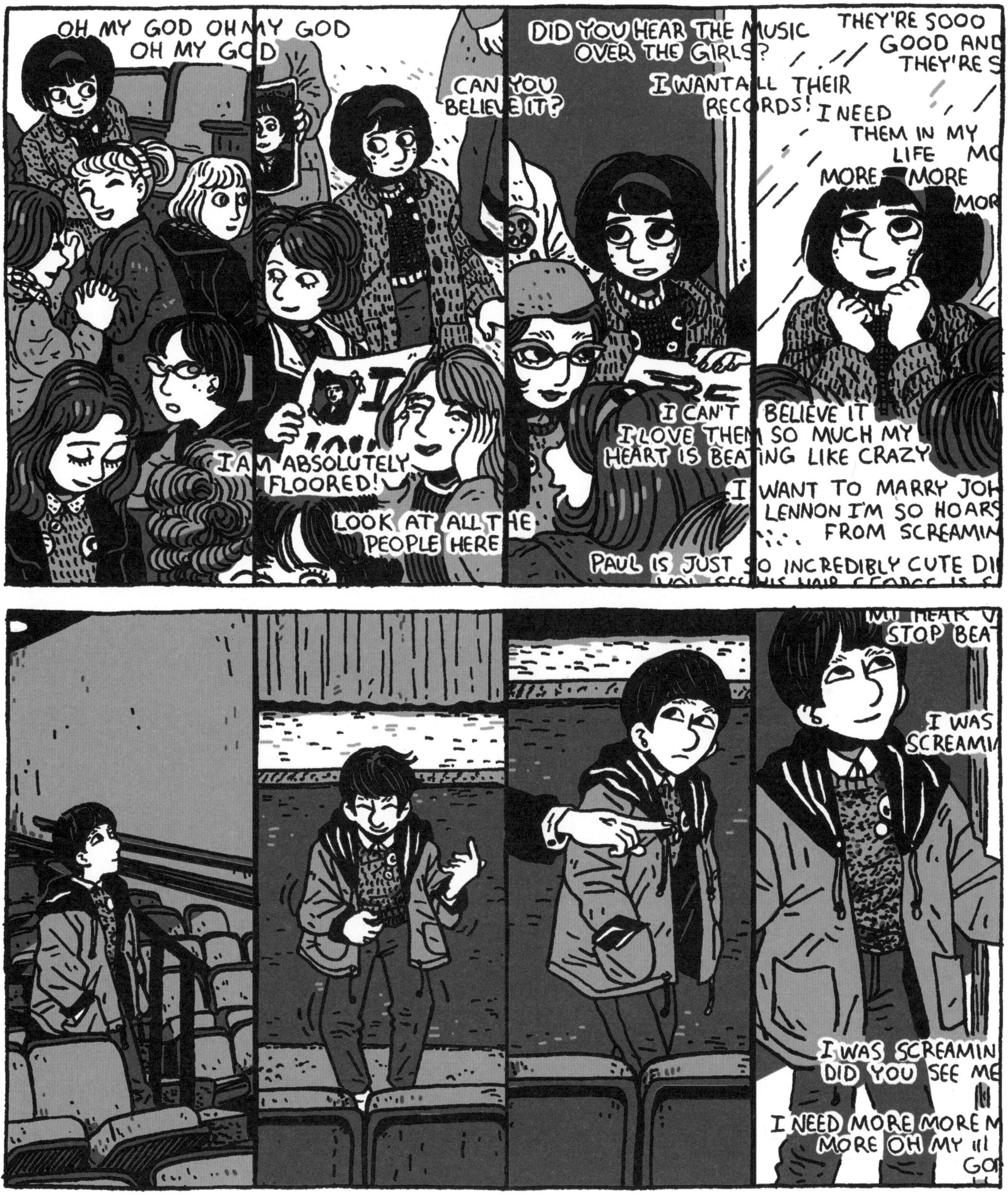
OH MY GOD OH MY GOD
OH MY GOD
CAN YOU BELIEVE IT?
I AM ABSOLUTELY FLOORED!
LOOK AT ALL THE PEOPLE HERE
DID YOU HEAR THE MUSIC OVER THE GIRLS?
I WANT ALL THEIR RECORDS!
THEY'RE SOOO GOOD AND THEY'RE S
I NEED THEM IN MY LIFE
MORE MORE
I CAN'T BELIEVE IT
I LOVE THEM SO MUCH MY HEART IS BEATING LIKE CRAZY
I WANT TO MARRY JOH LENNON I'M SO HOARS FROM SCREAMIN
PAUL IS JUST SO INCREDIBLY CUTE DI
STOP BEAT
I WAS SCREAMI
I WAS SCREAMIN DID YOU SEE ME
I NEED MORE MORE MORE OH MY

I'm sorry I got so nervous before...

But now those feelings have some meaning!

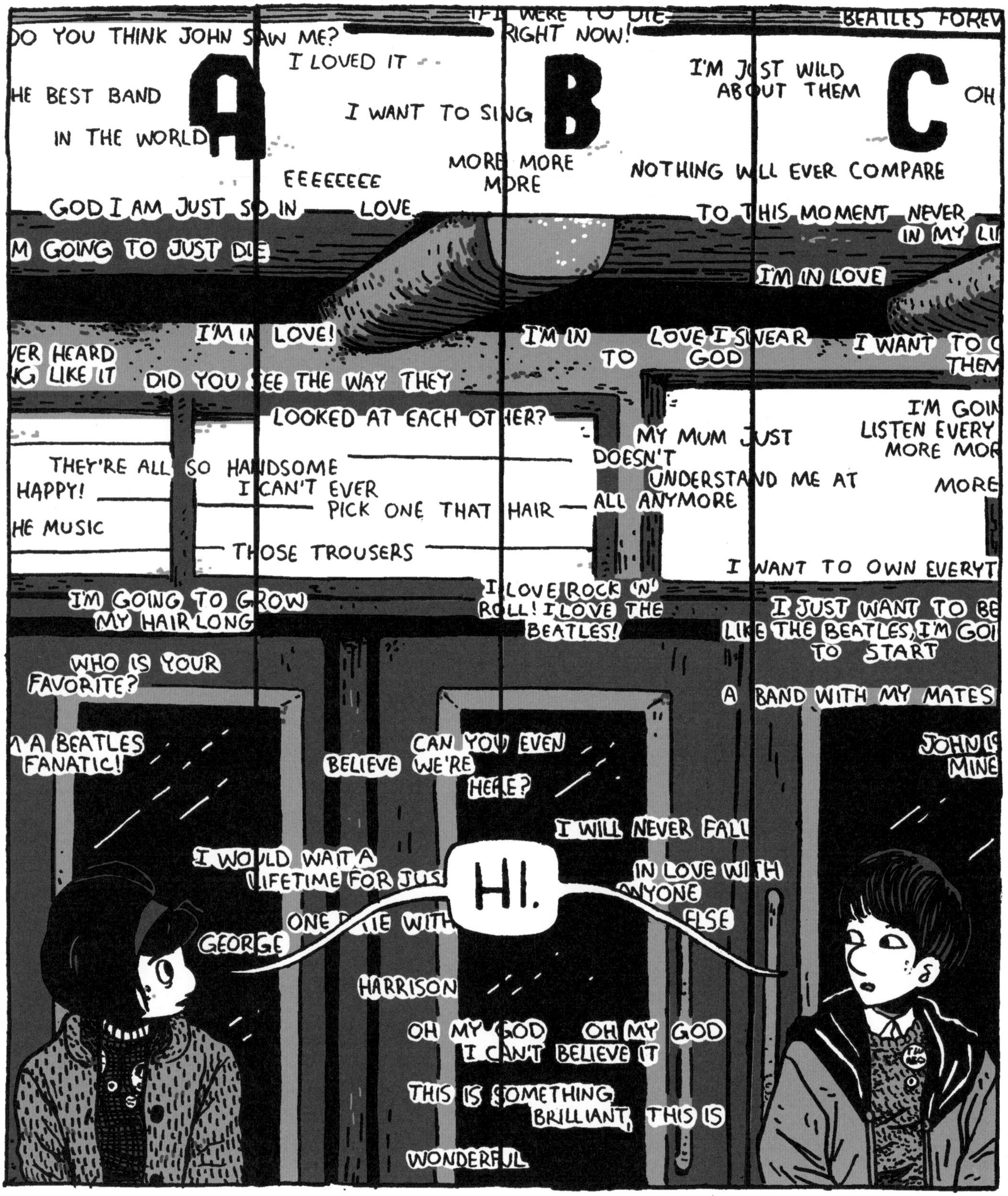
A B C
DO YOU THINK JOHN SAW ME?
I LOVED IT
IF I WERE TO DIE RIGHT NOW!
BEATLES FOREV
HE BEST BAND IN THE WORLD
I WANT TO SING
I'M JUST WILD ABOUT THEM
OH
EEEEEEEE
MORE MORE MORE
NOTHING WILL EVER COMPARE
GOD I AM JUST SO IN LOVE
TO THIS MOMENT NEVER IN MY LI
M GOING TO JUST DIE
I'M IN LOVE
I'M IN LOVE!
I'M IN LOVE I SWEAR TO GOD
I WANT TO THEM
ER HEARD G LIKE IT
DID YOU SEE THE WAY THEY LOOKED AT EACH OTHER?
MY MUM JUST DOESN'T UNDERSTAND ME AT ALL ANYMORE
I'M GOIN LISTEN EVERY MORE MOR MORE
THEY'RE ALL SO HANDSOME
HAPPY!
I CAN'T EVER PICK ONE THAT HAIR
HE MUSIC
THOSE TROUSERS
I WANT TO OWN EVERYT
I'M GOING TO GROW MY HAIR LONG
I LOVE ROCK 'N' ROLL! I LOVE THE BEATLES!
I JUST WANT TO BE LIKE THE BEATLES, I'M GOI TO START A BAND WITH MY MATES
WHO IS YOUR FAVORITE?
A BEATLES FANATIC!
CAN YOU EVEN BELIEVE WE'RE HERE?
JOHN IS MINE
I WILL NEVER FALL IN LOVE WITH ANYONE ELSE
I WOULD WAIT A LIFETIME FOR JUST ONE DATE WITH GEORGE HARRISON
HI.
OH MY GOD OH MY GOD I CAN'T BELIEVE IT
THIS IS SOMETHING BRILLIANT, THIS IS WONDERFUL

It felt like you could see rite into my sole!!!

It's all happened very quickly, but it's so real,

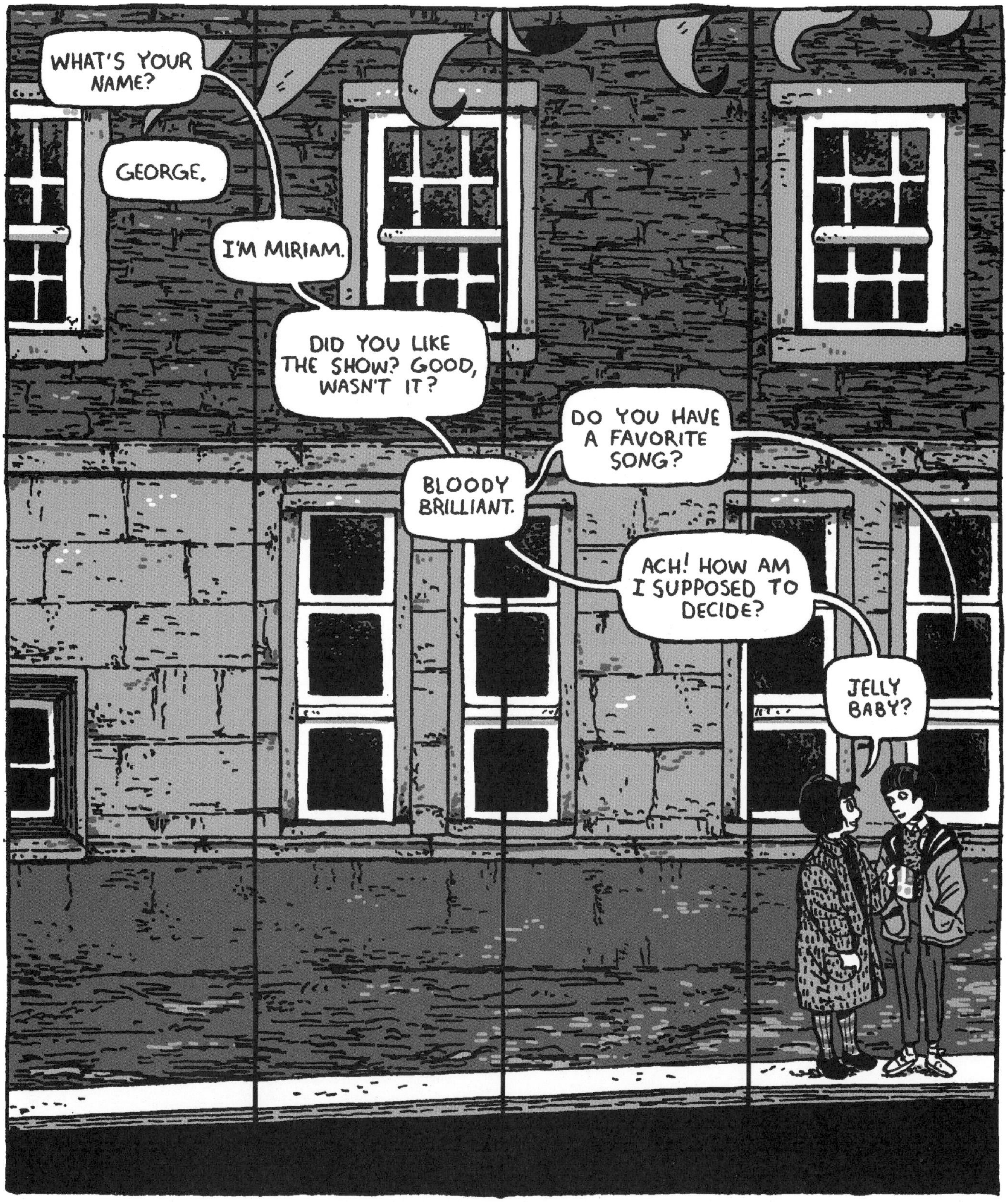

WHAT'S YOUR NAME?
GEORGE.
I'M MIRIAM.
DID YOU LIKE THE SHOW? GOOD, WASN'T IT?
BLOODY BRILLIANT.
DO YOU HAVE A FAVORITE SONG?
ACH! HOW AM I SUPPOSED TO DECIDE?
JELLY BABY?

I don't know if it makes any sense, but no one has ever listened to me before...

do I mean something to you, too?

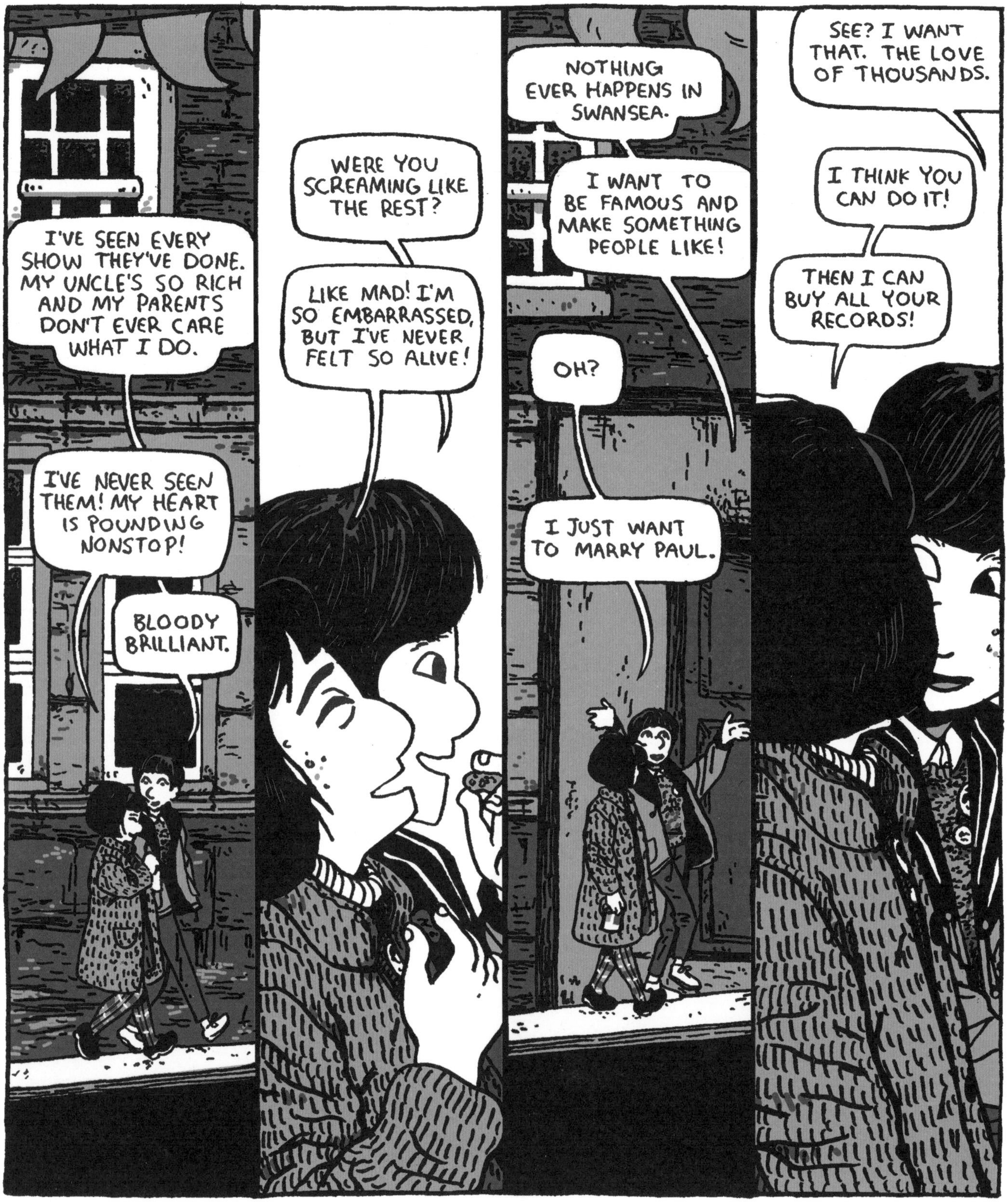
I'VE SEEN EVERY SHOW THEY'VE DONE. MY UNCLE'S SO RICH AND MY PARENTS DON'T EVER CARE WHAT I DO.
I'VE NEVER SEEN THEM! MY HEART IS POUNDING NONSTOP!
BLOODY BRILLIANT.
WERE YOU SCREAMING LIKE THE REST?
LIKE MAD! I'M SO EMBARRASSED, BUT I'VE NEVER FELT SO ALIVE!
NOTHING EVER HAPPENS IN SWANSEA.
I WANT TO BE FAMOUS AND MAKE SOMETHING PEOPLE LIKE!
OH?
I JUST WANT TO MARRY PAUL.
SEE? I WANT THAT. THE LOVE OF THOUSANDS.
I THINK YOU CAN DO IT!
THEN I CAN BUY ALL YOUR RECORDS!

anyway...
I hope you like me...

I think we had a special moment yesterday...

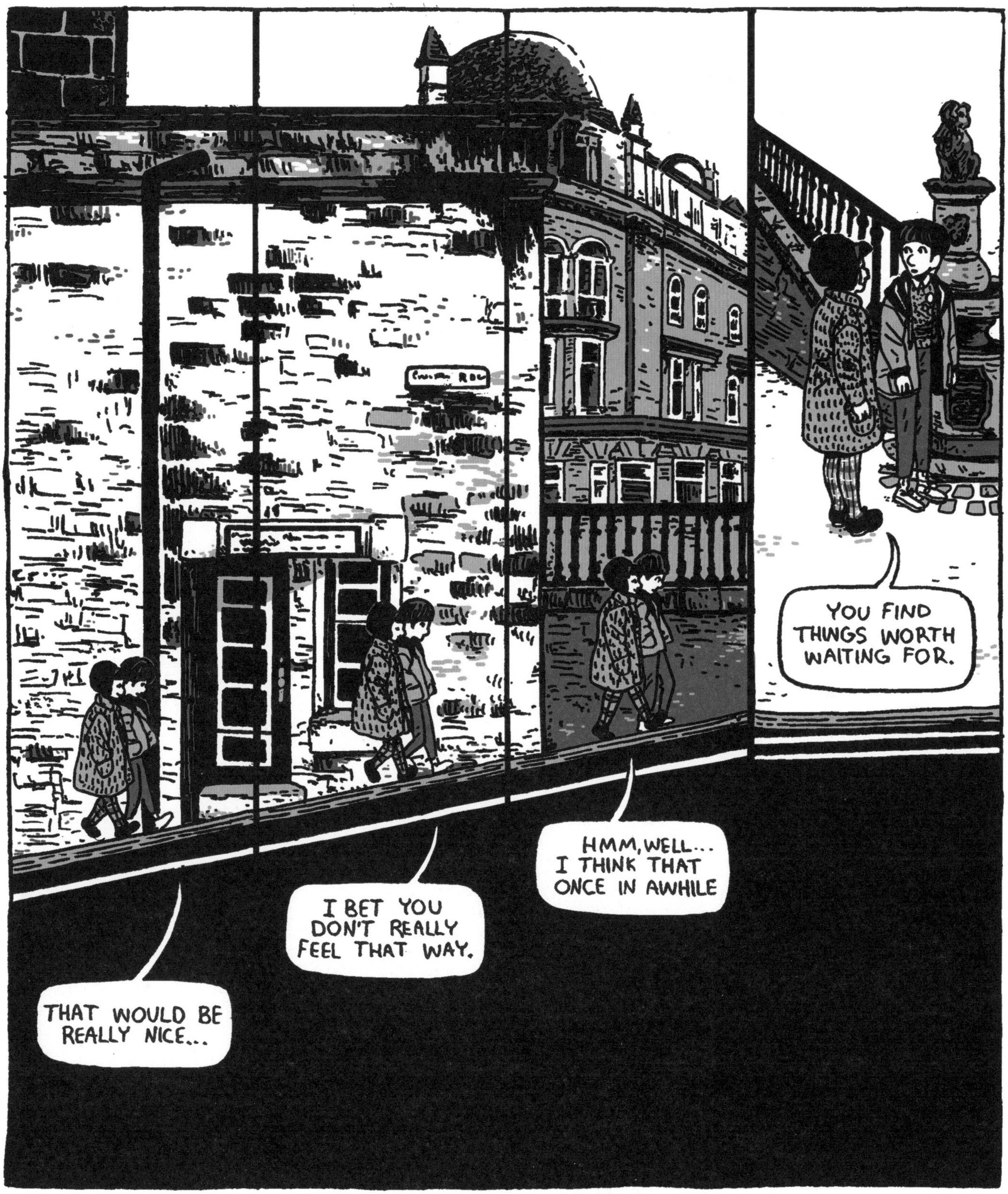
THAT WOULD BE REALLY NICE...
I BET YOU DON'T REALLY FEEL THAT WAY.
HMM, WELL... I THINK THAT ONCE IN AWHILE
YOU FIND THINGS WORTH WAITING FOR.

You know when you're mind goes to the same things over and over?

I cant get my mind off of it.

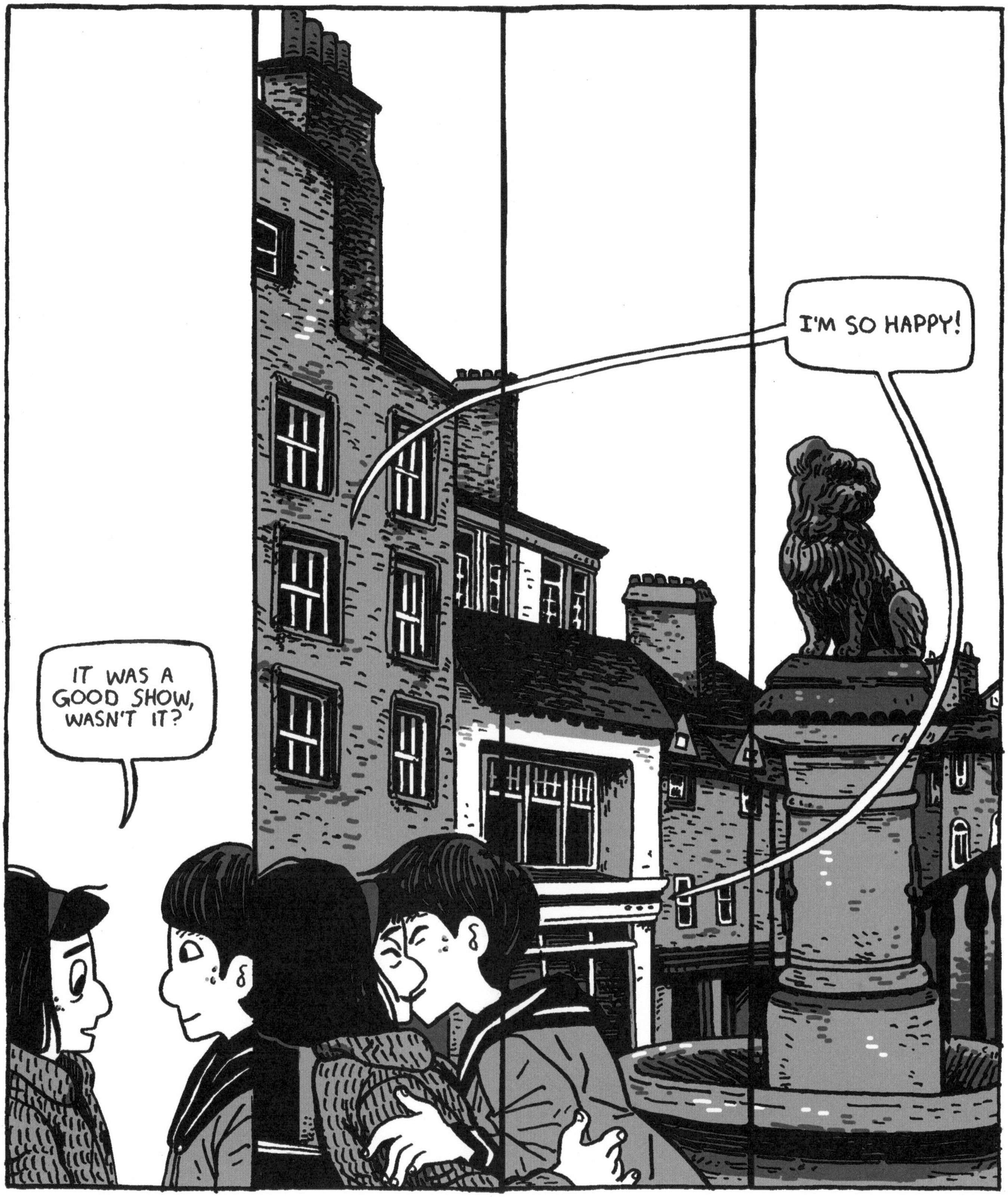
IT WAS A GOOD SHOW, WASN'T IT?
I'M SO HAPPY!

That's like the day we met.

I want to feel that way again.

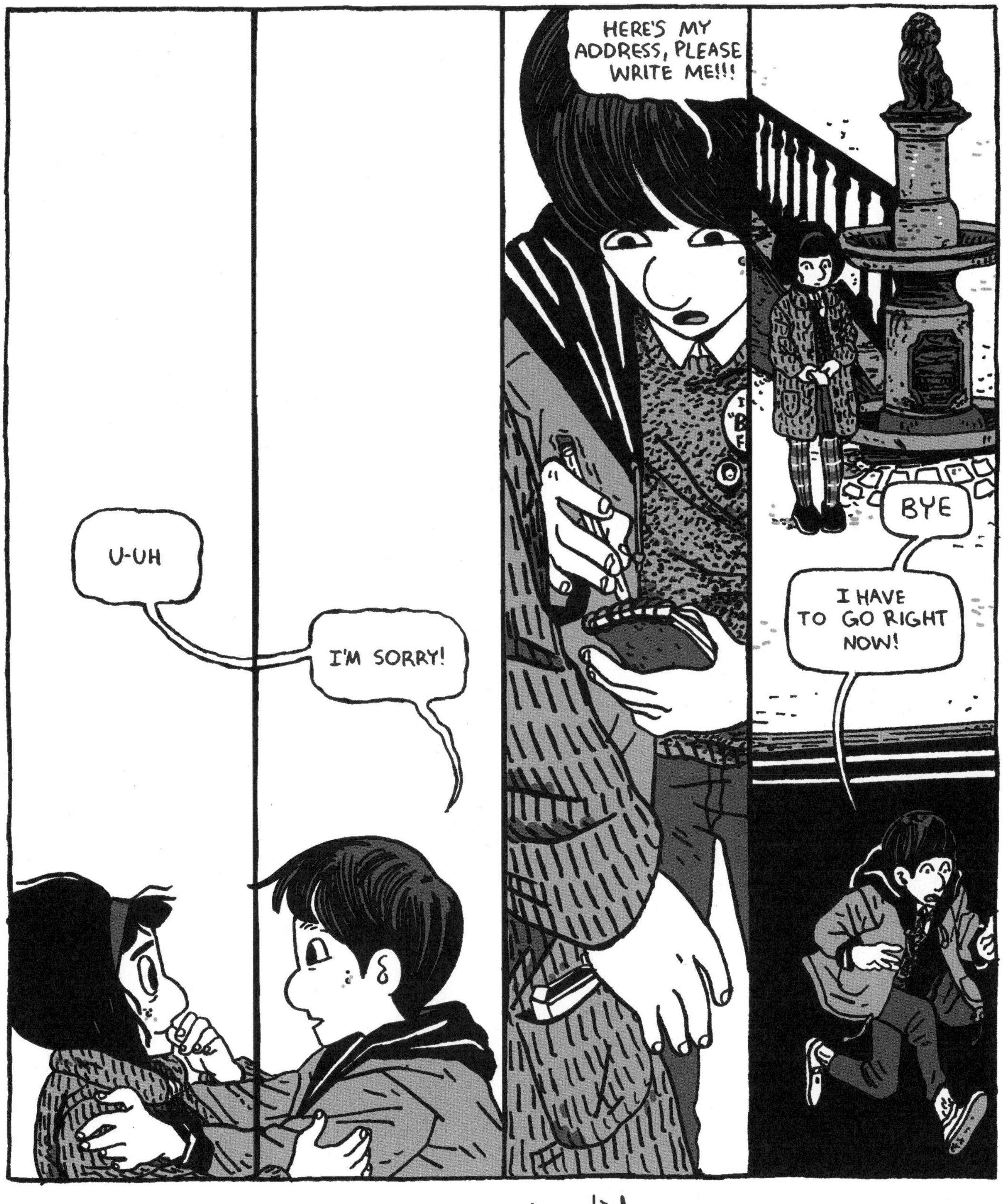
U-UH
I'M SORRY!
HERE'S MY ADDRESS, PLEASE WRITE ME!!!
BYE
I HAVE TO GO RIGHT NOW!

You make me feel spetial.

Sincerely,
Miriam K.

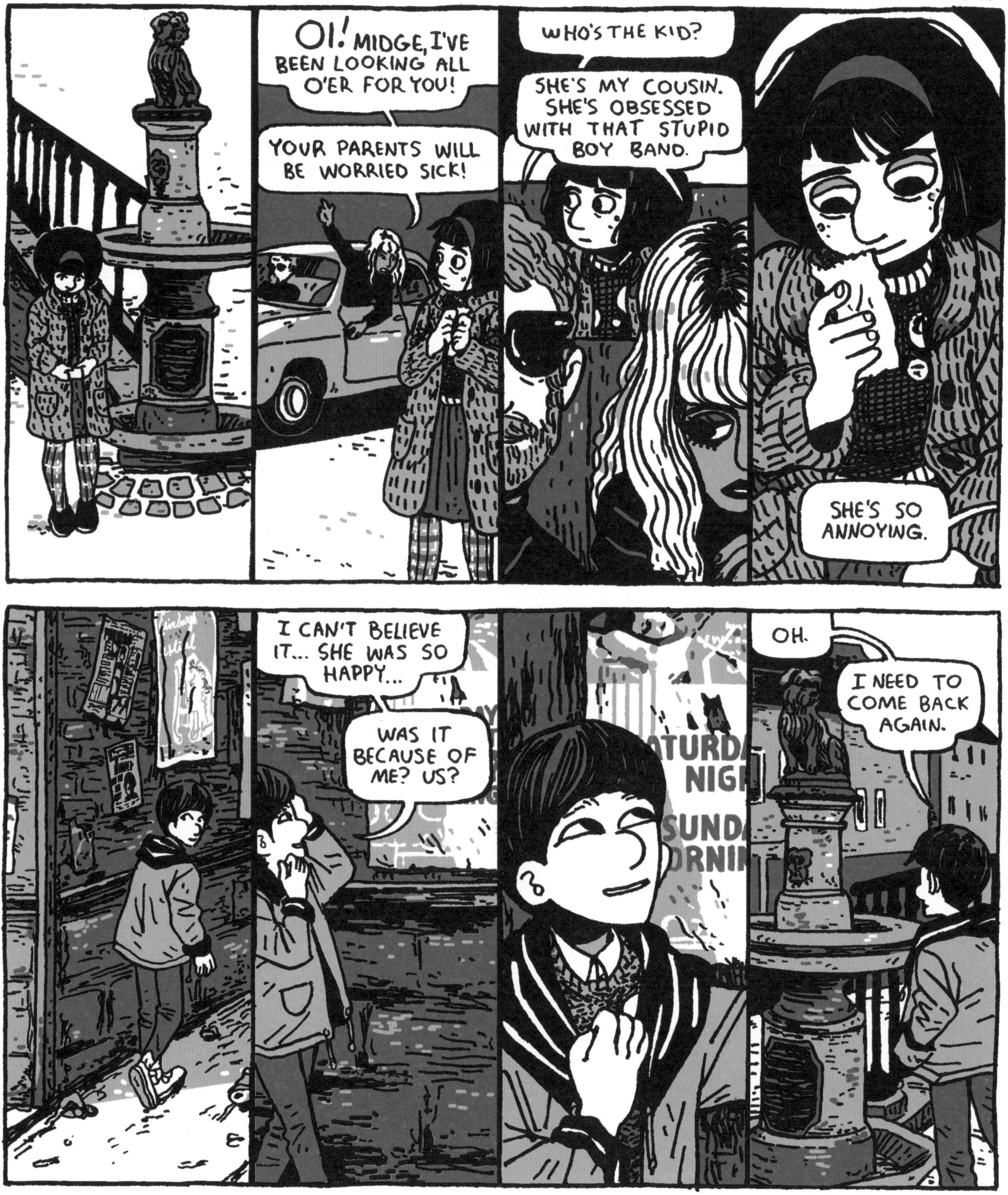

OI! MIDGE, I'VE BEEN LOOKING ALL O'ER FOR YOU!
YOUR PARENTS WILL BE WORRIED SICK!
WHO'S THE KID?
SHE'S MY COUSIN. SHE'S OBSESSED WITH THAT STUPID BOY BAND.
SHE'S SO ANNOYING.
I CAN'T BELIEVE IT... SHE WAS SO HAPPY...
WAS IT BECAUSE OF ME? US?
SATURDA
NIG
SUNDA
ORNIN
OH.
I NEED TO COME BACK AGAIN.

Sincerely yours,
George

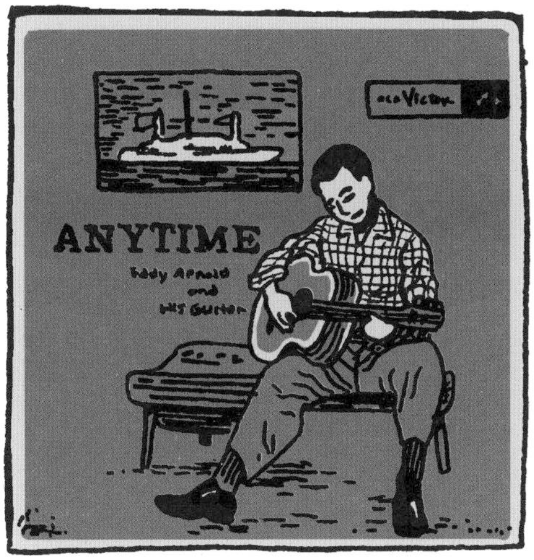
ANYTIME

"Baby Fat"

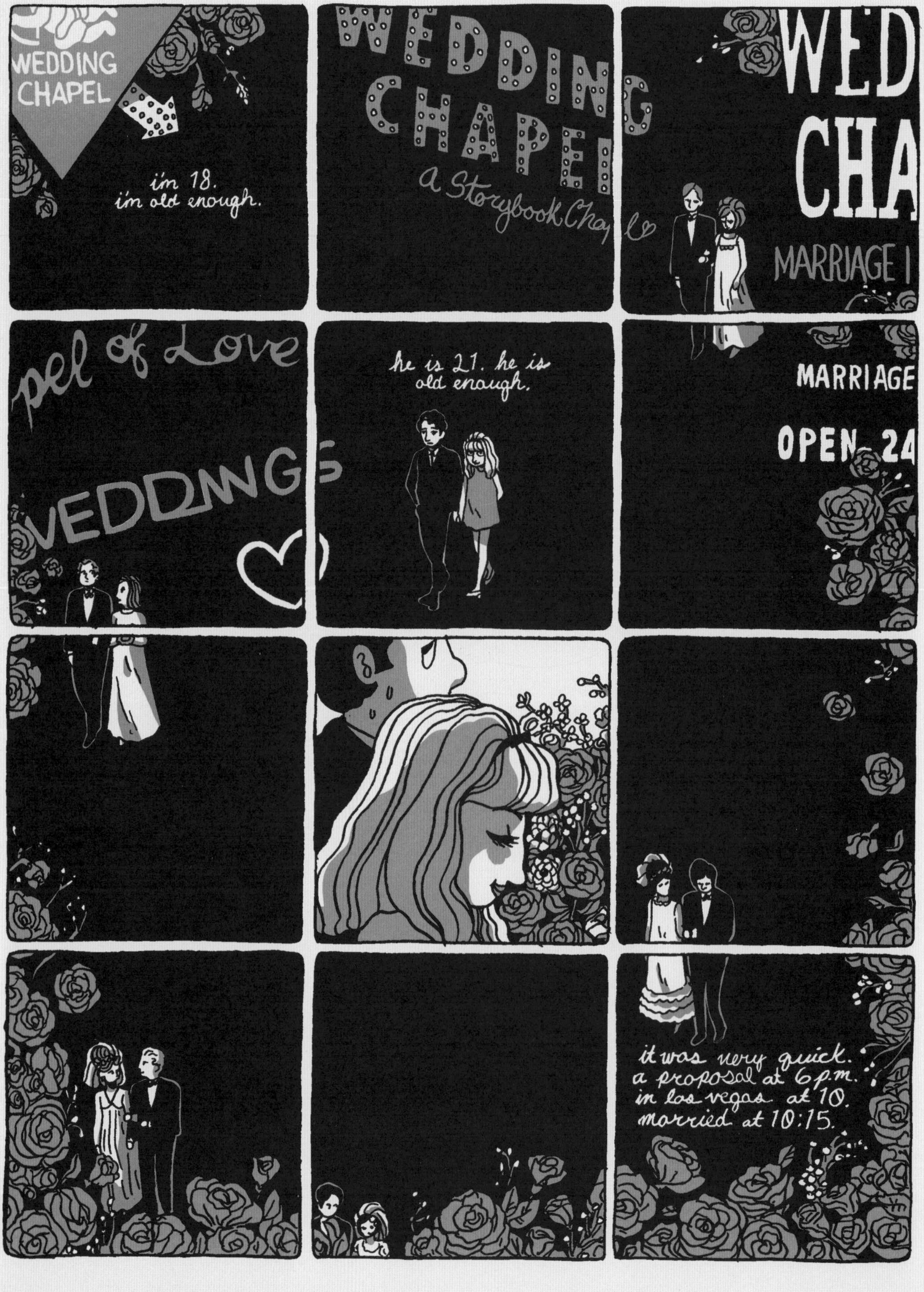
WEDDING CHAPEL
im 18.
im old enough.
WEDDING CHAPEL
a Storybook Chapel
WED
CHA
MARRIAGE I
pel of Love
WEDDINGS
he is 21. he is old enough.
MARRIAGE
OPEN 24
it was very quick.
a proposal at 6 p.m.
in las vegas at 10.
married at 10:15.

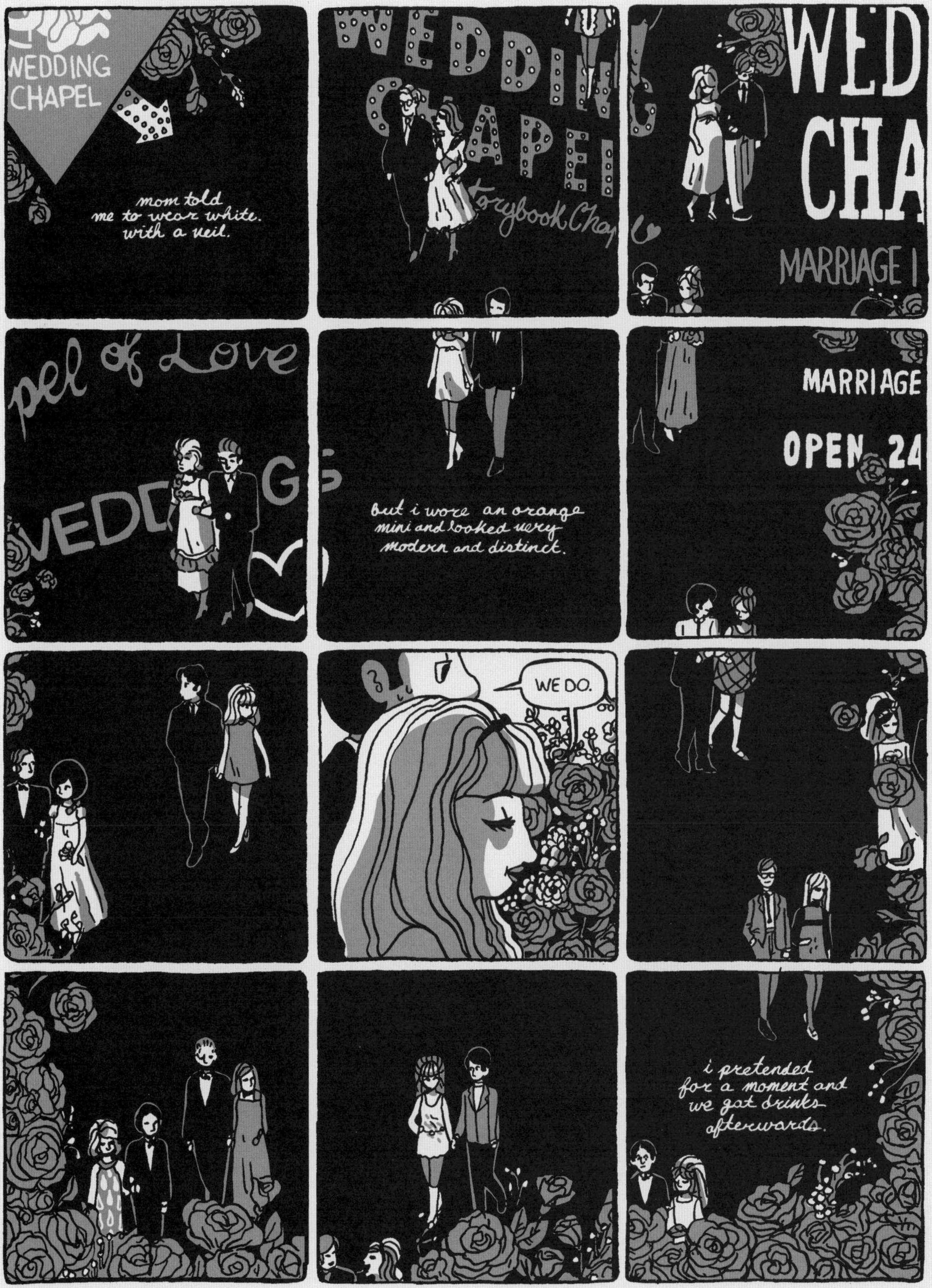
WEDDING CHAPEL
mom told me to wear white. with a veil.
WED
CHA
MARRIAGE
pel of Love
but i wore an orange mini and looked very modern and distinct.
MARRIAGE
OPEN 24
WE DO.
i pretended for a moment and we got drinks afterwards.

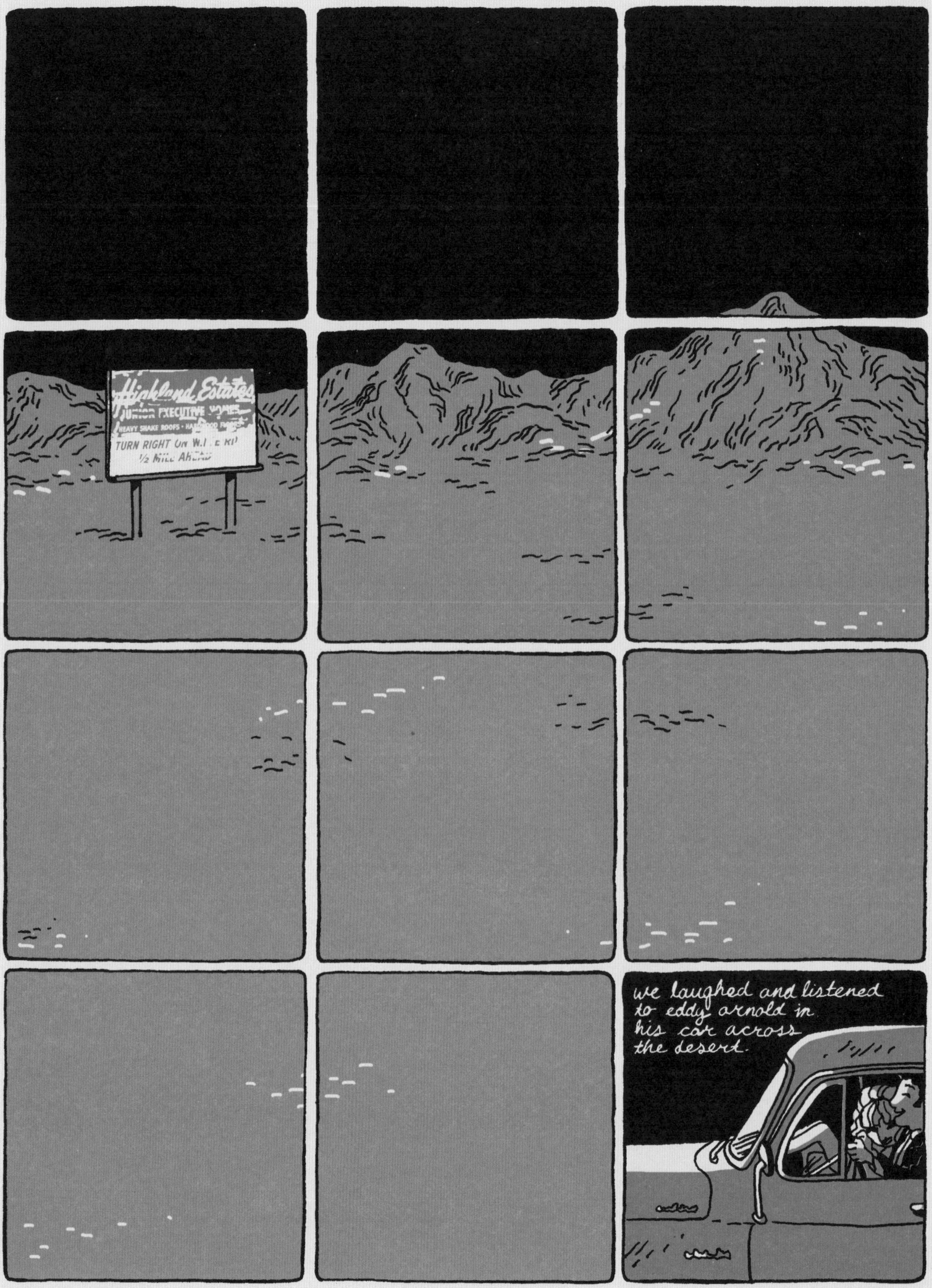
Highland Estates
JUNIOR EXECUTIVE
HEAVY SHAKE ROOFS
TURN RIGHT
we laughed and listened to eddy arnold in his car across the desert.

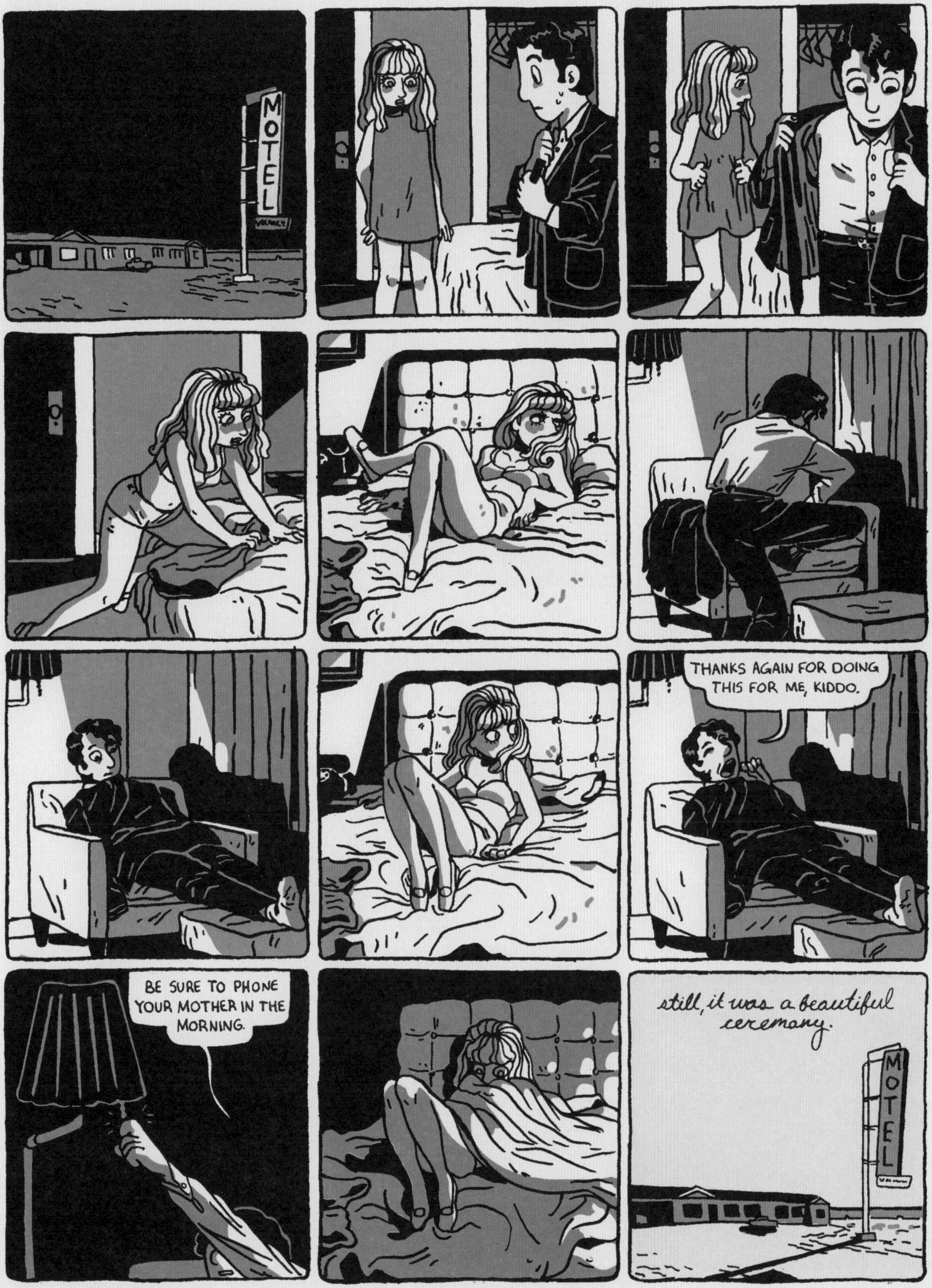
MOTEL
THANKS AGAIN FOR DOING THIS FOR ME, KIDDO.
BE SURE TO PHONE YOUR MOTHER IN THE MORNING.
still, it was a beautiful ceremony.
MOTEL

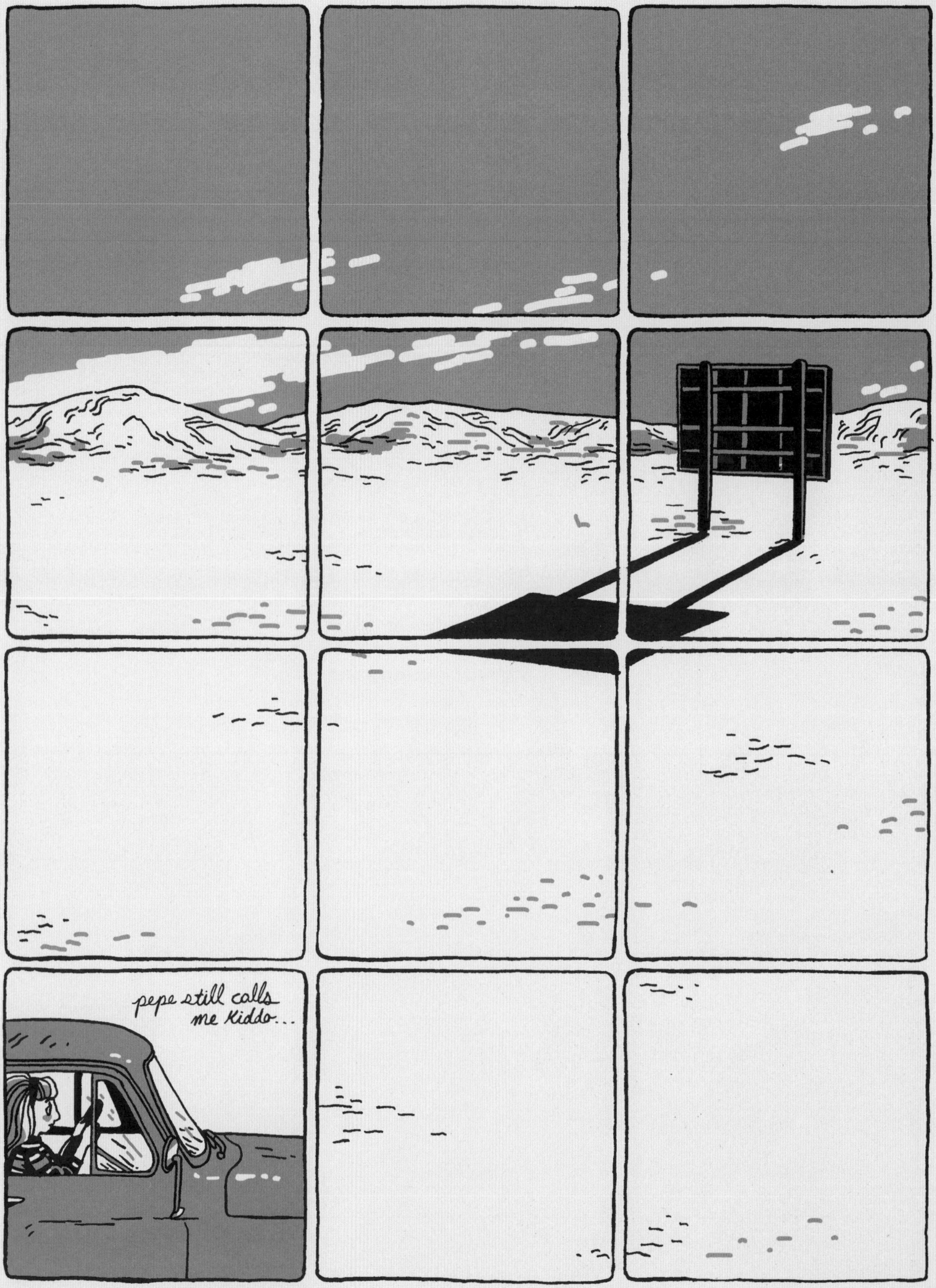
pepe still calls
me kiddo...

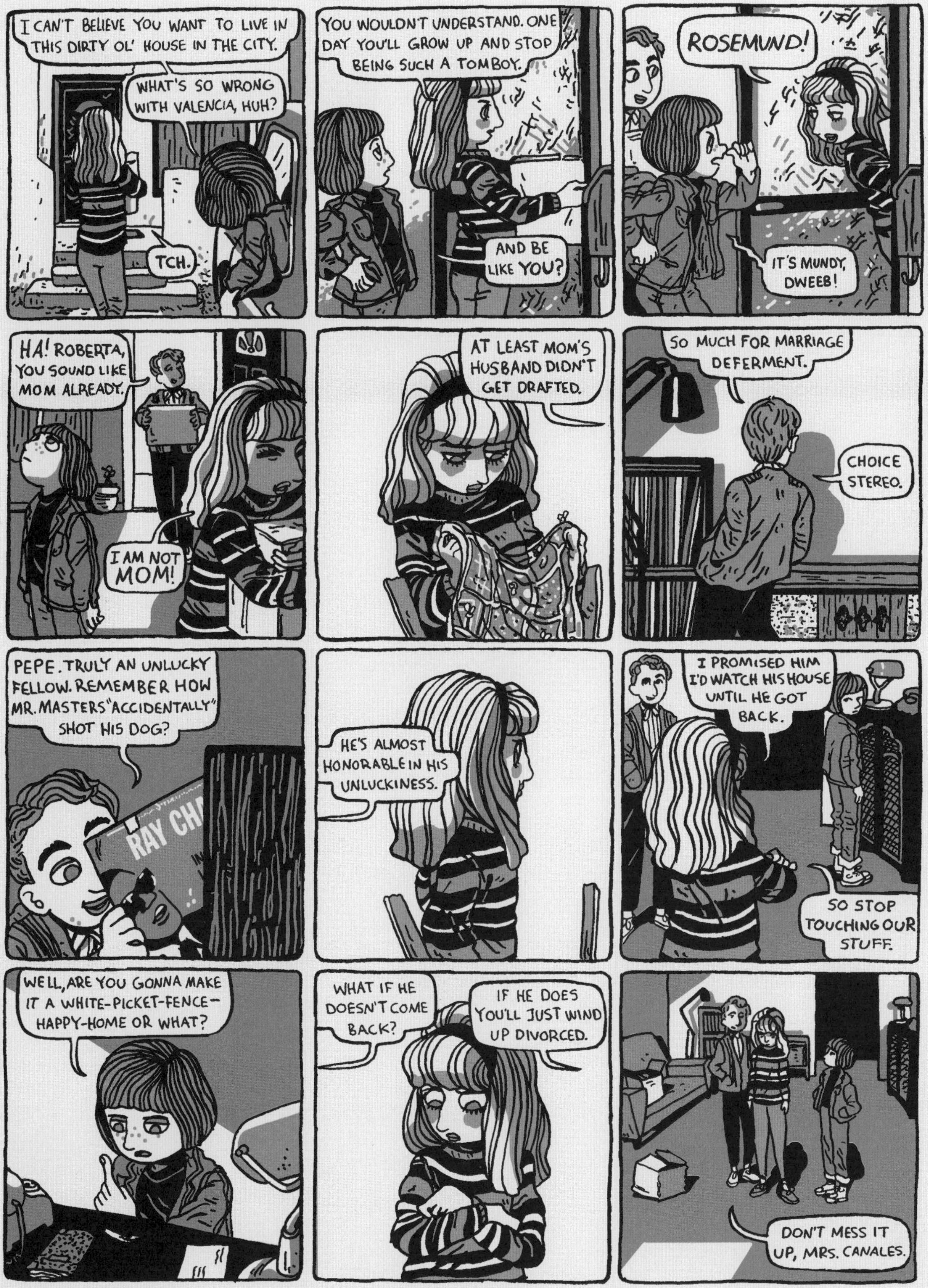
I CAN'T BELIEVE YOU WANT TO LIVE IN THIS DIRTY OL' HOUSE IN THE CITY.
WHAT'S SO WRONG WITH VALENCIA, HUH?
TCH.
YOU WOULDN'T UNDERSTAND. ONE DAY YOU'LL GROW UP AND STOP BEING SUCH A TOMBOY.
AND BE LIKE YOU?
ROSEMUND!
IT'S MUNDY, DWEEB!
HA! ROBERTA, YOU SOUND LIKE MOM ALREADY.
I AM NOT MOM!
AT LEAST MOM'S HUSBAND DIDN'T GET DRAFTED.
SO MUCH FOR MARRIAGE DEFERMENT.
CHOICE STEREO.
PEPE. TRULY AN UNLUCKY FELLOW. REMEMBER HOW MR. MASTERS "ACCIDENTALLY" SHOT HIS DOG?
RAY CH
HE'S ALMOST HONORABLE IN HIS UNLUCKINESS.
I PROMISED HIM I'D WATCH HIS HOUSE UNTIL HE GOT BACK.
SO STOP TOUCHING OUR STUFF.
WELL, ARE YOU GONNA MAKE IT A WHITE-PICKET-FENCE-HAPPY-HOME OR WHAT?
WHAT IF HE DOESN'T COME BACK?
IF HE DOES YOU'LL JUST WIND UP DIVORCED.
DON'T MESS IT UP, MRS. CANALES.

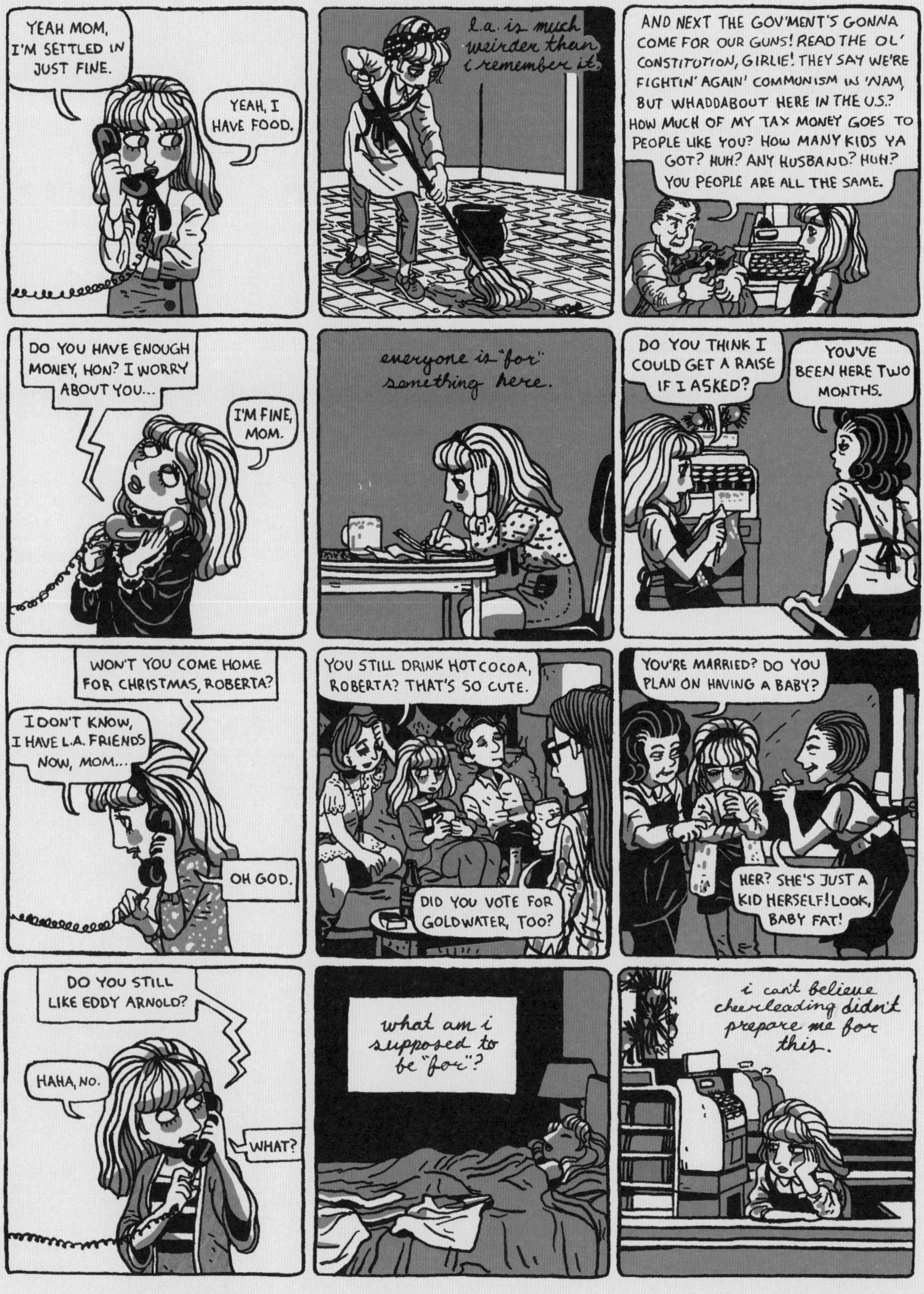
YEAH MOM, I'M SETTLED IN JUST FINE.
YEAH, I HAVE FOOD.
l.a. is much weirder than i remember it.
AND NEXT THE GOV'MENT'S GONNA COME FOR OUR GUNS! READ THE OL' CONSTITUTION, GIRLIE! THEY SAY WE'RE FIGHTIN' AGAIN' COMMUNISM IN 'NAM, BUT WHADDABOUT HERE IN THE U.S.? HOW MUCH OF MY TAX MONEY GOES TO PEOPLE LIKE YOU? HOW MANY KIDS YA GOT? HUH? ANY HUSBAND? HUH? YOU PEOPLE ARE ALL THE SAME.
DO YOU HAVE ENOUGH MONEY, HON? I WORRY ABOUT YOU...
I'M FINE, MOM.
everyone is "for" something here.
DO YOU THINK I COULD GET A RAISE IF I ASKED?
YOU'VE BEEN HERE TWO MONTHS.
WON'T YOU COME HOME FOR CHRISTMAS, ROBERTA?
I DON'T KNOW, I HAVE L.A. FRIENDS NOW, MOM...
OH GOD.
YOU STILL DRINK HOT COCOA, ROBERTA? THAT'S SO CUTE.
DID YOU VOTE FOR GOLDWATER, TOO?
YOU'RE MARRIED? DO YOU PLAN ON HAVING A BABY?
HER? SHE'S JUST A KID HERSELF! LOOK, BABY FAT!
DO YOU STILL LIKE EDDY ARNOLD?
HAHA, NO.
WHAT?
what am i supposed to be "for"?
i can't believe cheerleading didn't prepare me for this.

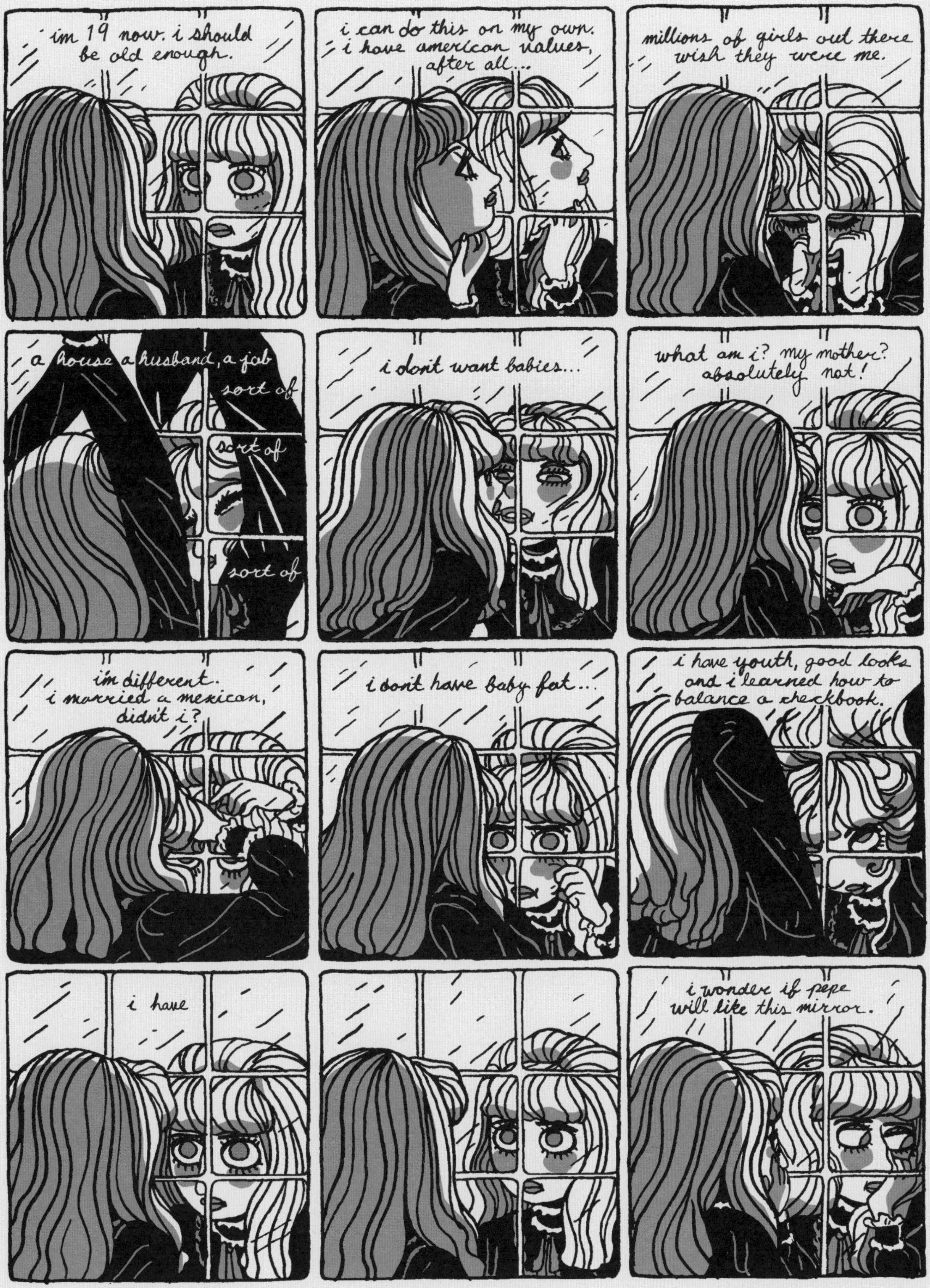
im 19 now. i should be old enough.
i can do this on my own. i have american values, after all...
millions of girls out there wish they were me.
a house a husband, a job
sort of
sort of
sort of
i dont want babies...
what am i? my mother? absolutely not!
im different. i married a mexican, didn't i?
i dont have baby fat...
i have youth, good looks and i learned how to balance a checkbook.
i have
i wonder if pepe will like this mirror.

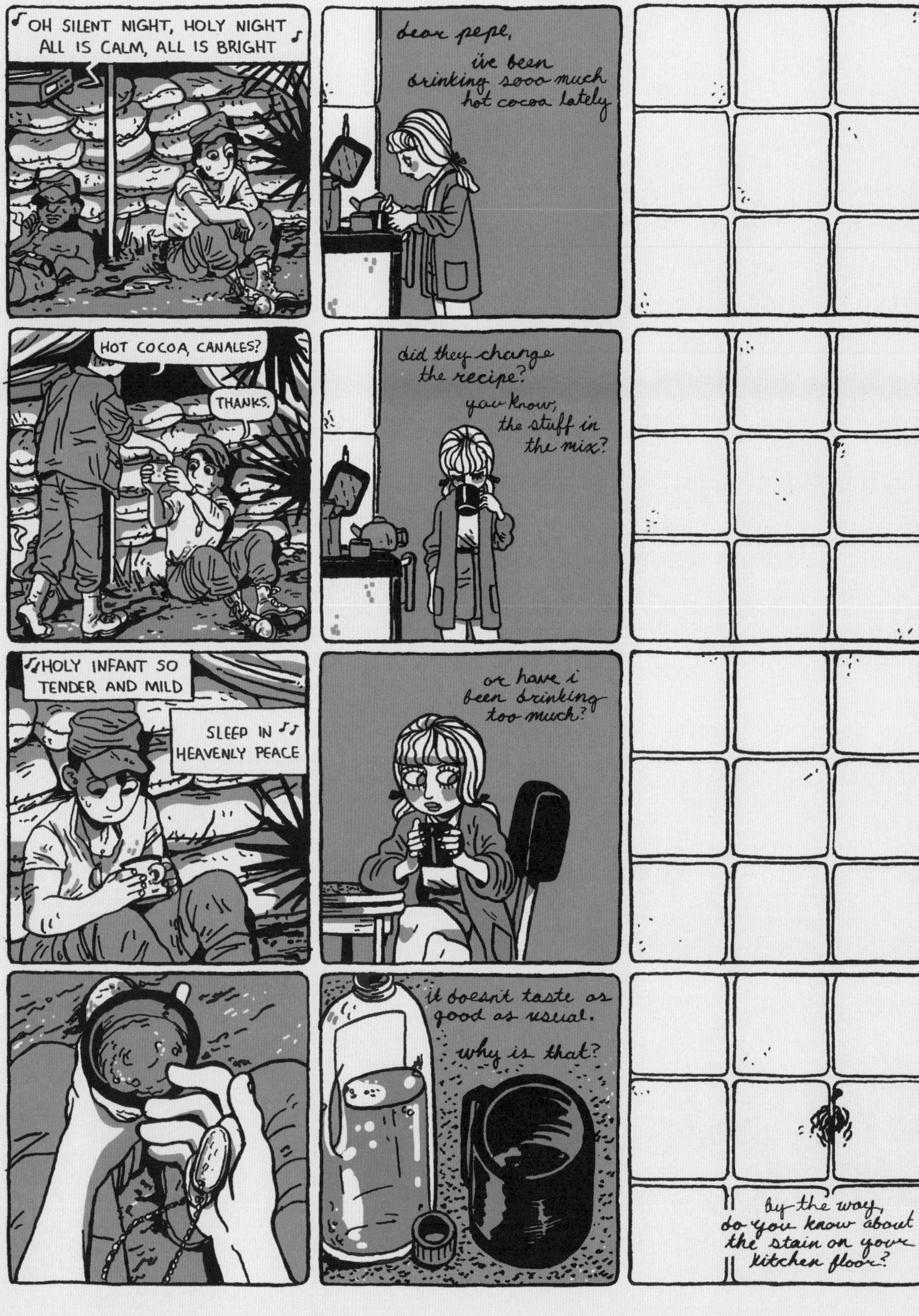

OH SILENT NIGHT, HOLY NIGHT
ALL IS CALM, ALL IS BRIGHT
dear pepe,
ive been drinking sooo much hot cocoa lately
HOT COCOA, CANALES?
THANKS.
did they change the recipe?
you know, the stuff in the mix?
HOLY INFANT SO TENDER AND MILD
SLEEP IN HEAVENLY PEACE
or have i been drinking too much?
it doesnt taste as good as usual.
why is that?
by the way, do you know about the stain on your kitchen floor?

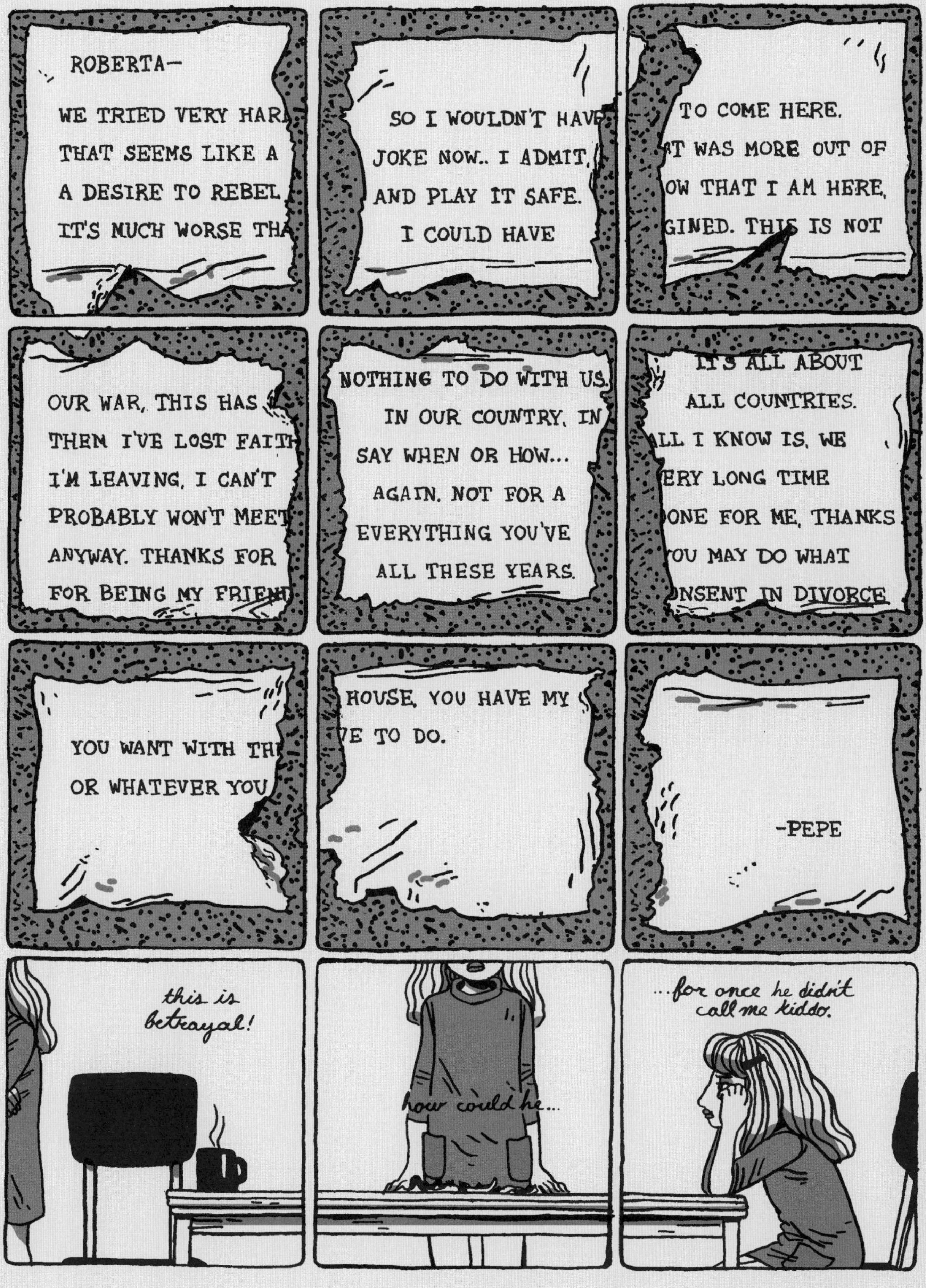
ROBERTA—
WE TRIED VERY HAR
THAT SEEMS LIKE A
A DESIRE TO REBEL
IT'S MUCH WORSE THA
SO I WOULDN'T HAVE
JOKE NOW.. I ADMIT,
AND PLAY IT SAFE.
I COULD HAVE
TO COME HERE.
T WAS MORE OUT OF
OW THAT I AM HERE,
GINED. THIS IS NOT
OUR WAR, THIS HAS
THEN I'VE LOST FAIT
I'M LEAVING, I CAN'T
PROBABLY WON'T MEET
ANYWAY. THANKS FOR
FOR BEING MY FRIEND
NOTHING TO DO WITH US.
IN OUR COUNTRY, IN
SAY WHEN OR HOW...
AGAIN, NOT FOR A
EVERYTHING YOU'VE
ALL THESE YEARS.
IT'S ALL ABOUT
ALL COUNTRIES.
LL I KNOW IS, WE
ERY LONG TIME
ONE FOR ME, THANKS
OU MAY DO WHAT
NSENT IN DIVORCE
YOU WANT WITH TH
OR WHATEVER YOU
HOUSE, YOU HAVE MY
E TO DO.
-PEPE
this is betrayal!
how could he...
...for once he didn't call me kiddo.

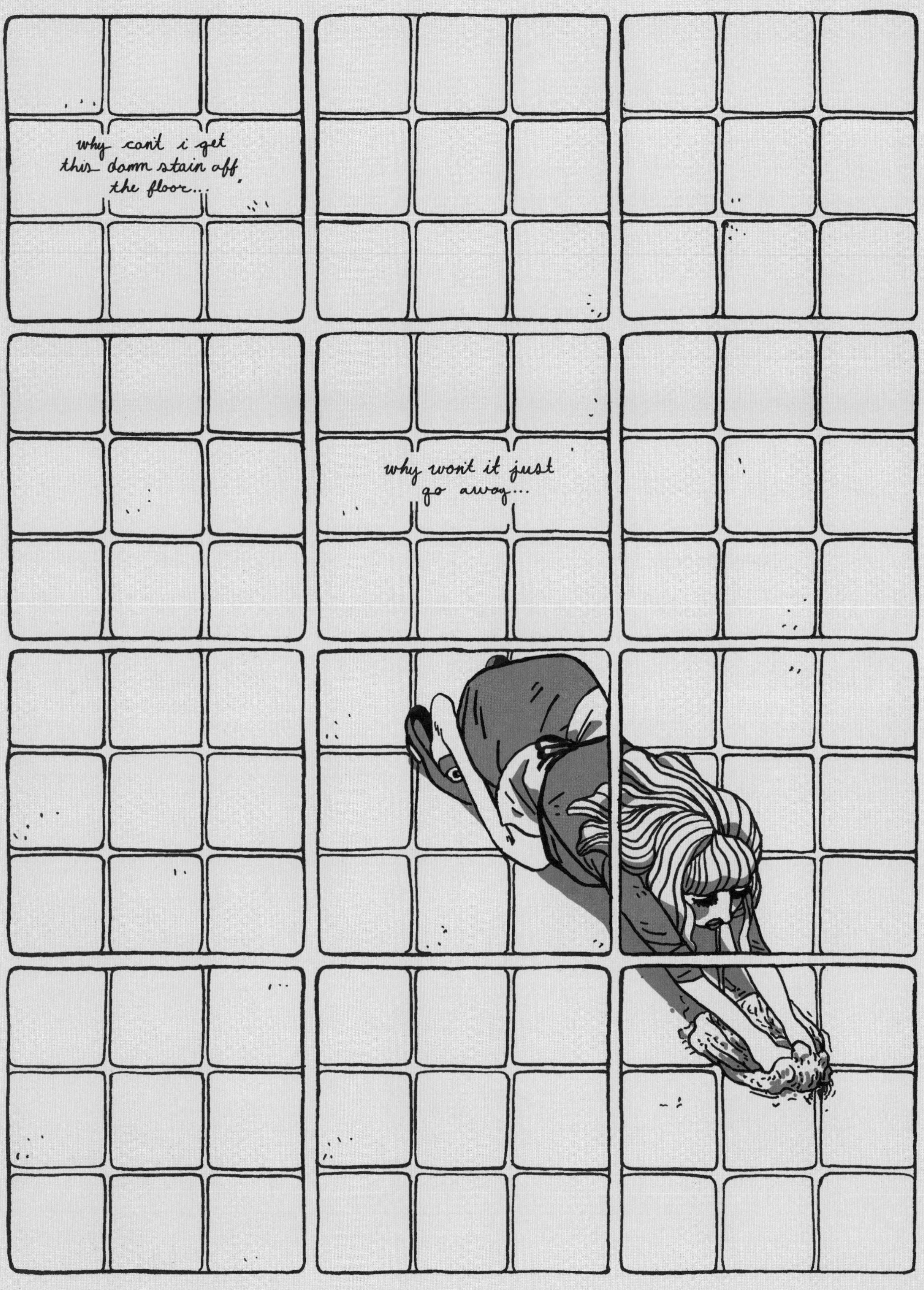
why can't i get this damn stain off the floor...
why won't it just go away...

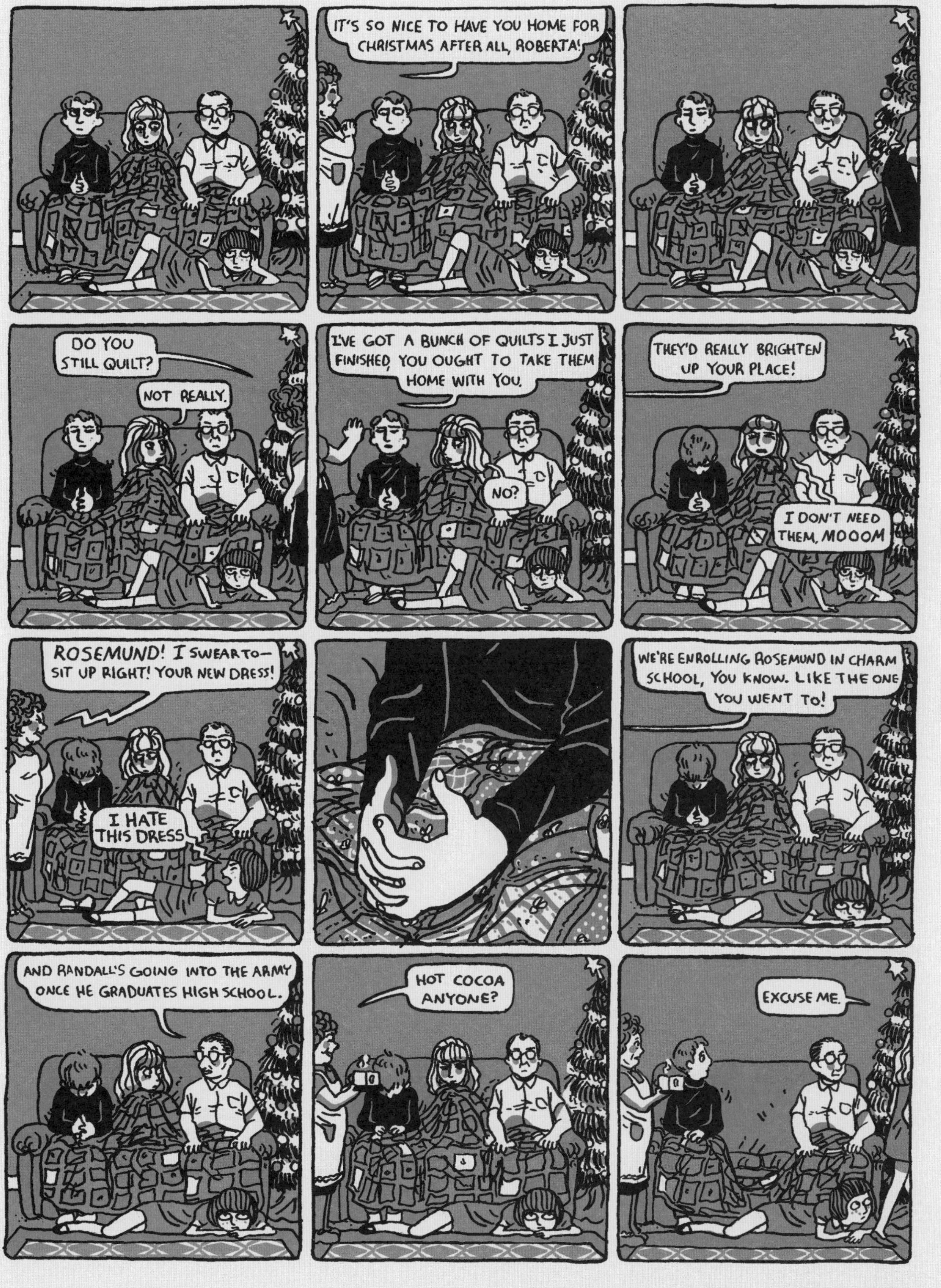
IT'S SO NICE TO HAVE YOU HOME FOR CHRISTMAS AFTER ALL, ROBERTA!
DO YOU STILL QUILT?
NOT REALLY.
I'VE GOT A BUNCH OF QUILTS I JUST FINISHED, YOU OUGHT TO TAKE THEM HOME WITH YOU.
NO?
THEY'D REALLY BRIGHTEN UP YOUR PLACE!
I DON'T NEED THEM, MOOOM
ROSEMUND! I SWEAR TO— SIT UP RIGHT! YOUR NEW DRESS!
I HATE THIS DRESS
WE'RE ENROLLING ROSEMUND IN CHARM SCHOOL, YOU KNOW. LIKE THE ONE YOU WENT TO!
AND RANDALL'S GOING INTO THE ARMY ONCE HE GRADUATES HIGH SCHOOL.
HOT COCOA ANYONE?
EXCUSE ME.

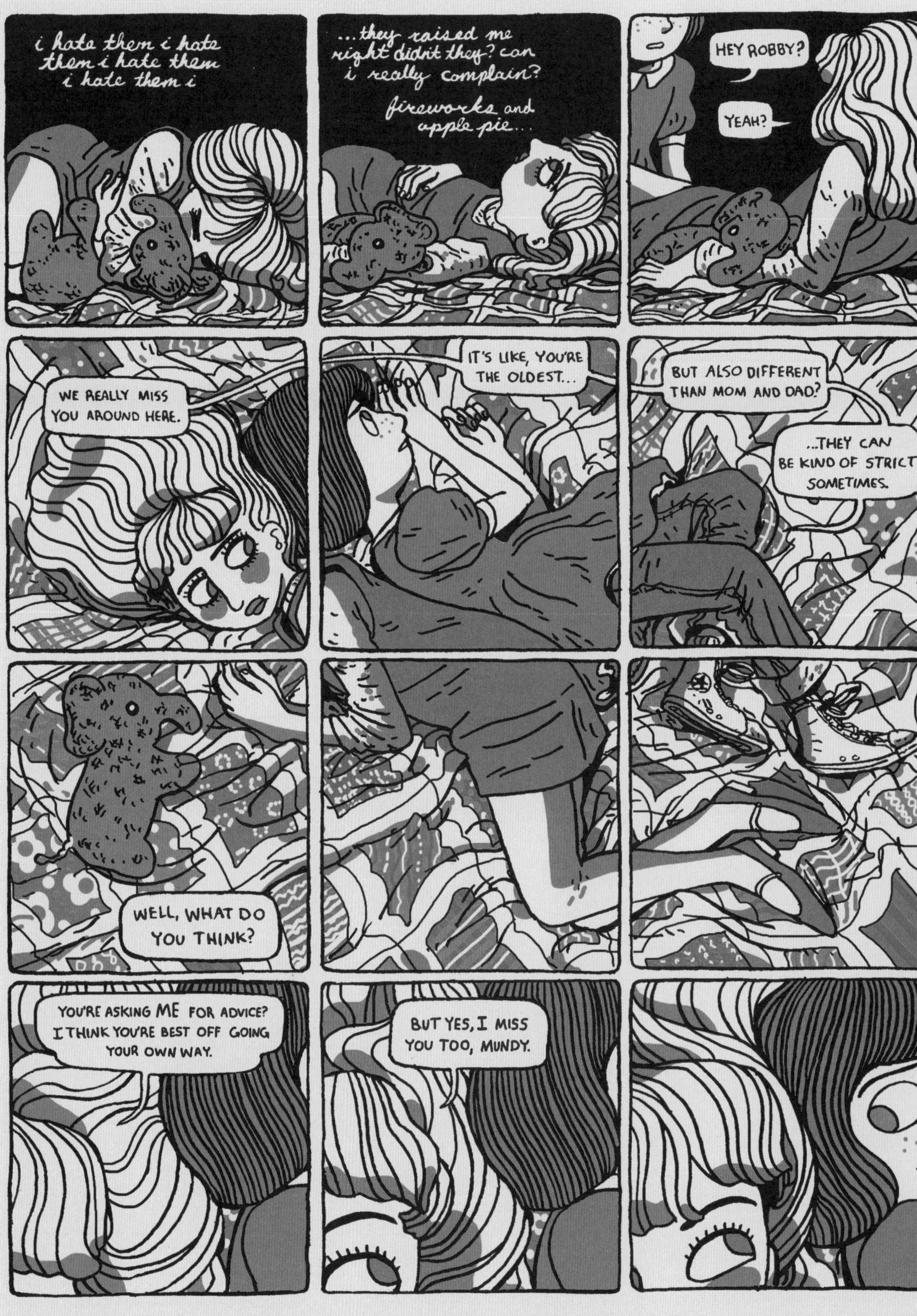
i hate them i hate them i hate them i hate them i
...they raised me right didn't they? can i really complain?
fireworks and apple pie...
HEY ROBBY?
YEAH?
WE REALLY MISS YOU AROUND HERE.
IT'S LIKE, YOU'RE THE OLDEST...
BUT ALSO DIFFERENT THAN MOM AND DAD?
...THEY CAN BE KIND OF STRICT SOMETIMES.
WELL, WHAT DO YOU THINK?
YOU'RE ASKING ME FOR ADVICE? I THINK YOU'RE BEST OFF GOING YOUR OWN WAY.
BUT YES, I MISS YOU TOO, MUNDY.

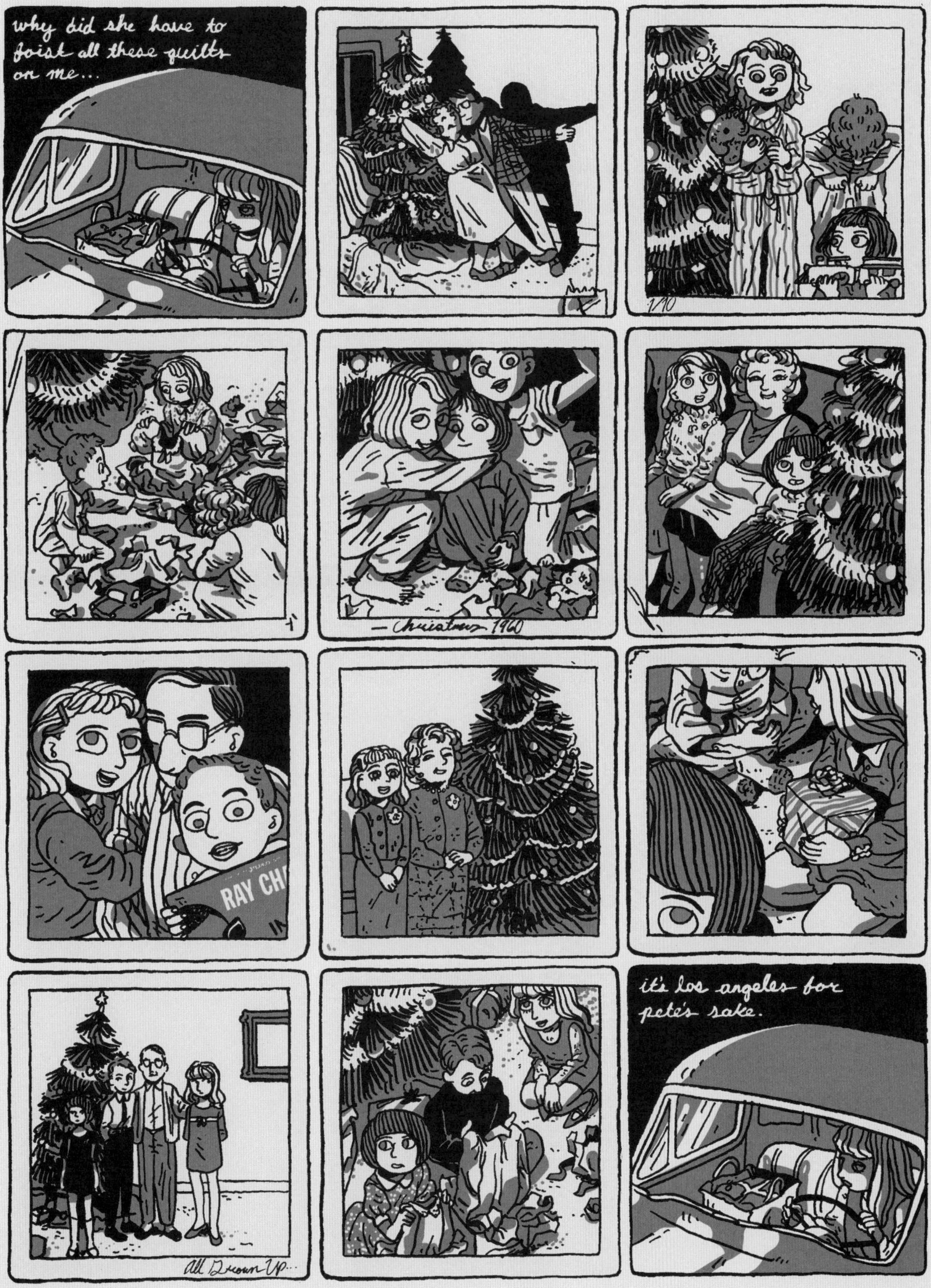
why did she have to foist all these quilts on me...
1/10
—Christmas 1960
RAY CH
All Grown Up...
it's los angeles for pete's sake.

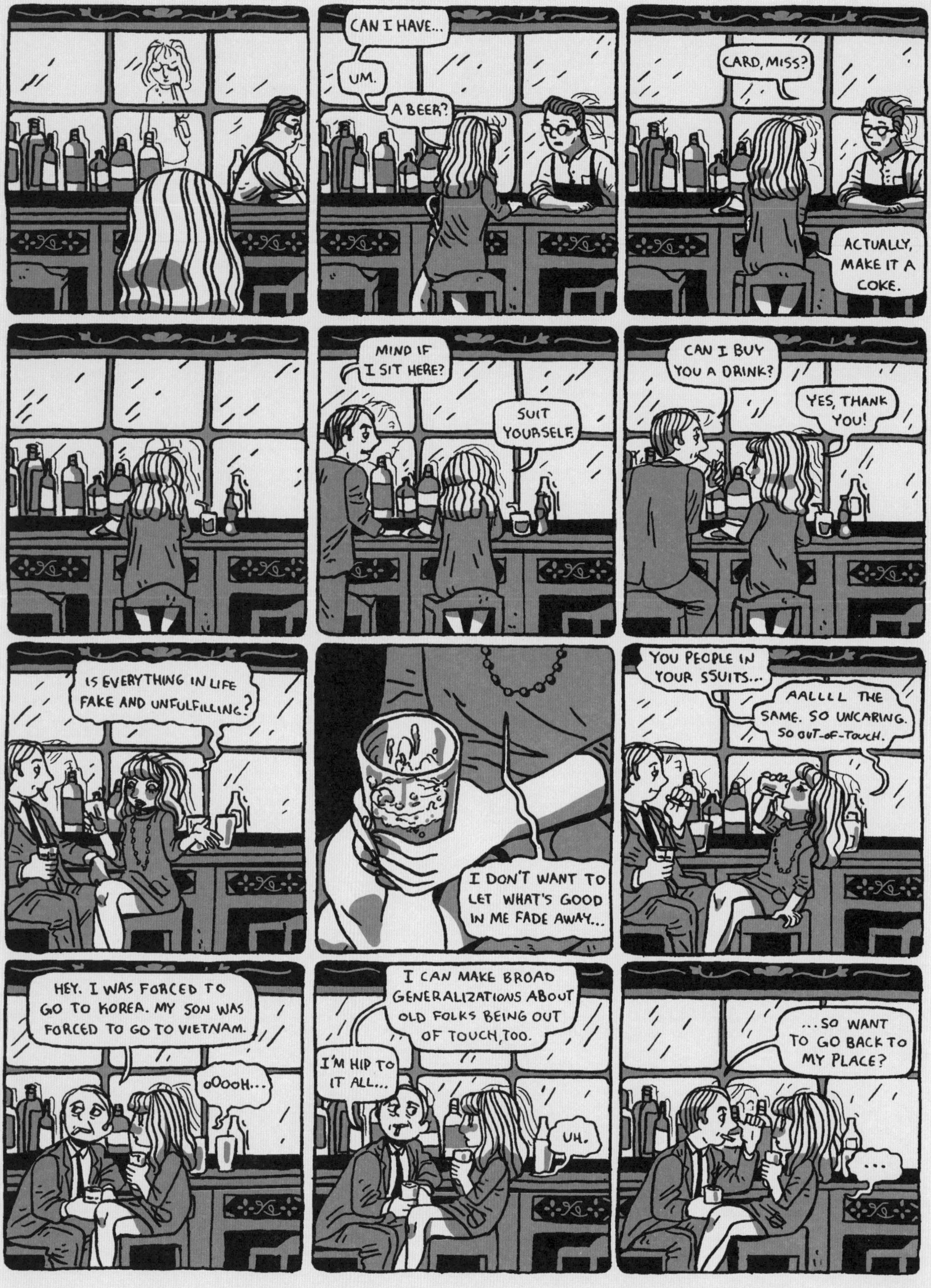
CAN I HAVE...
UM.
A BEER?
CARD, MISS?
ACTUALLY, MAKE IT A COKE.
MIND IF I SIT HERE?
SUIT YOURSELF.
CAN I BUY YOU A DRINK?
YES, THANK YOU!
IS EVERYTHING IN LIFE FAKE AND UNFULFILLING?
I DON'T WANT TO LET WHAT'S GOOD IN ME FADE AWAY...
YOU PEOPLE IN YOUR SSUITS...
AALLLL THE SAME. SO UNCARING. SO OUT-OF-TOUCH.
HEY. I WAS FORCED TO GO TO KOREA. MY SON WAS FORCED TO GO TO VIETNAM.
OOOOH...
I CAN MAKE BROAD GENERALIZATIONS ABOUT OLD FOLKS BEING OUT OF TOUCH, TOO.
I'M HIP TO IT ALL...
UH.
...SO WANT TO GO BACK TO MY PLACE?
...

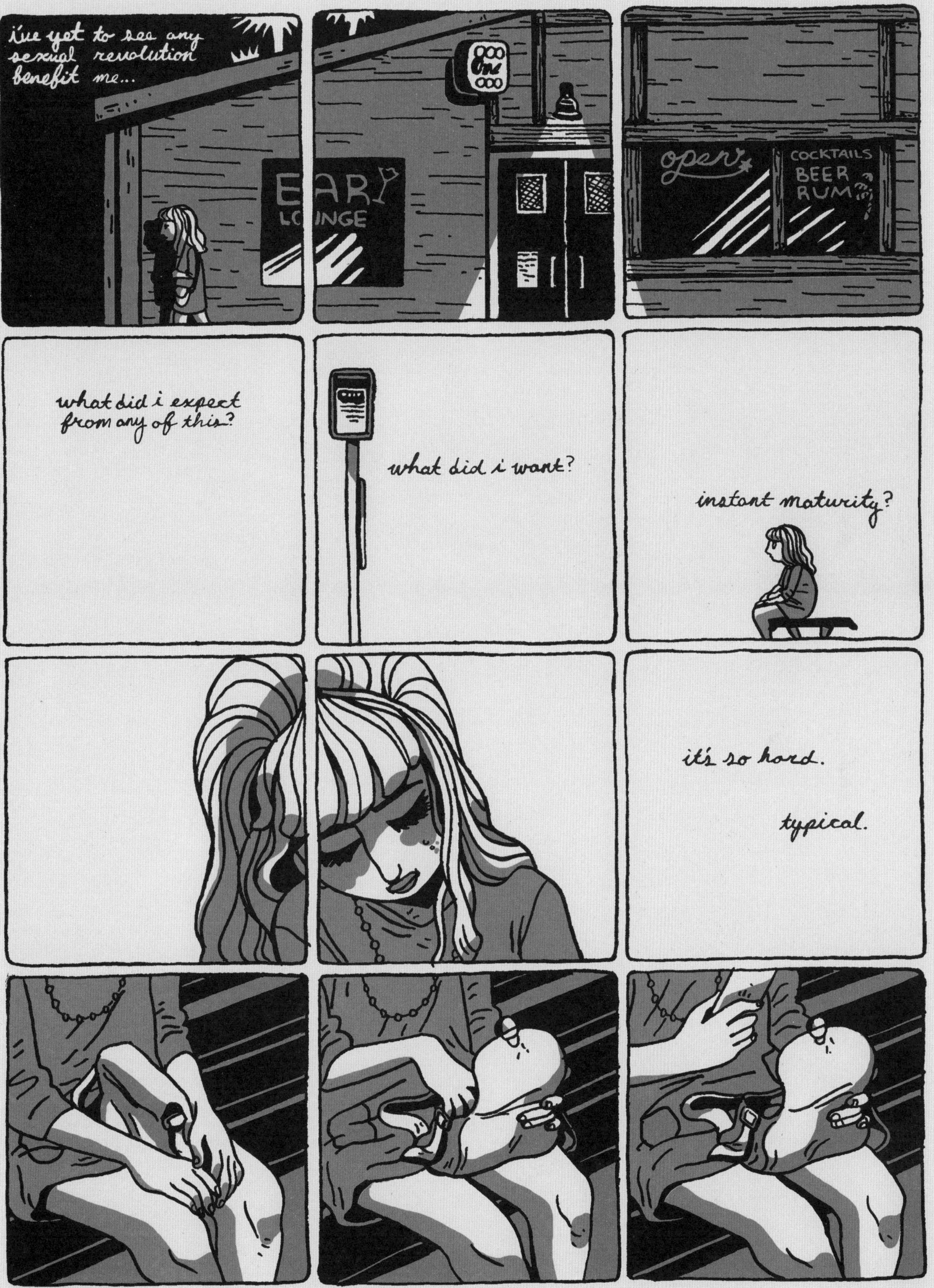

i've yet to see any sexual revolution benefit me...
COCKTAILS
BEER
RUM
what did i expect from any of this?
what did i want?
instant maturity?
it's so hard.
typical.

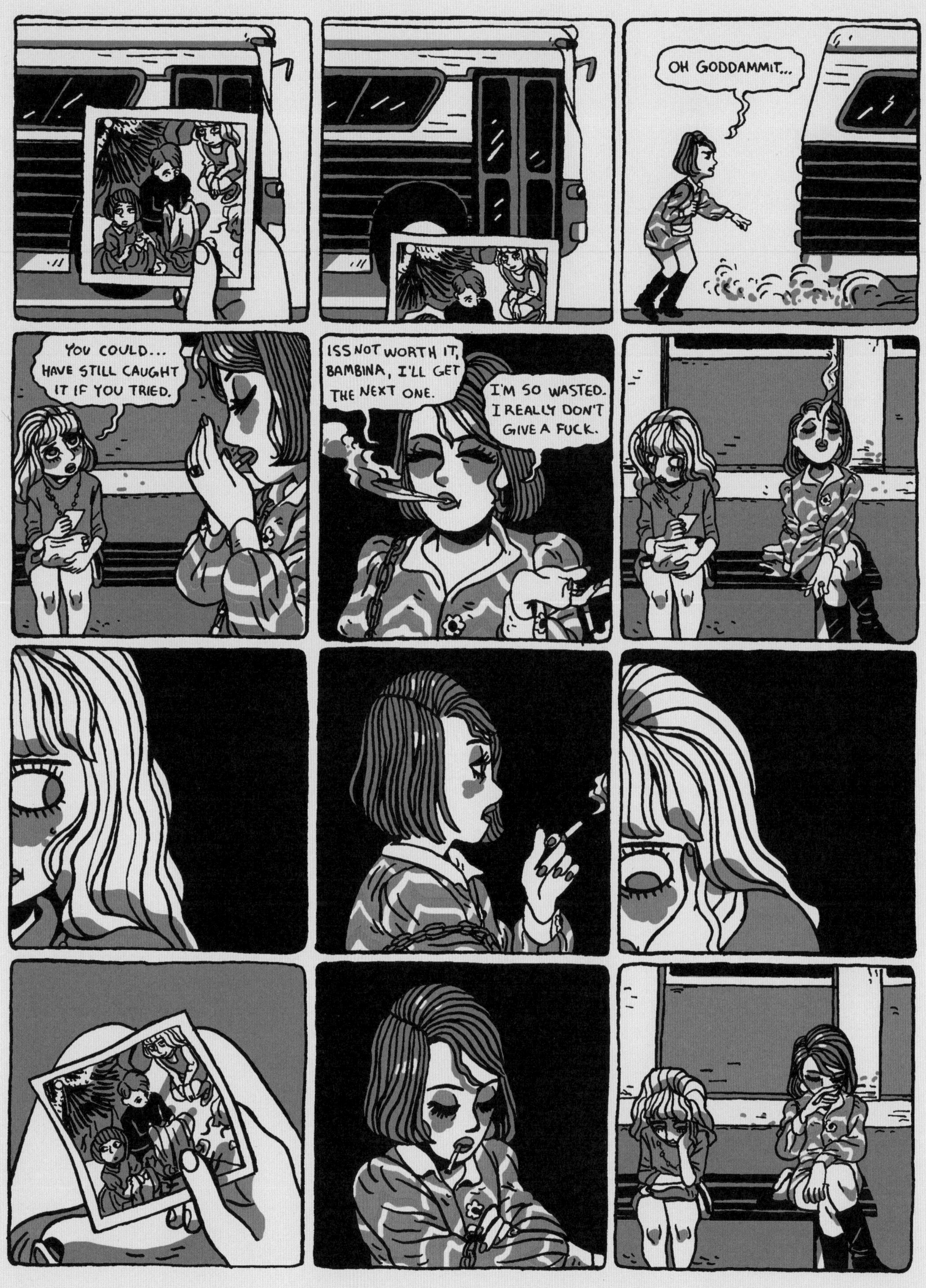
OH GODDAMMIT...
YOU COULD... HAVE STILL CAUGHT IT IF YOU TRIED.
ISS NOT WORTH IT, BAMBINA, I'LL GET THE NEXT ONE.
I'M SO WASTED. I REALLY DON'T GIVE A FUCK.

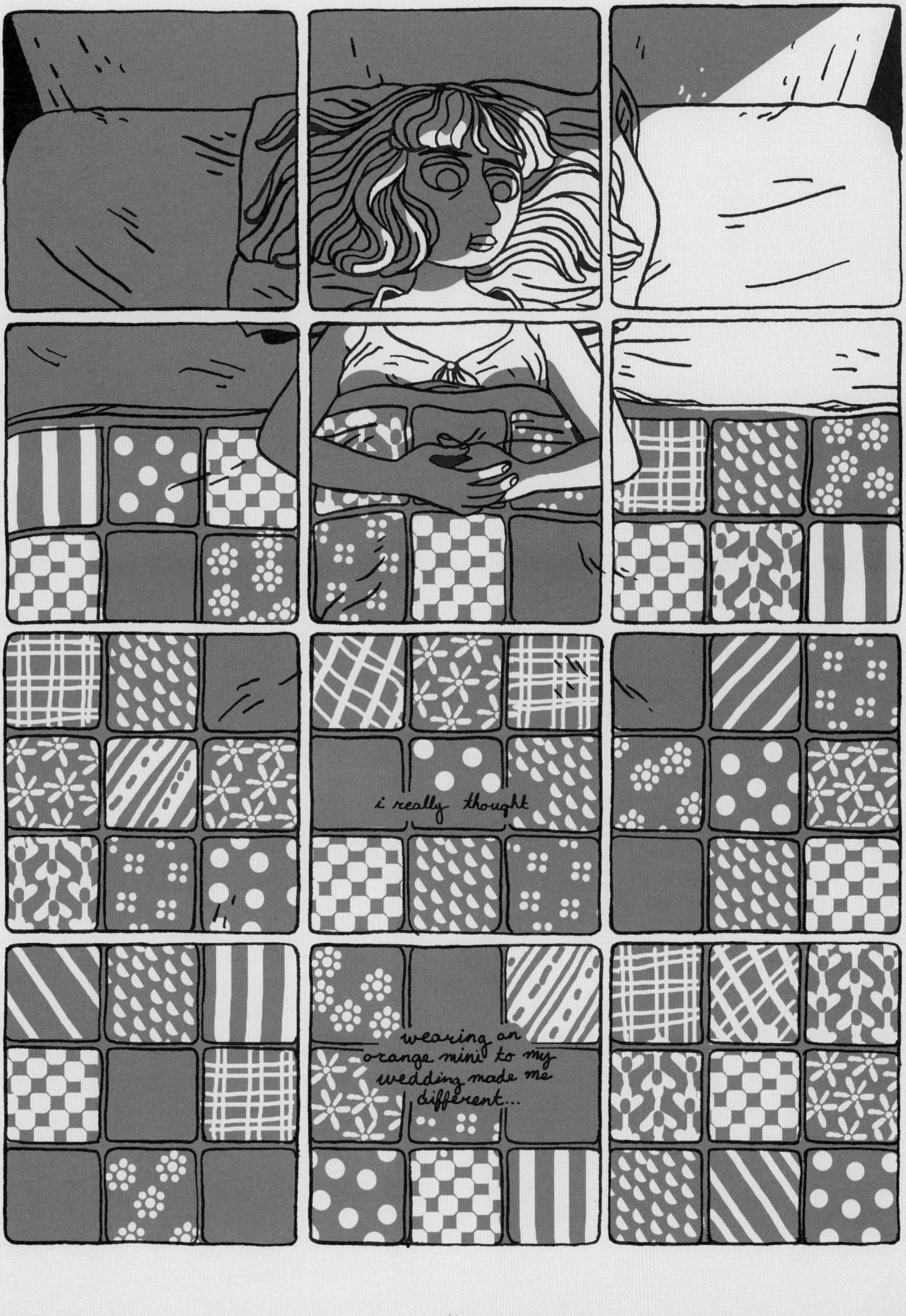
i really thought
wearing an orange mini to my wedding made me different...

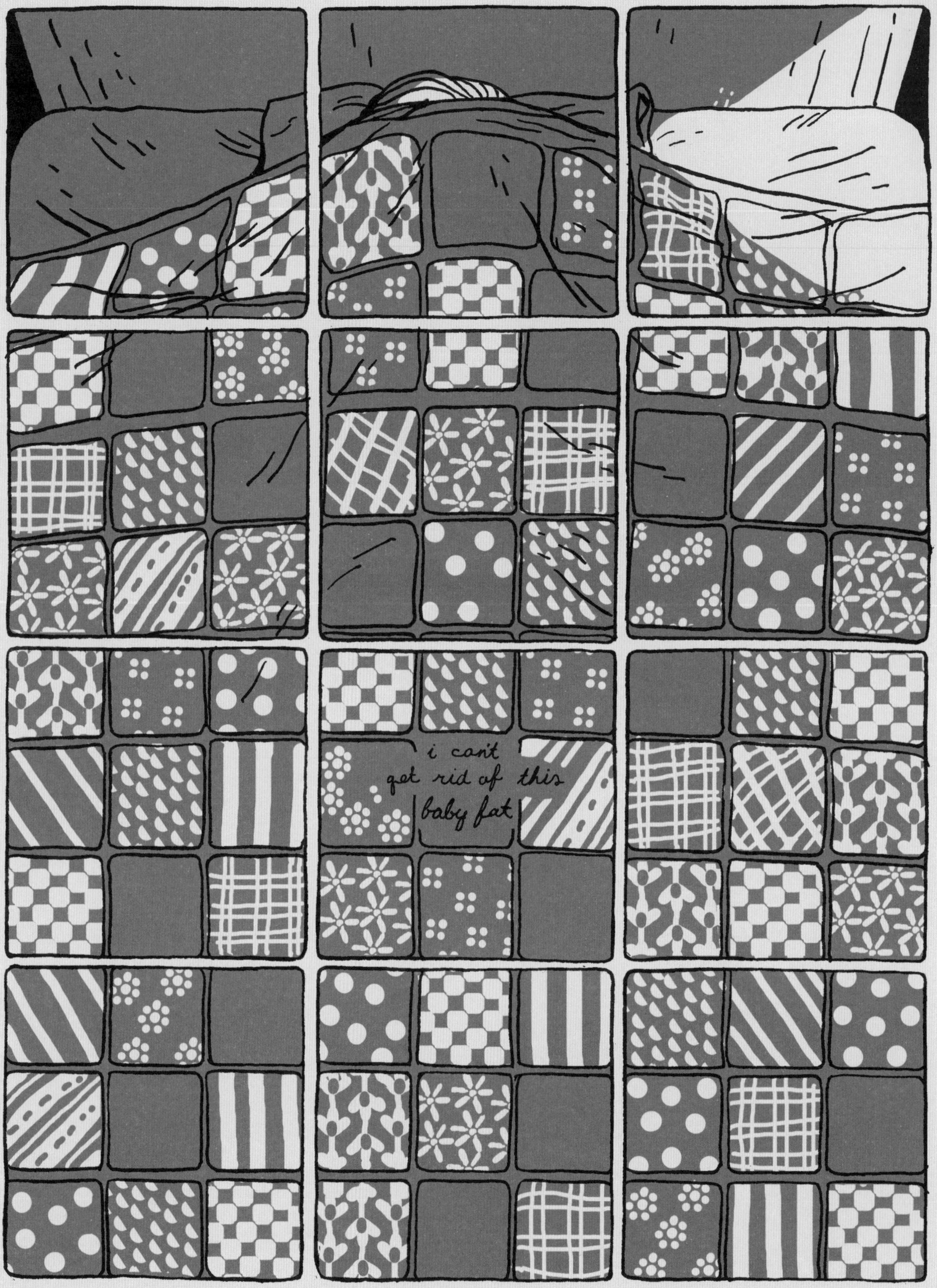
i can't get rid of this baby fat

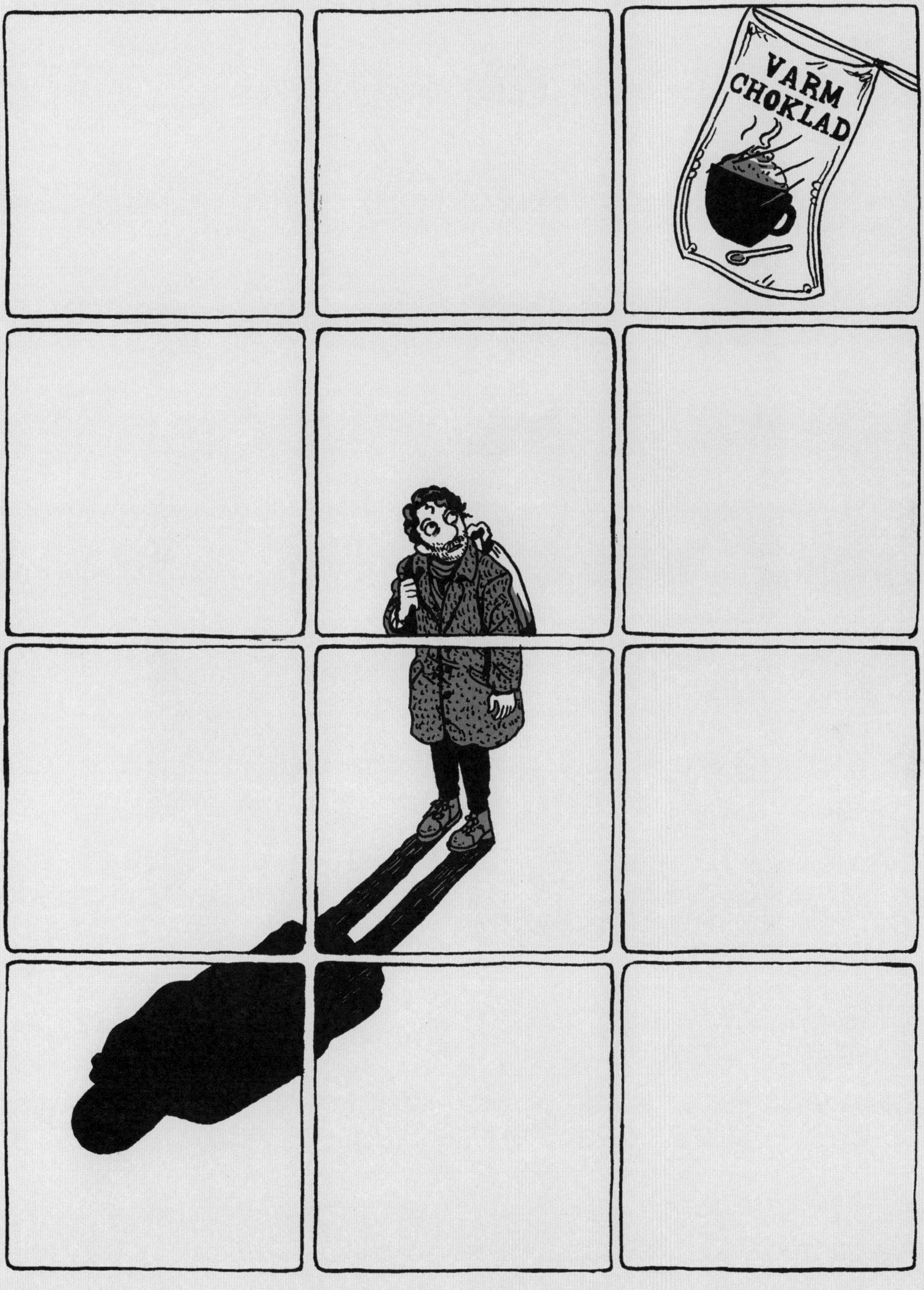
VARM
CHOKLAD

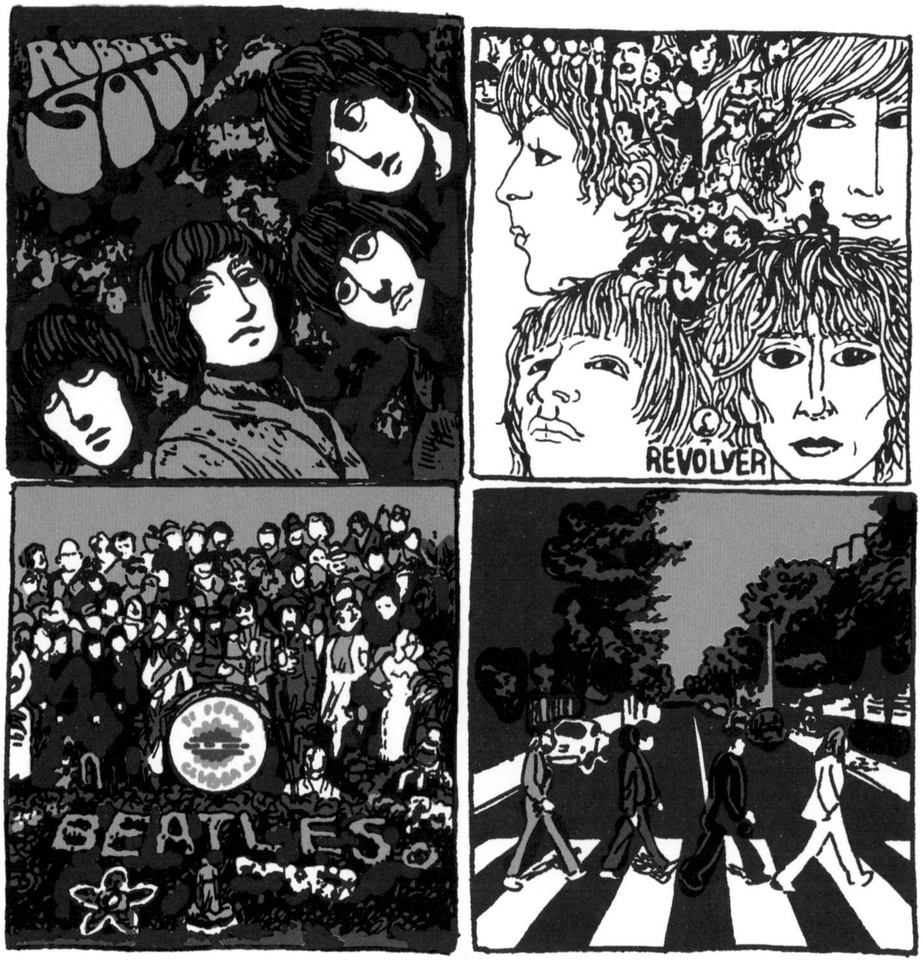
RUBBER SOUL
REVOLVER
BEATLES

Dear George,

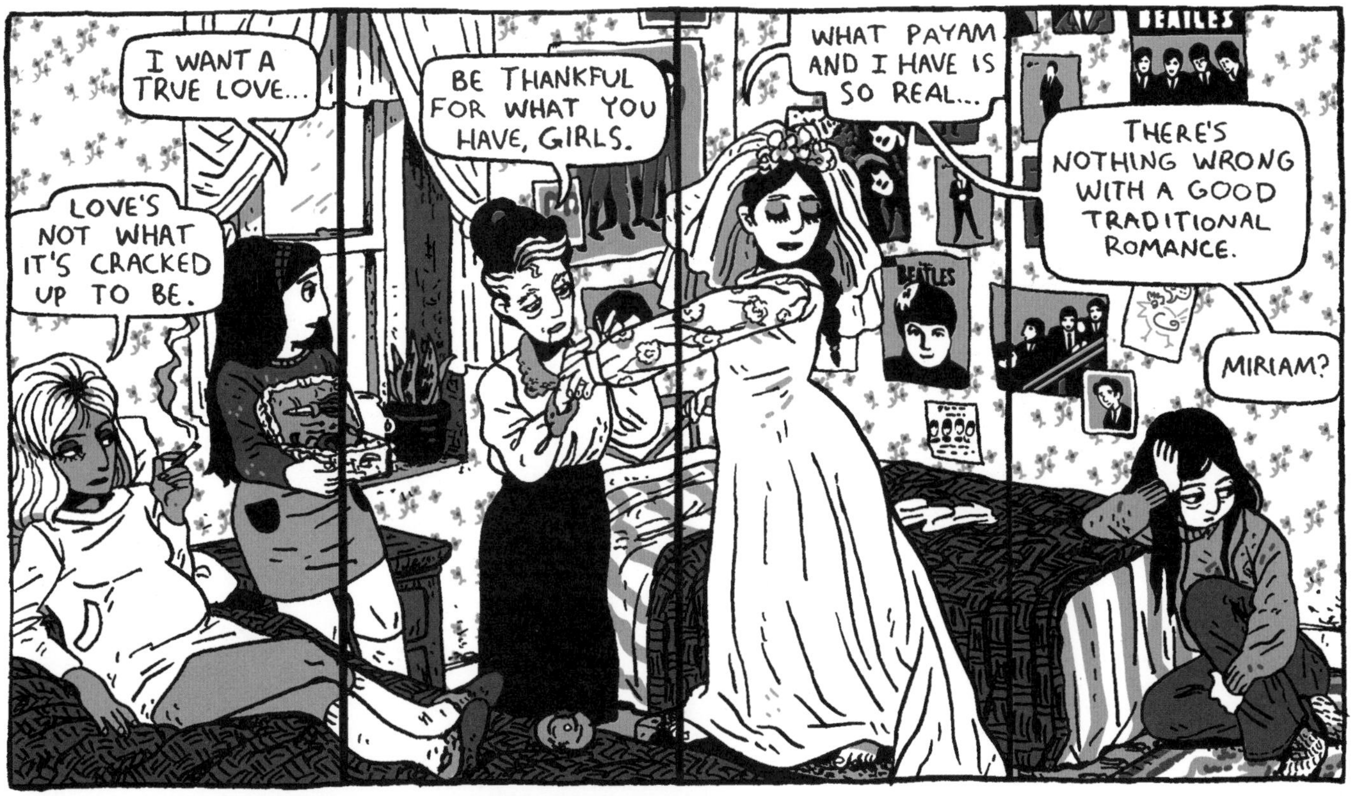
I WANT A TRUE LOVE...
LOVE'S NOT WHAT IT'S CRACKED UP TO BE.
BE THANKFUL FOR WHAT YOU HAVE, GIRLS.
WHAT PAYAM AND I HAVE IS SO REAL...
THERE'S NOTHING WRONG WITH A GOOD TRADITIONAL ROMANCE.
MIRIAM?
BEATLES
BEATLES

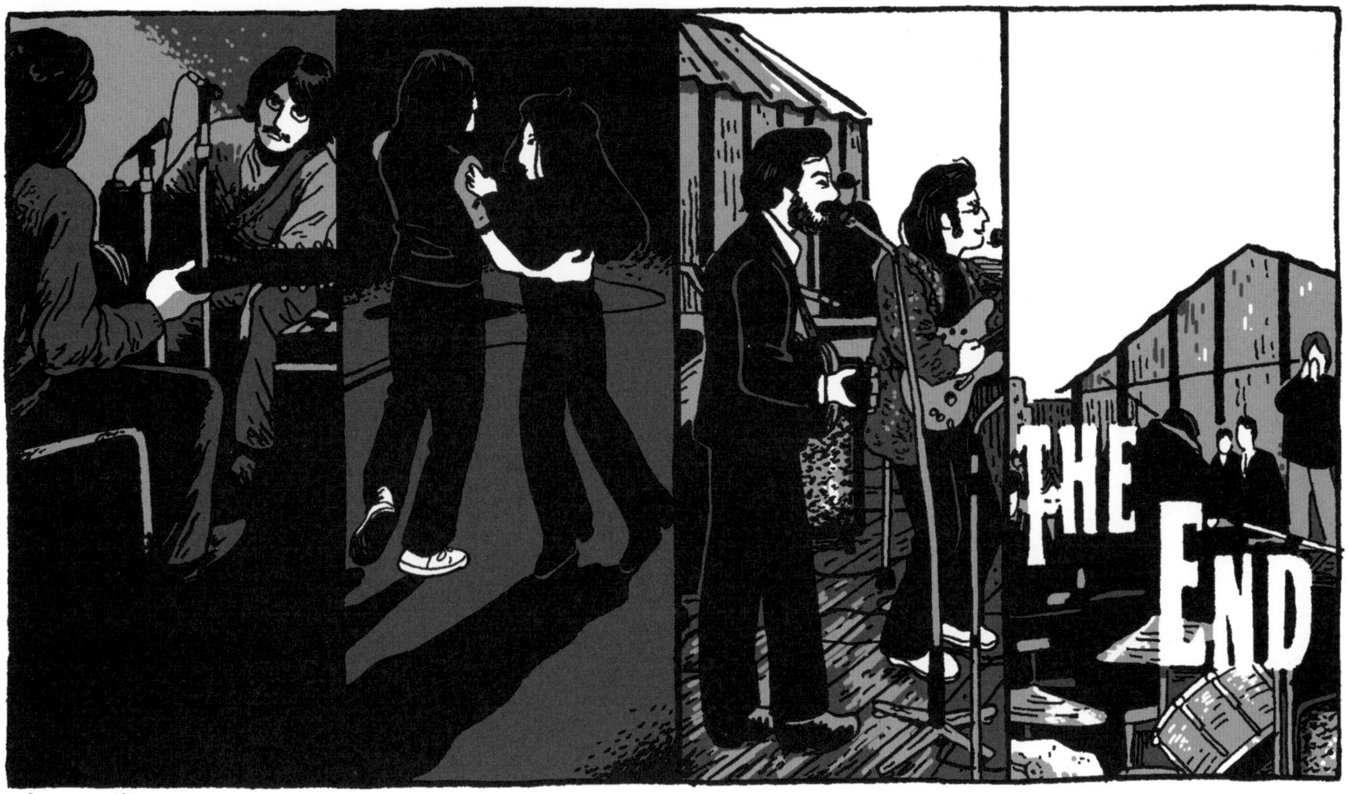
THE END

Dear Mir,

Sometimes...
the distance between us
feels more than physical.

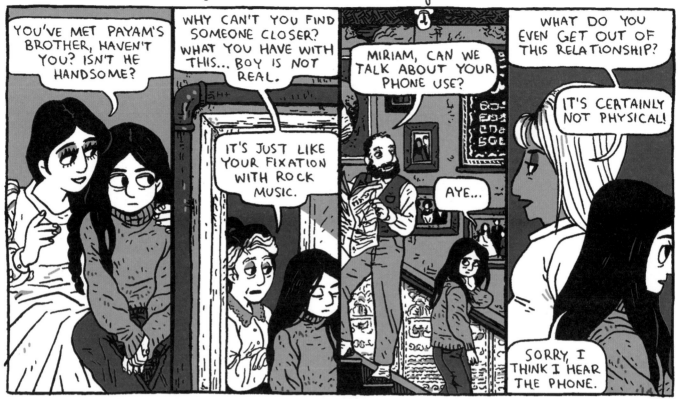

YOU'VE MET PAYAM'S BROTHER, HAVEN'T YOU? ISN'T HE HANDSOME?

WHY CAN'T YOU FIND SOMEONE CLOSER? WHAT YOU HAVE WITH THIS... BOY IS NOT REAL.

IT'S JUST LIKE YOUR FIXATION WITH ROCK MUSIC.

MIRIAM, CAN WE TALK ABOUT YOUR PHONE USE?

AYE...

WHAT DO YOU EVEN GET OUT OF THIS RELATIONSHIP?

IT'S CERTAINLY NOT PHYSICAL!

SORRY, I THINK I HEAR THE PHONE.

THE BEAT

"Let it be

TELEPHONE

You're asking
a lot of me again...

46

I really believe being together will make it better. We can be ourselves.

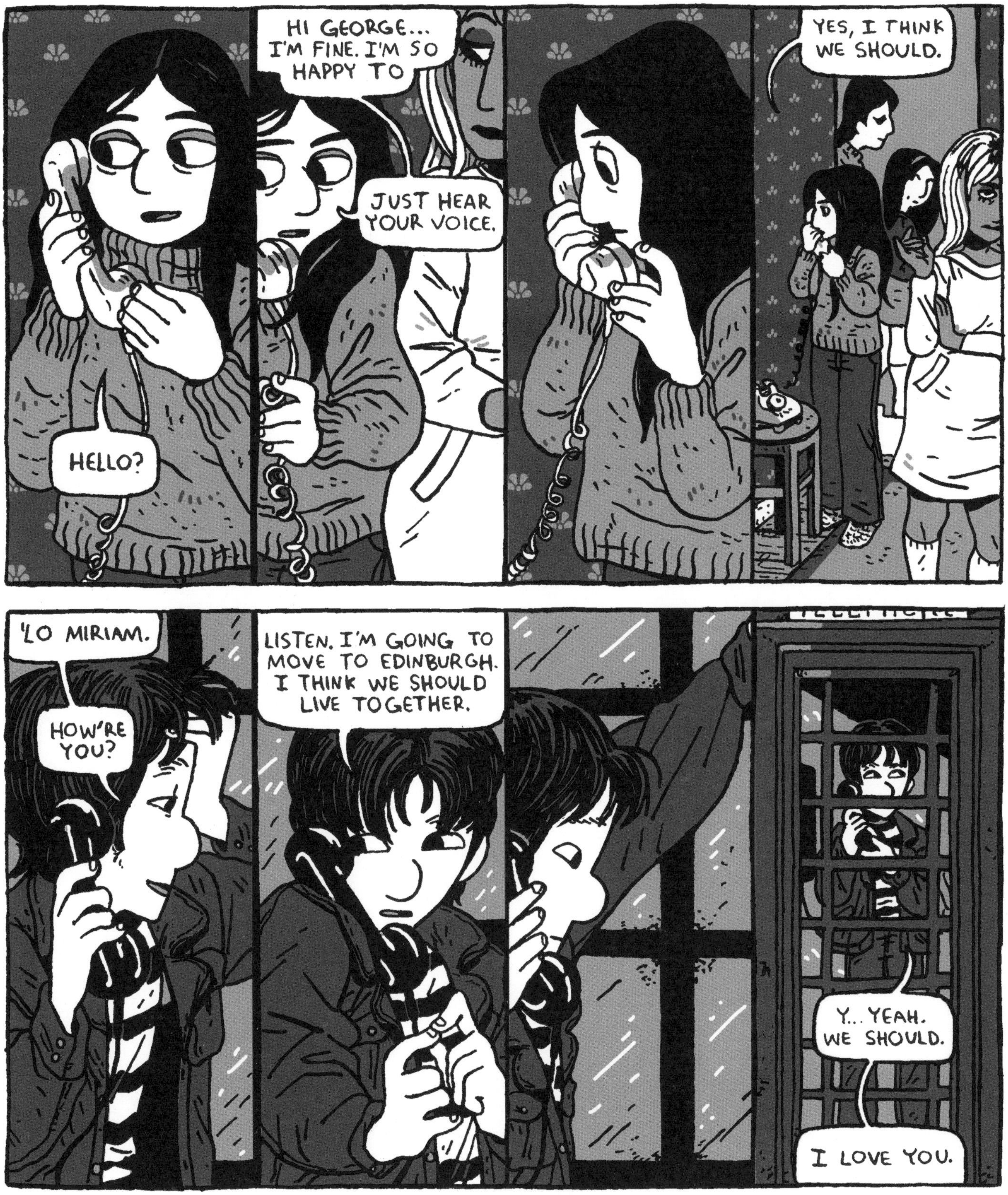
HELLO?
HI GEORGE... I'M FINE. I'M SO HAPPY TO
JUST HEAR YOUR VOICE.
YES, I THINK WE SHOULD.
'LO MIRIAM.
HOW'RE YOU?
LISTEN. I'M GOING TO MOVE TO EDINBURGH. I THINK WE SHOULD LIVE TOGETHER.
Y... YEAH. WE SHOULD.
I LOVE YOU.

I have your letters. I want more of you... but I want my freedom too.

I want it to be just like when we first met...

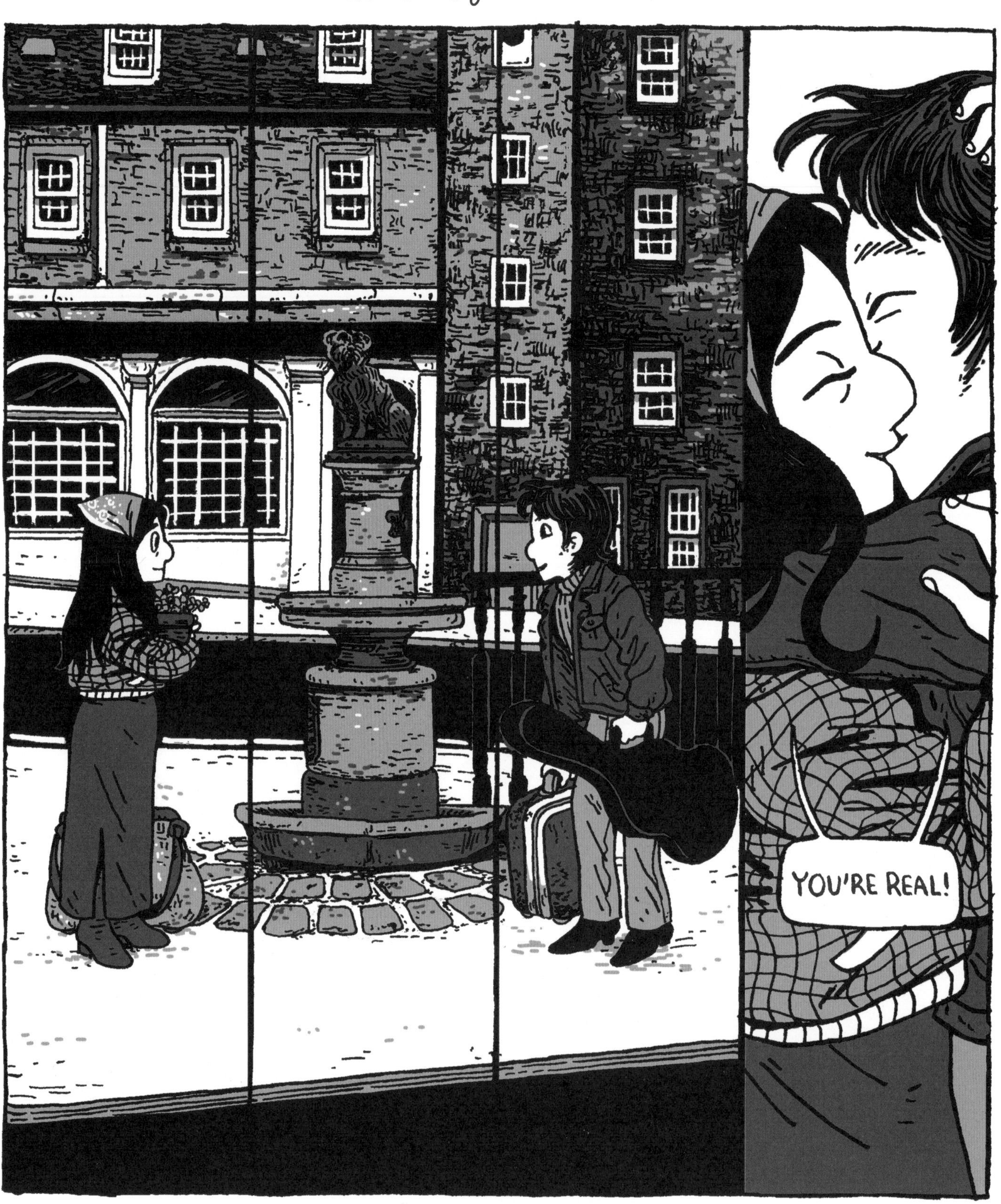
YOU'RE REAL!

I want too many things... I want to touch you, be close to you.

Are you just like the boy in the pictures you send me?

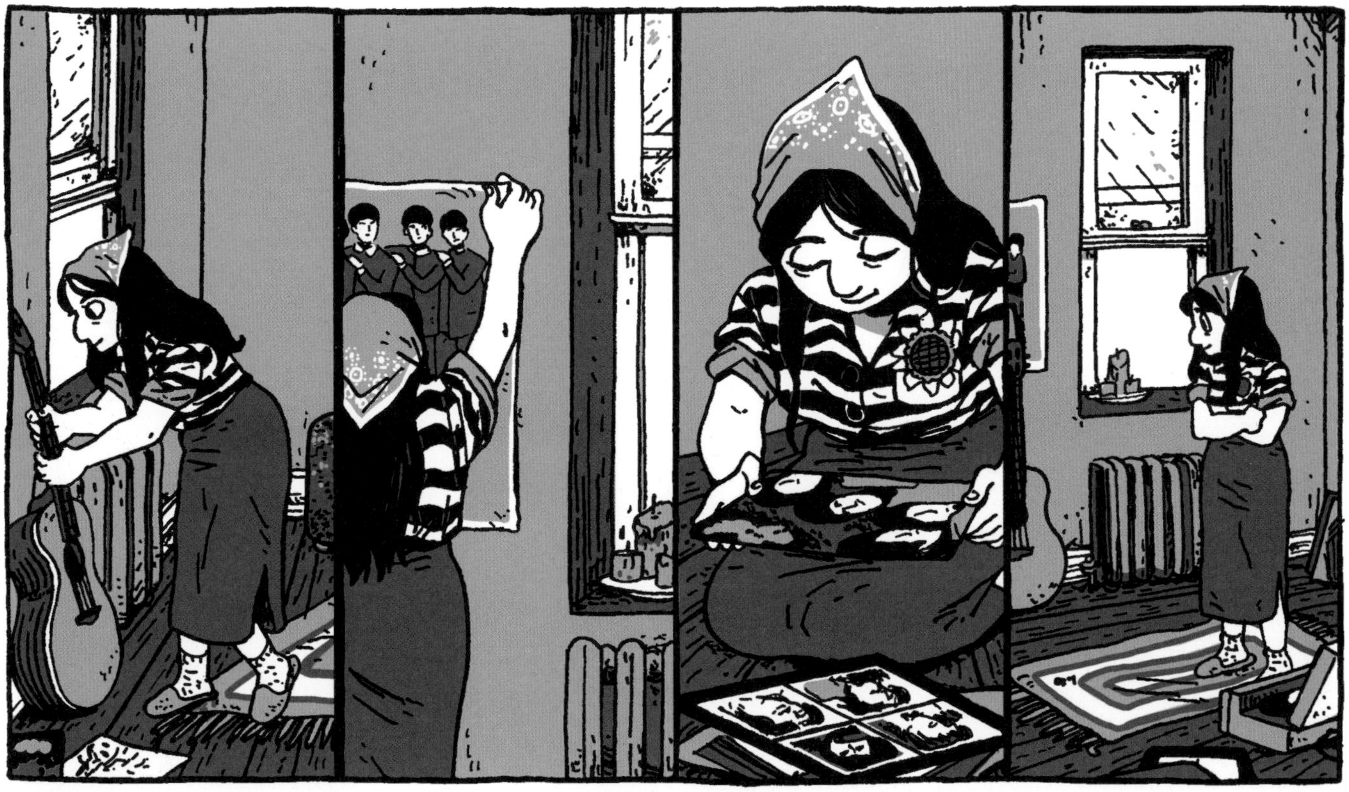

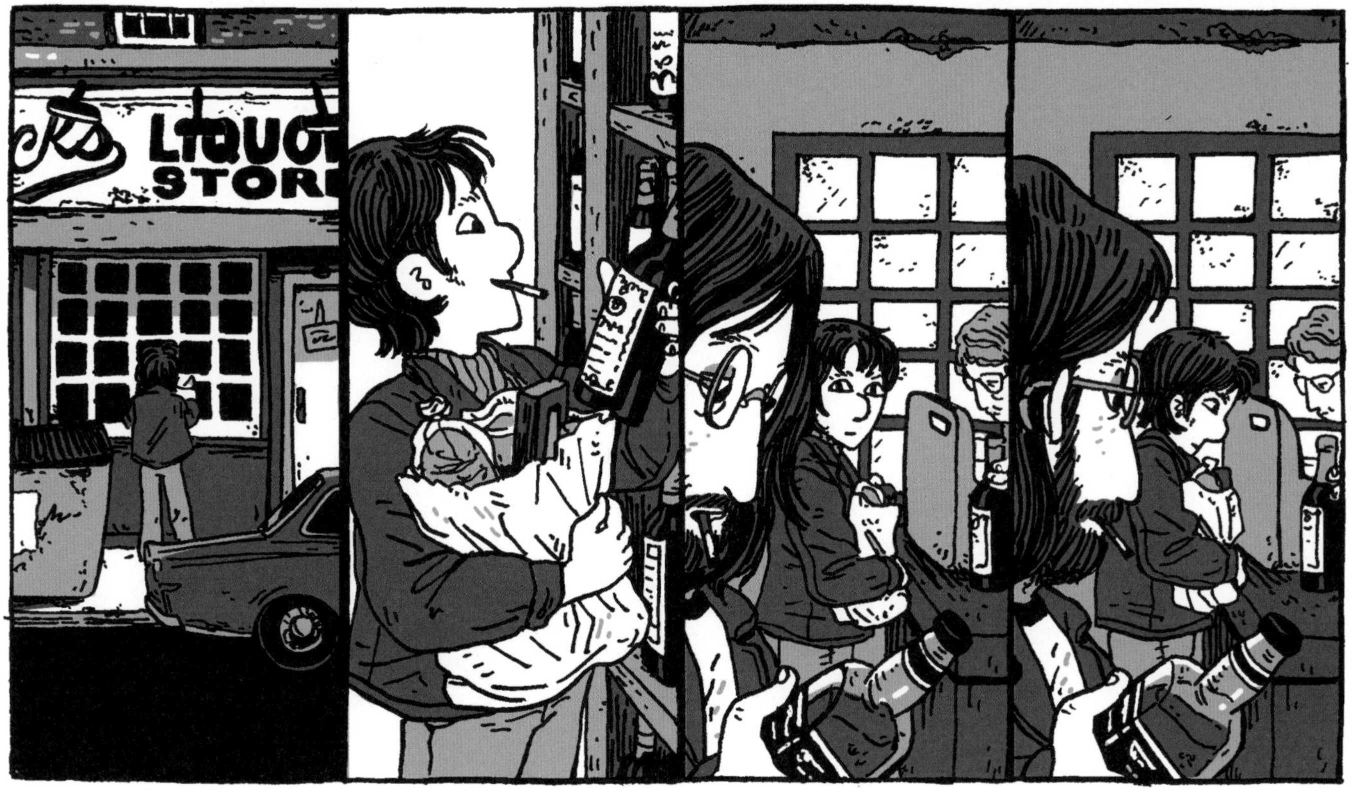
LIQUO
STOR

But I don't know if that's always enough. We're not kids.

There's so many things we've never had. We can get our own room, even a telly.

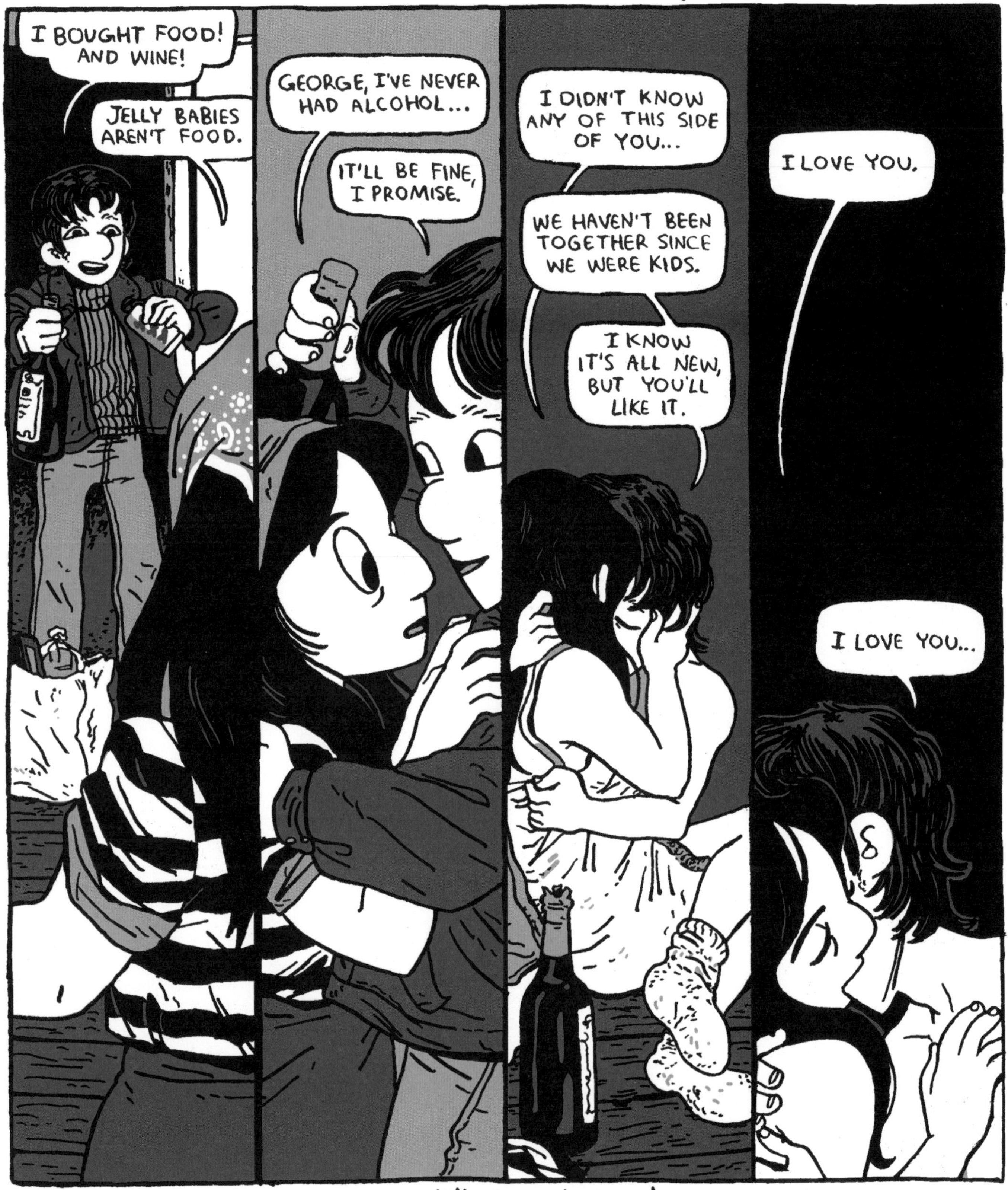
I BOUGHT FOOD! AND WINE!
JELLY BABIES AREN'T FOOD.
GEORGE, I'VE NEVER HAD ALCOHOL...
IT'LL BE FINE, I PROMISE.
I DIDN'T KNOW ANY OF THIS SIDE OF YOU...
WE HAVEN'T BEEN TOGETHER SINCE WE WERE KIDS.
I KNOW IT'S ALL NEW, BUT YOU'LL LIKE IT.
I LOVE YOU.
I LOVE YOU...

You're still immature and obsessive. I don't think you know anything about the world.

It's so easy for you, you've
had everything you ever wanted
and don't even enjoy it.

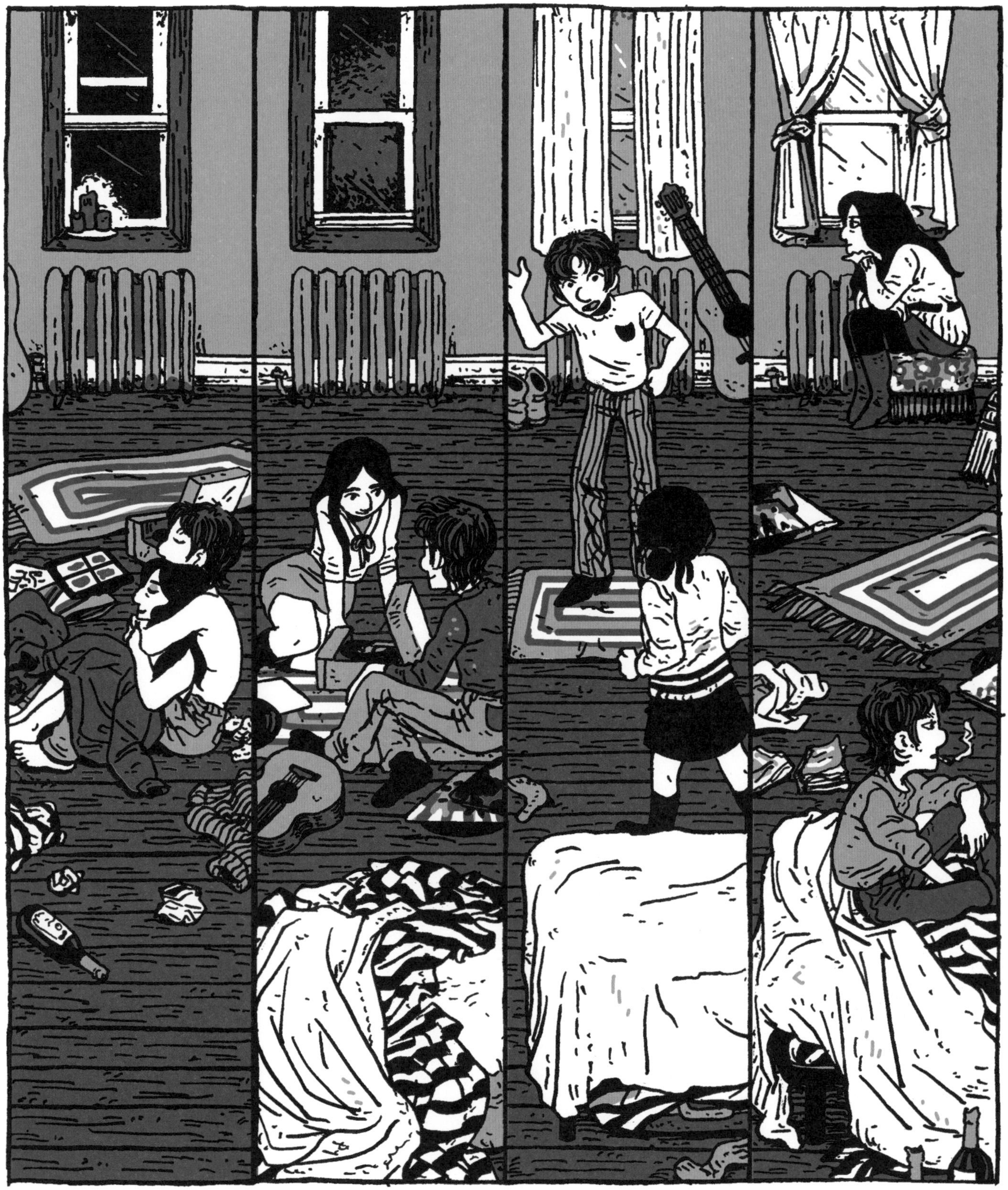

I want to put good in the world.
I want you to be happy, too.

Do I make you happy enough?

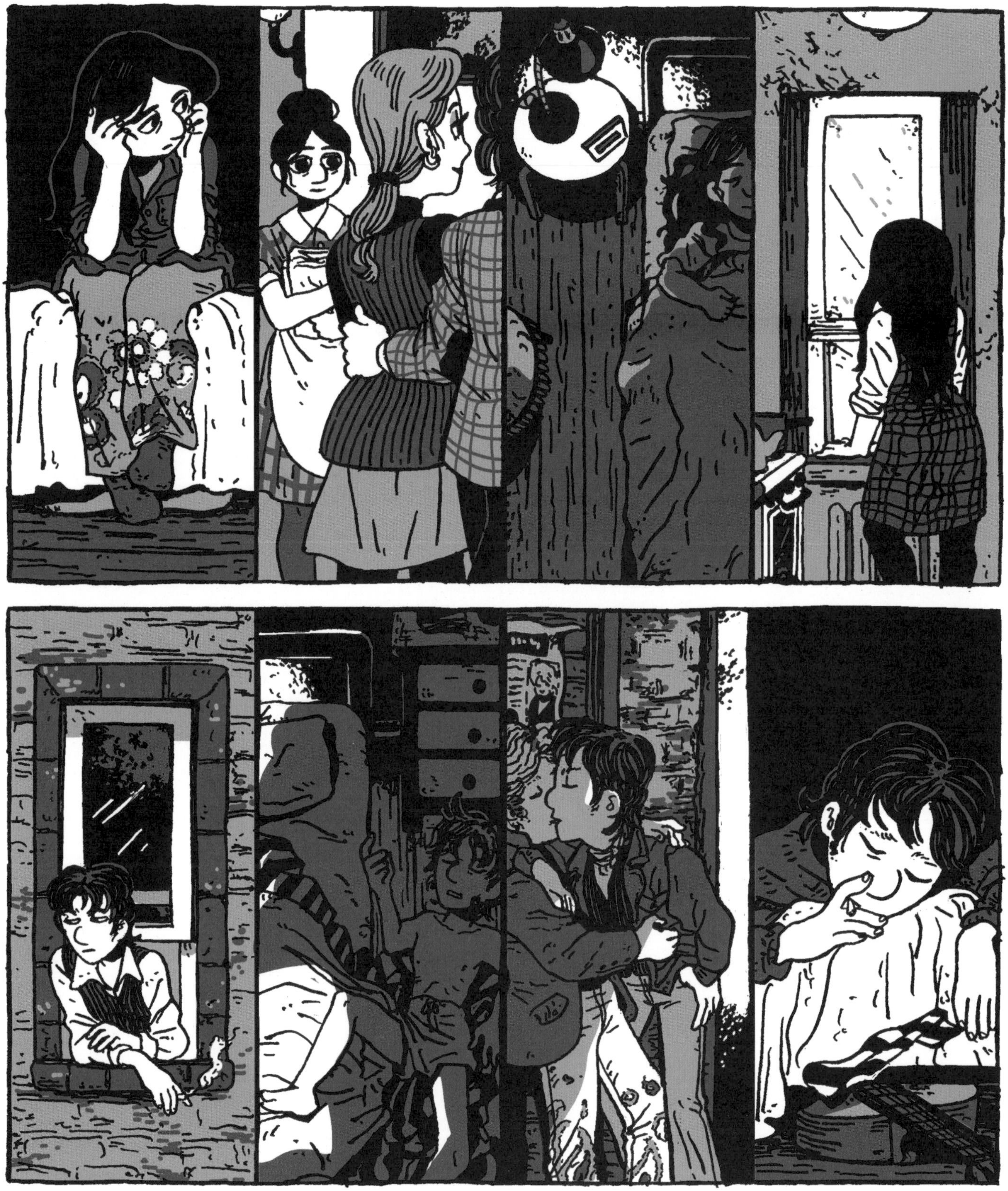

And God!... If you only knew
how much I need you...

you still make me happy...

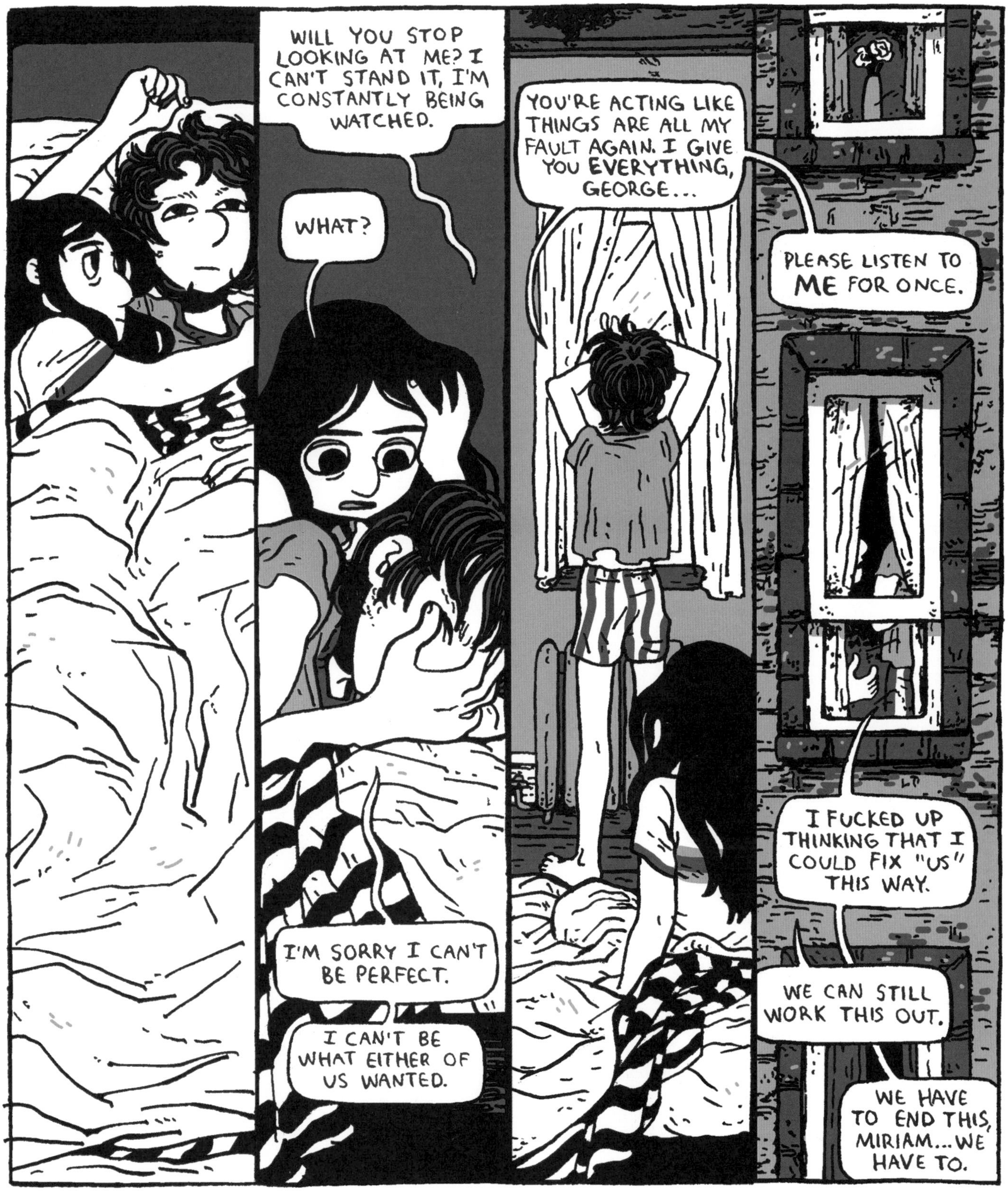
WILL YOU STOP LOOKING AT ME? I CAN'T STAND IT, I'M CONSTANTLY BEING WATCHED.
WHAT?
I'M SORRY I CAN'T BE PERFECT.
I CAN'T BE WHAT EITHER OF US WANTED.
YOU'RE ACTING LIKE THINGS ARE ALL MY FAULT AGAIN. I GIVE YOU EVERYTHING, GEORGE...
PLEASE LISTEN TO ME FOR ONCE.
I FUCKED UP THINKING THAT I COULD FIX "US" THIS WAY.
WE CAN STILL WORK THIS OUT.
WE HAVE TO END THIS, MIRIAM... WE HAVE TO.

What am I without you?

Love,
Miriam

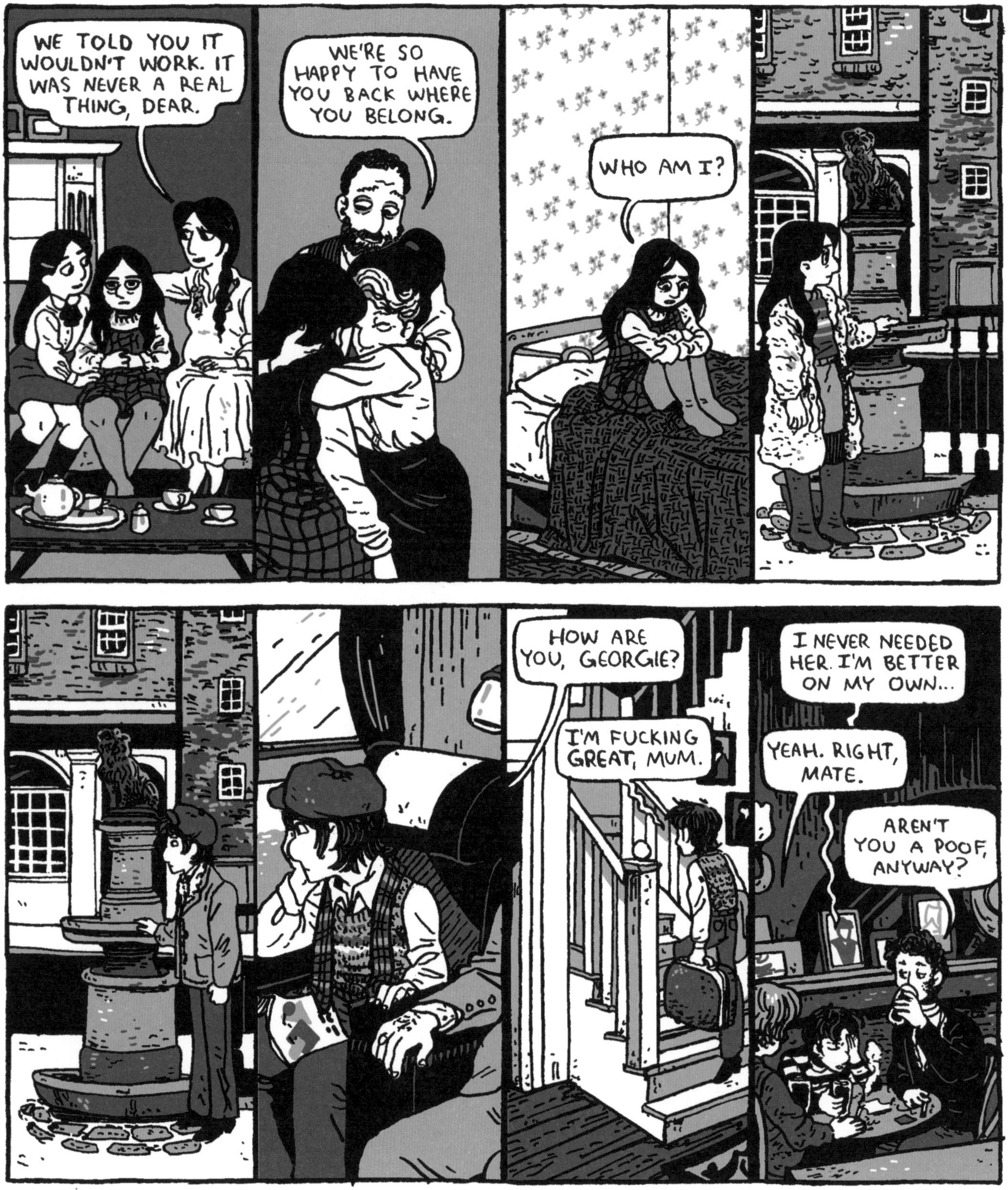
WE TOLD YOU IT WOULDN'T WORK. IT WAS NEVER A REAL THING, DEAR.
WE'RE SO HAPPY TO HAVE YOU BACK WHERE YOU BELONG.
WHO AM I?
HOW ARE YOU, GEORGIE?
I'M FUCKING GREAT, MUM.
I NEVER NEEDED HER. I'M BETTER ON MY OWN...
YEAH. RIGHT, MATE.
AREN'T YOU A POOF, ANYWAY?

Love,
George

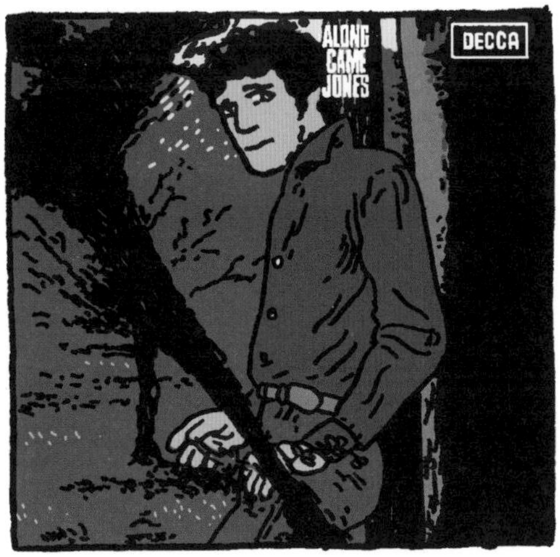
ALONG CAME JONES
DECCA

"K.M. & R.P.
& MCMLXXL
(1971)"

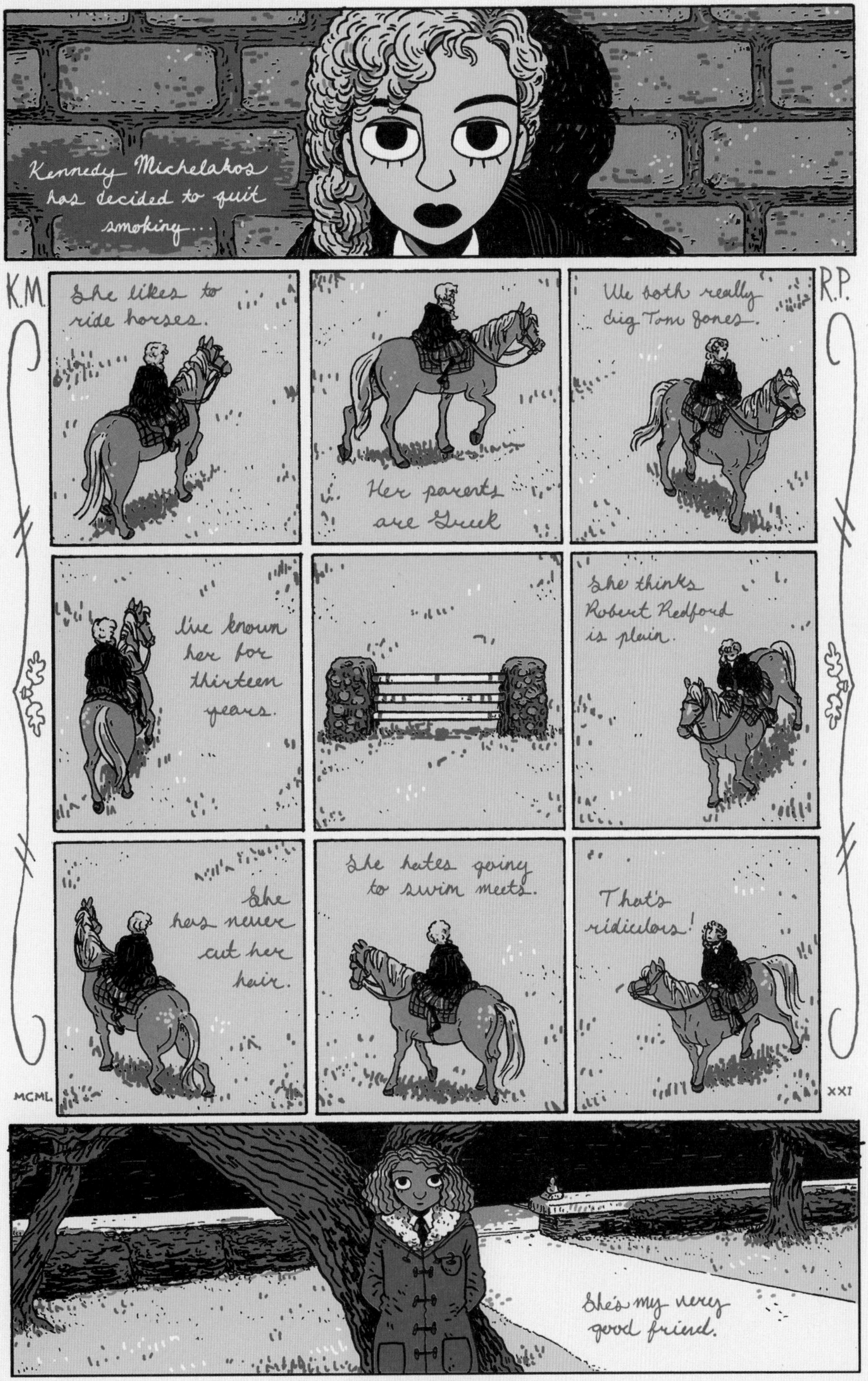
Kennedy Michelakos has decided to quit smoking...
K.M.
R.P.
She likes to ride horses.
Her parents are Greek
We both really dig Tom Jones.
I've known her for thirteen years.
She thinks Robert Redford is plain.
She has never cut her hair.
She hates going to swim meets.
That's ridiculous!
MCML
XXI
She's my very good friend.

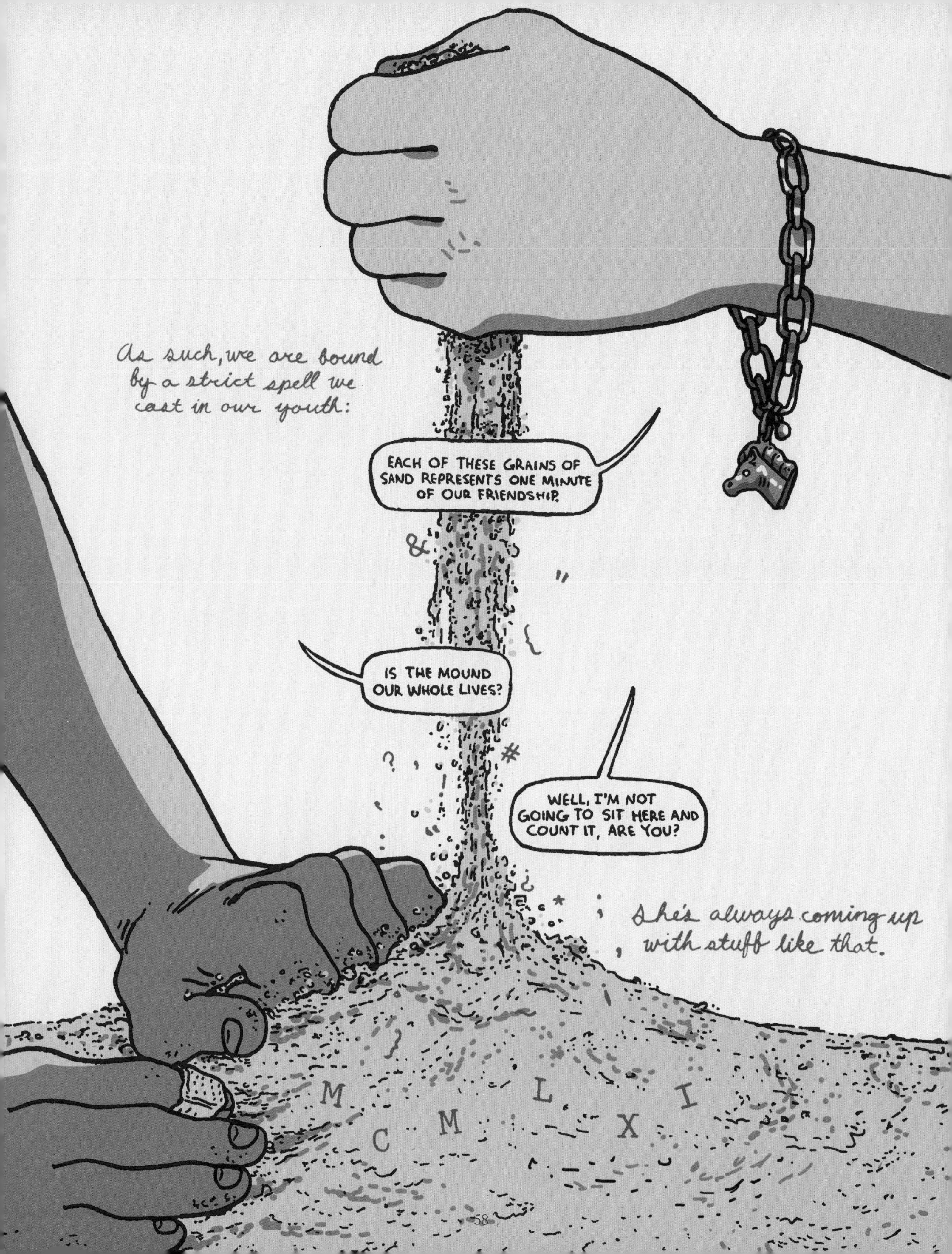
As such, we are bound by a strict spell we cast in our youth:
EACH OF THESE GRAINS OF SAND REPRESENTS ONE MINUTE OF OUR FRIENDSHIP.
IS THE MOUND OUR WHOLE LIVES?
WELL, I'M NOT GOING TO SIT HERE AND COUNT IT, ARE YOU?
She's always coming up with stuff like that.
MCMLXI

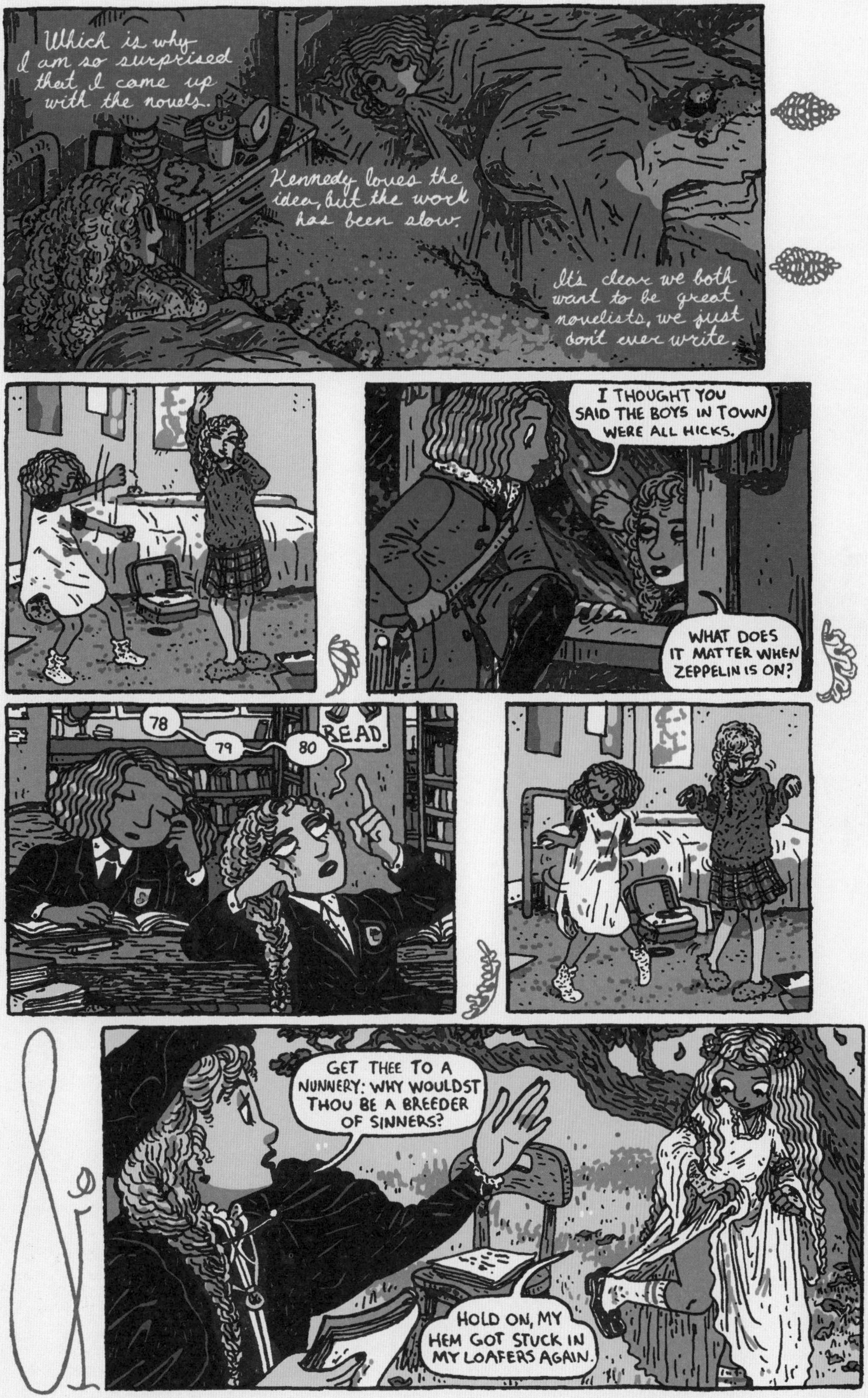
Which is why I am so surprised that I came up with the novels.
Kennedy loves the idea, but the work has been slow.
It's clear we both want to be great novelists, we just don't ever write.
I THOUGHT YOU SAID THE BOYS IN TOWN WERE ALL HICKS.
WHAT DOES IT MATTER WHEN ZEPPELIN IS ON?
78
79
80
READ
GET THEE TO A NUNNERY: WHY WOULDST THOU BE A BREEDER OF SINNERS?
HOLD ON, MY HEM GOT STUCK IN MY LOAFERS AGAIN.

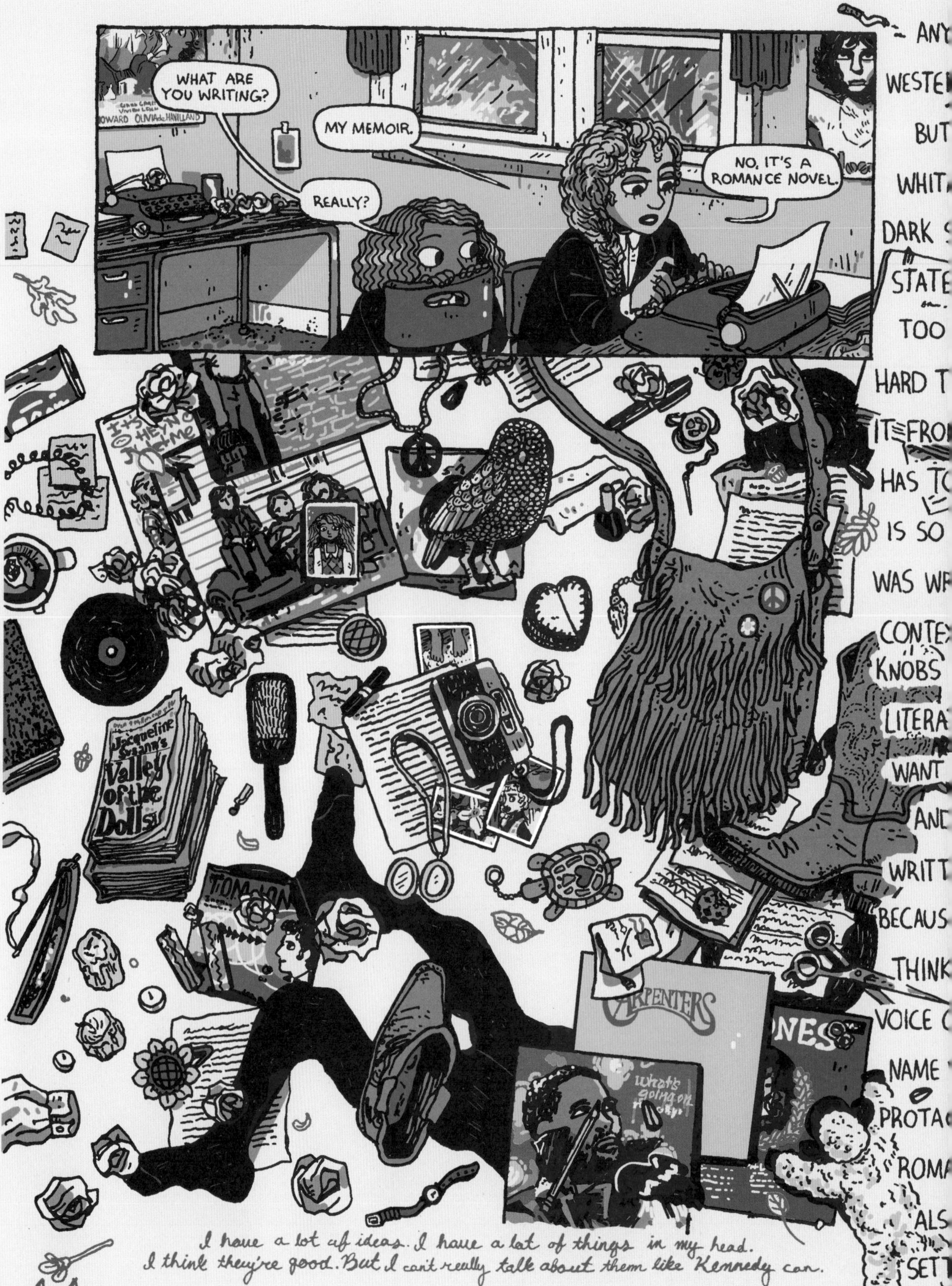
WHAT ARE YOU WRITING?
MY MEMOIR.
REALLY?
NO, IT'S A ROMANCE NOVEL.
I have a lot of ideas. I have a lot of things in my head.
I think they're good. But I can't really talk about them like Kennedy can.

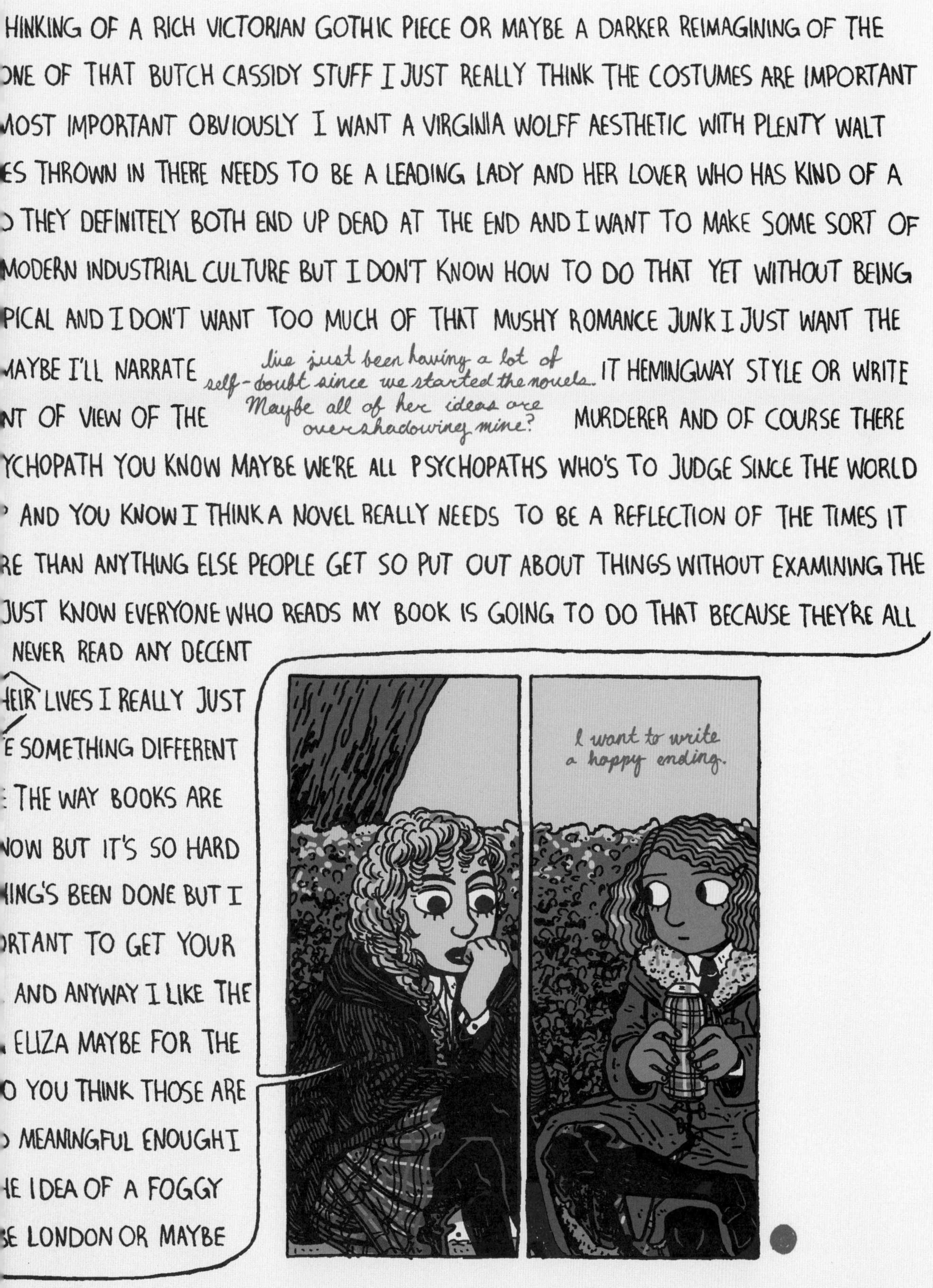
HINKING OF A RICH VICTORIAN GOTHIC PIECE OR MAYBE A DARKER REIMAGINING OF THE
ONE OF THAT BUTCH CASSIDY STUFF I JUST REALLY THINK THE COSTUMES ARE IMPORTANT
MOST IMPORTANT OBVIOUSLY I WANT A VIRGINIA WOLFF AESTHETIC WITH PLENTY WALT
ES THROWN IN THERE NEEDS TO BE A LEADING LADY AND HER LOVER WHO HAS KIND OF A
THEY DEFINITELY BOTH END UP DEAD AT THE END AND I WANT TO MAKE SOME SORT OF
MODERN INDUSTRIAL CULTURE BUT I DON'T KNOW HOW TO DO THAT YET WITHOUT BEING
PICAL AND I DON'T WANT TOO MUCH OF THAT MUSHY ROMANCE JUNK I JUST WANT THE
MAYBE I'LL NARRATE IT HEMINGWAY STYLE OR WRITE
NT OF VIEW OF THE MURDERER AND OF COURSE THERE
YCHOPATH YOU KNOW MAYBE WE'RE ALL PSYCHOPATHS WHO'S TO JUDGE SINCE THE WORLD
AND YOU KNOW I THINK A NOVEL REALLY NEEDS TO BE A REFLECTION OF THE TIMES IT
RE THAN ANYTHING ELSE PEOPLE GET SO PUT OUT ABOUT THINGS WITHOUT EXAMINING THE
JUST KNOW EVERYONE WHO READS MY BOOK IS GOING TO DO THAT BECAUSE THEY'RE ALL
NEVER READ ANY DECENT
HEIR LIVES I REALLY JUST
E SOMETHING DIFFERENT
THE WAY BOOKS ARE
NOW BUT IT'S SO HARD
HING'S BEEN DONE BUT I
RTANT TO GET YOUR
AND ANYWAY I LIKE THE
ELIZA MAYBE FOR THE
O YOU THINK THOSE ARE
MEANINGFUL ENOUGH I
HE IDEA OF A FOGGY
E LONDON OR MAYBE
I've just been having a lot of self-doubt since we started the novels. Maybe all of her ideas are overshadowing mine?
I want to write a happy ending.

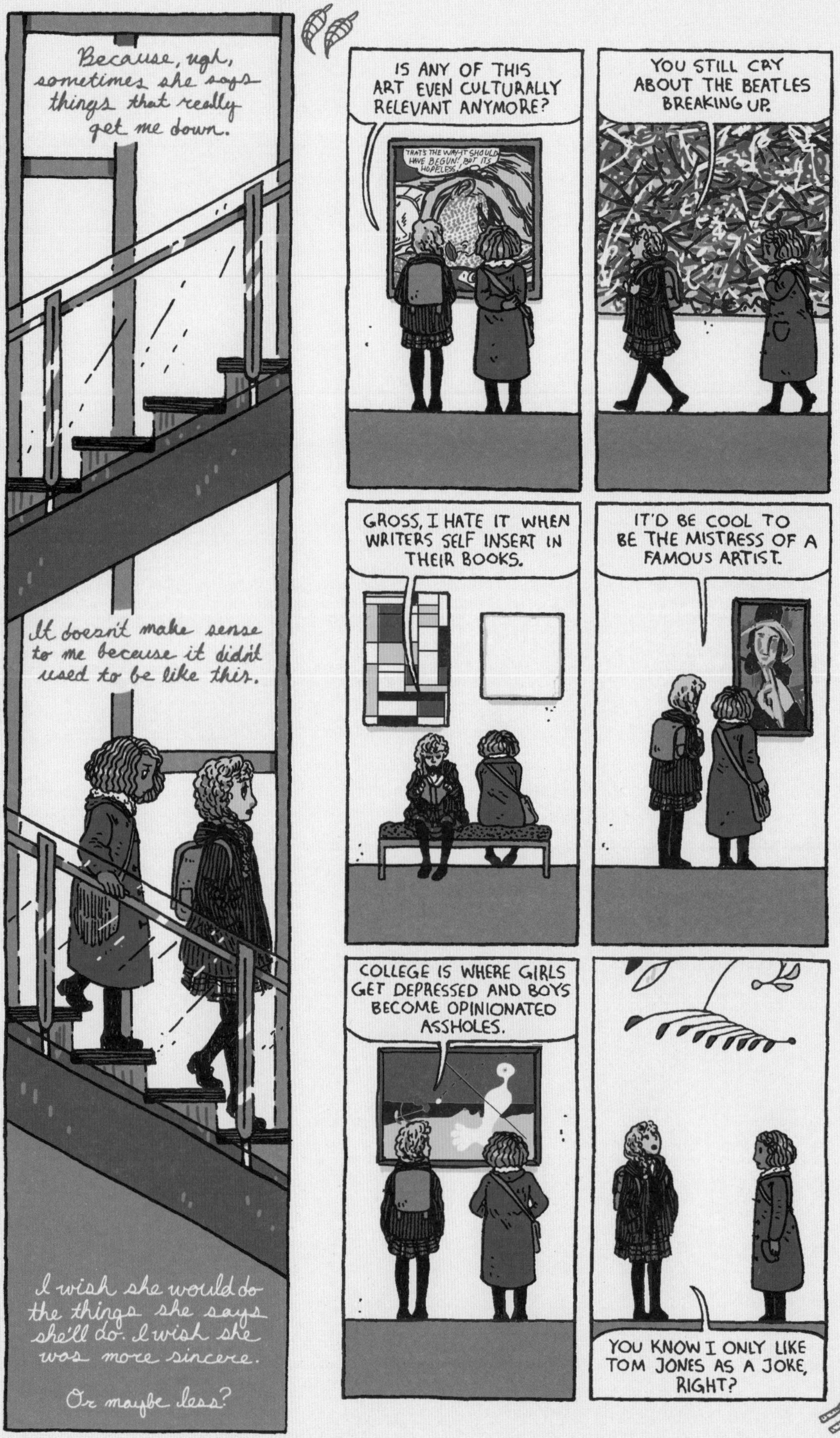
Because, ugh, sometimes she says things that really get me down.
It doesn't make sense to me because it didn't used to be like this.
I wish she would do the things she says she'll do. I wish she was more sincere.
Or maybe less?
IS ANY OF THIS ART EVEN CULTURALLY RELEVANT ANYMORE?
THAT'S THE WAY IT SHOULD HAVE BEGUN! BUT IT'S HOPELESS!
YOU STILL CRY ABOUT THE BEATLES BREAKING UP.
GROSS, I HATE IT WHEN WRITERS SELF INSERT IN THEIR BOOKS.
IT'D BE COOL TO BE THE MISTRESS OF A FAMOUS ARTIST.
COLLEGE IS WHERE GIRLS GET DEPRESSED AND BOYS BECOME OPINIONATED ASSHOLES.
YOU KNOW I ONLY LIKE TOM JONES AS A JOKE, RIGHT?

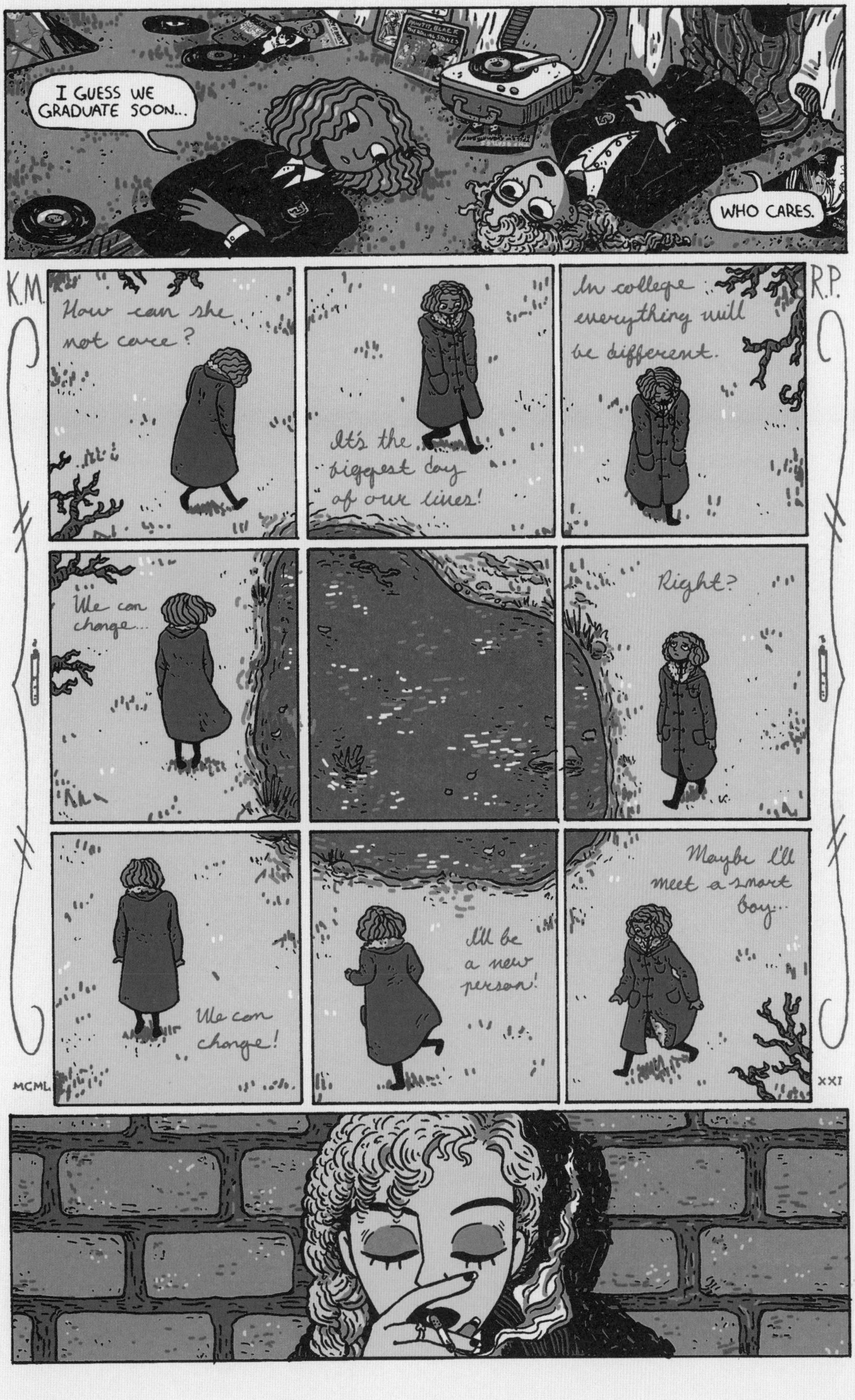

I GUESS WE GRADUATE SOON...
WHO CARES.
K.M.
R.P.
How can she not care?
It's the biggest day of our lives!
In college everything will be different.
We can change...
Right?
We can change!
I'll be a new person!
Maybe I'll meet a smart boy...
MCML
XXI

I just want to write something really good.

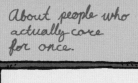
About people who actually care for once.

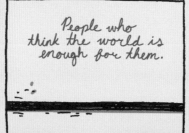
People who think the world is enough for them.

Where everything actually matters.

CLK CLK
CLK Smith-Co

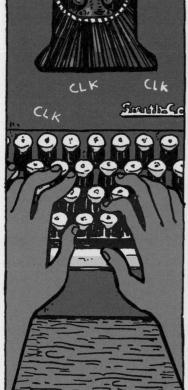

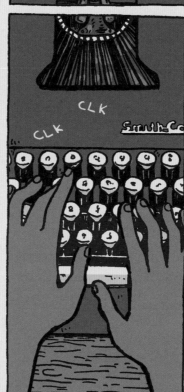

CLK CLK
CLK Smith-Co

CLK
CLK Smith-Co

The End.

Kennedy thinks she's so smart because she kisses boys and saw a dead person once and read a book by Camus.

And besides, people find naïveté charming, right?

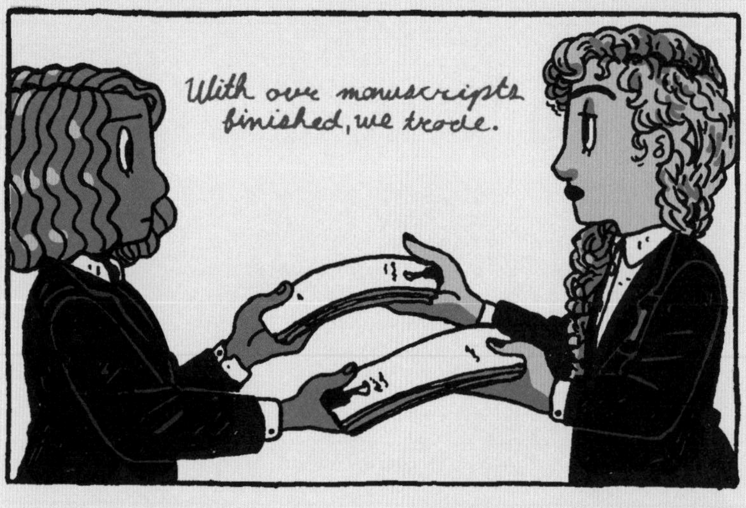
With our manuscripts finished, we trade.

And they both stink.

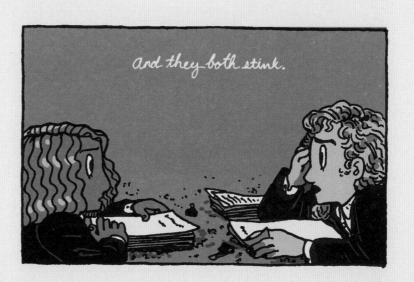

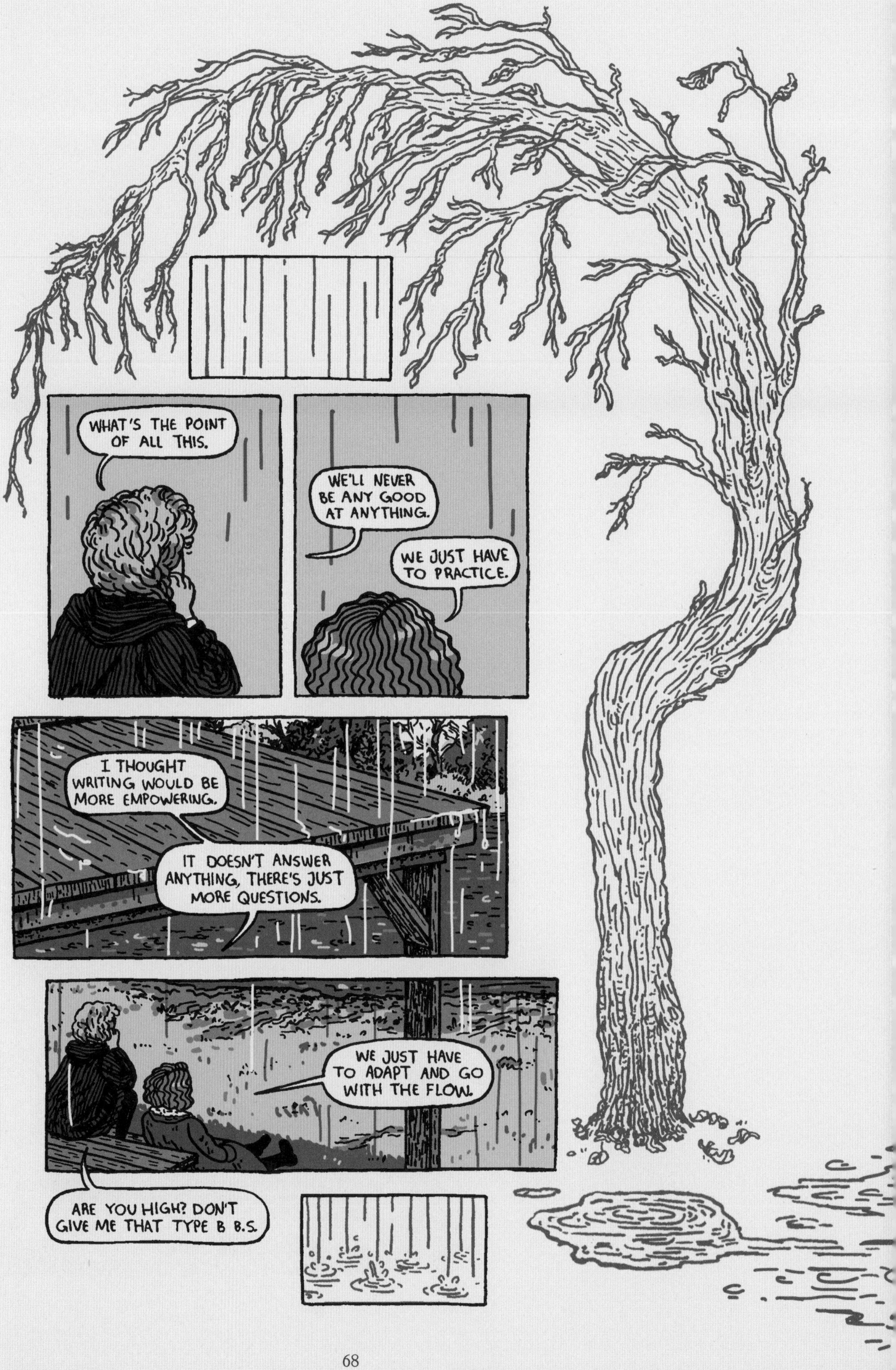

WHAT'S THE POINT OF ALL THIS.
WE'LL NEVER BE ANY GOOD AT ANYTHING.
WE JUST HAVE TO PRACTICE.
I THOUGHT WRITING WOULD BE MORE EMPOWERING.
IT DOESN'T ANSWER ANYTHING, THERE'S JUST MORE QUESTIONS.
WE JUST HAVE TO ADAPT AND GO WITH THE FLOW.
ARE YOU HIGH? DON'T GIVE ME THAT TYPE B B.S.

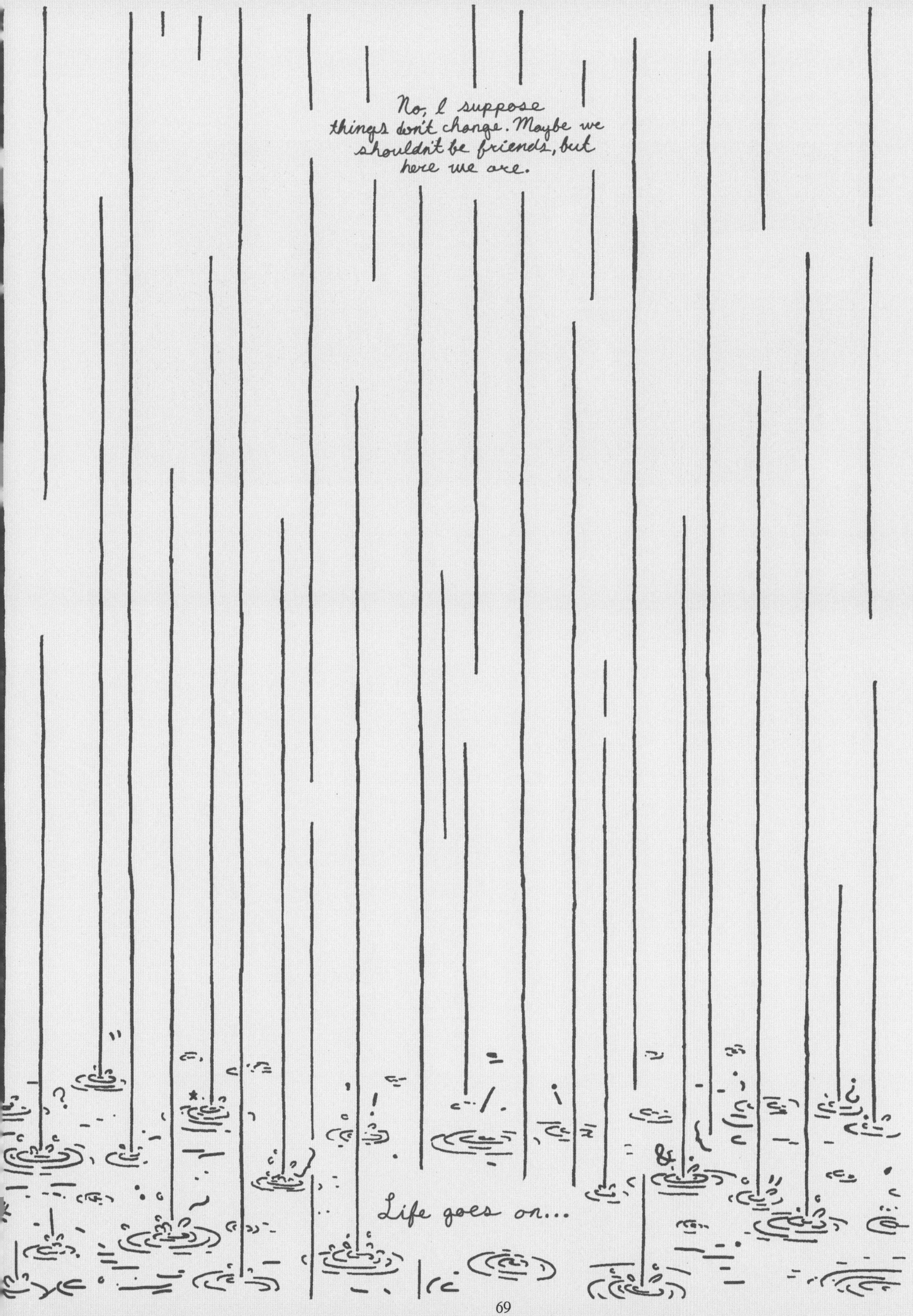
No, I suppose things don't change. Maybe we shouldn't be friends, but here we are.
Life goes on...

And maybe,
even if she doesn't admit it, Kennedy is
actually happiest knowing there are no real   answers

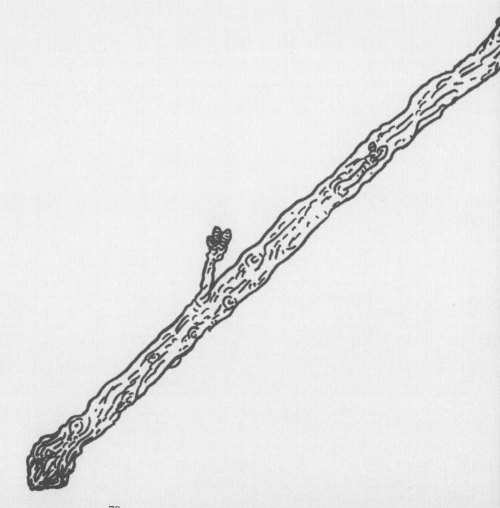

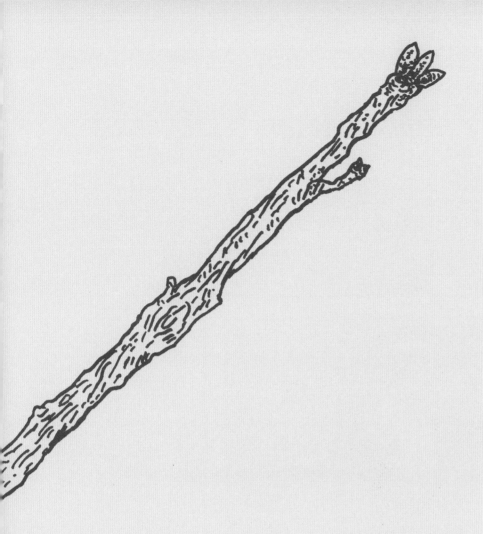

endings.

I think I am, anyway.

*

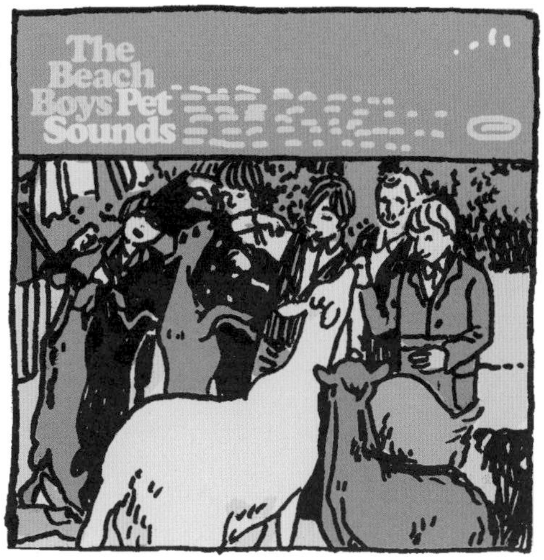
The Beach Boys Pet Sounds

"Strange Magic"

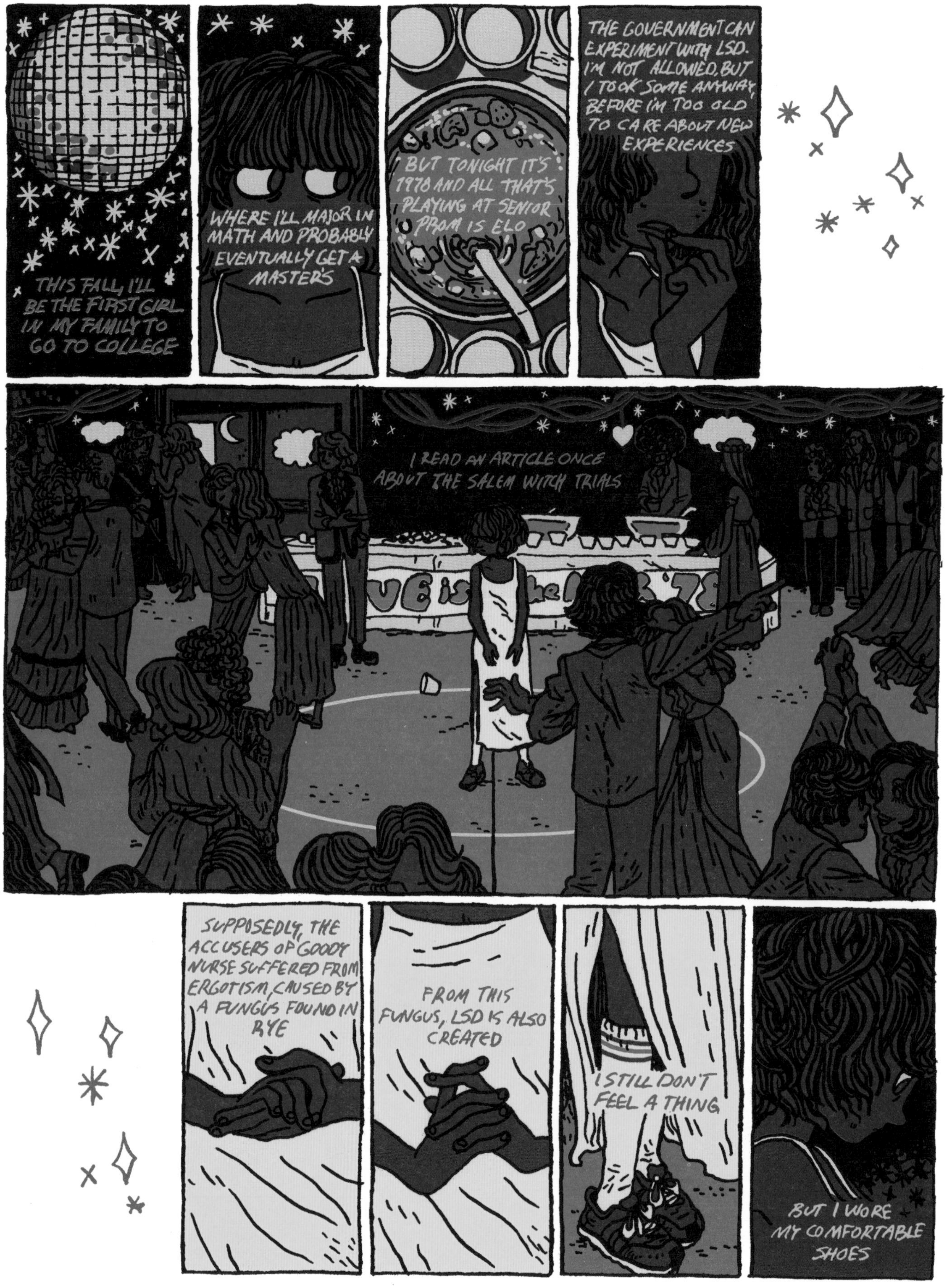
THIS FALL, I'LL BE THE FIRST GIRL IN MY FAMILY TO GO TO COLLEGE
WHERE I'LL MAJOR IN MATH AND PROBABLY EVENTUALLY GET A MASTER'S
BUT TONIGHT IT'S 1978 AND ALL THAT'S PLAYING AT SENIOR PROM IS ELO
THE GOVERNMENT CAN EXPERIMENT WITH LSD. I'M NOT ALLOWED, BUT I TOOK SOME ANYWAY, BEFORE I'M TOO OLD TO CARE ABOUT NEW EXPERIENCES
I READ AN ARTICLE ONCE ABOUT THE SALEM WITCH TRIALS
SUPPOSEDLY, THE ACCUSERS OF GOODY NURSE SUFFERED FROM ERGOTISM, CAUSED BY A FUNGUS FOUND IN RYE
FROM THIS FUNGUS, LSD IS ALSO CREATED
I STILL DON'T FEEL A THING
BUT I WORE MY COMFORTABLE SHOES

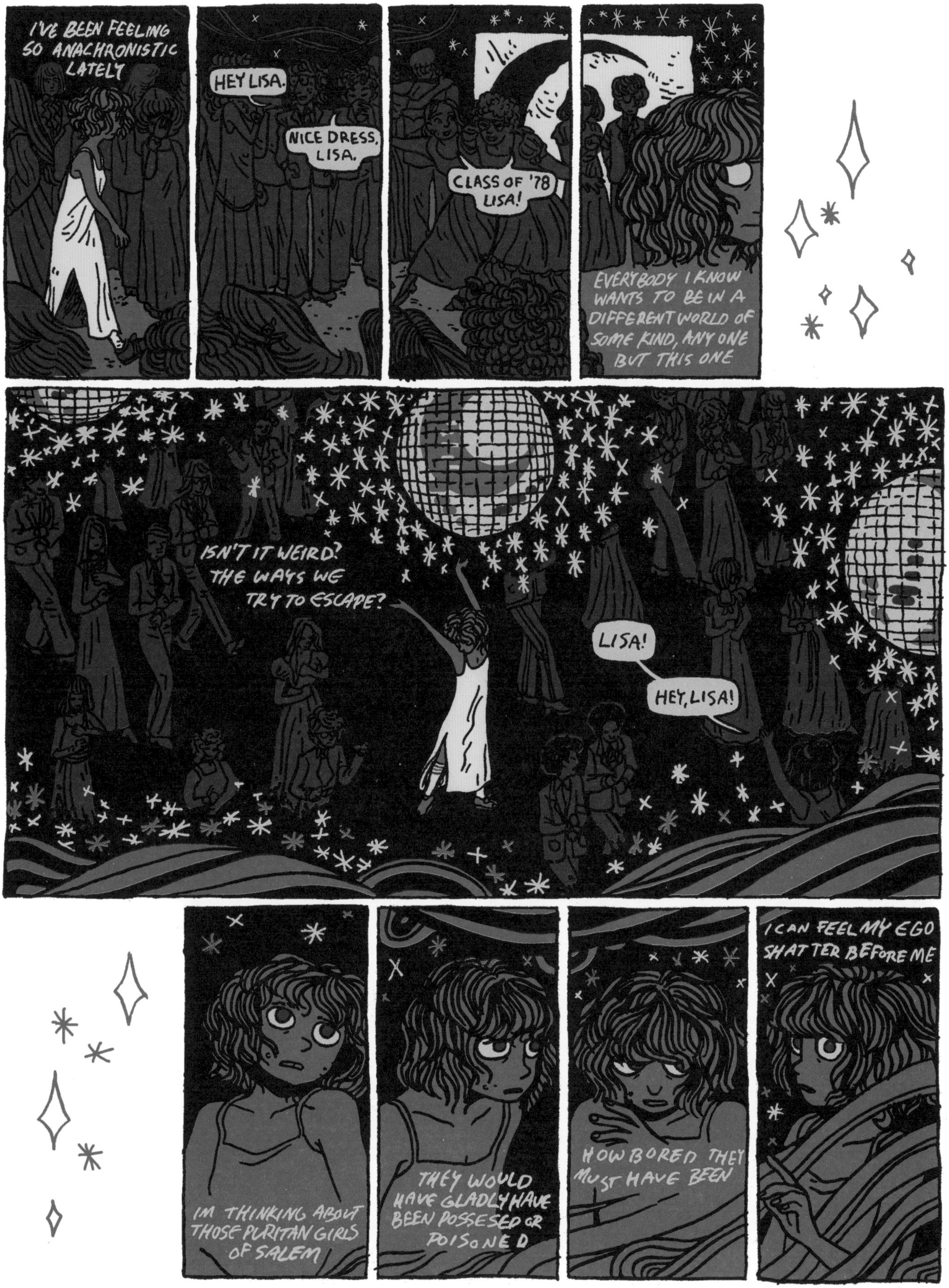
I'VE BEEN FEELING SO ANACHRONISTIC LATELY
HEY LISA.
NICE DRESS, LISA.
CLASS OF '78 LISA!
EVERYBODY I KNOW WANTS TO BE IN A DIFFERENT WORLD OF SOME KIND, ANY ONE BUT THIS ONE
ISN'T IT WEIRD? THE WAYS WE TRY TO ESCAPE?
LISA!
HEY, LISA!
IM THINKING ABOUT THOSE PURITAN GIRLS OF SALEM
THEY WOULD HAVE GLADLY HAVE BEEN POSSESED OR POISONED
HOW BORED THEY MUST HAVE BEEN
I CAN FEEL MY EGO SHATTER BEFORE ME

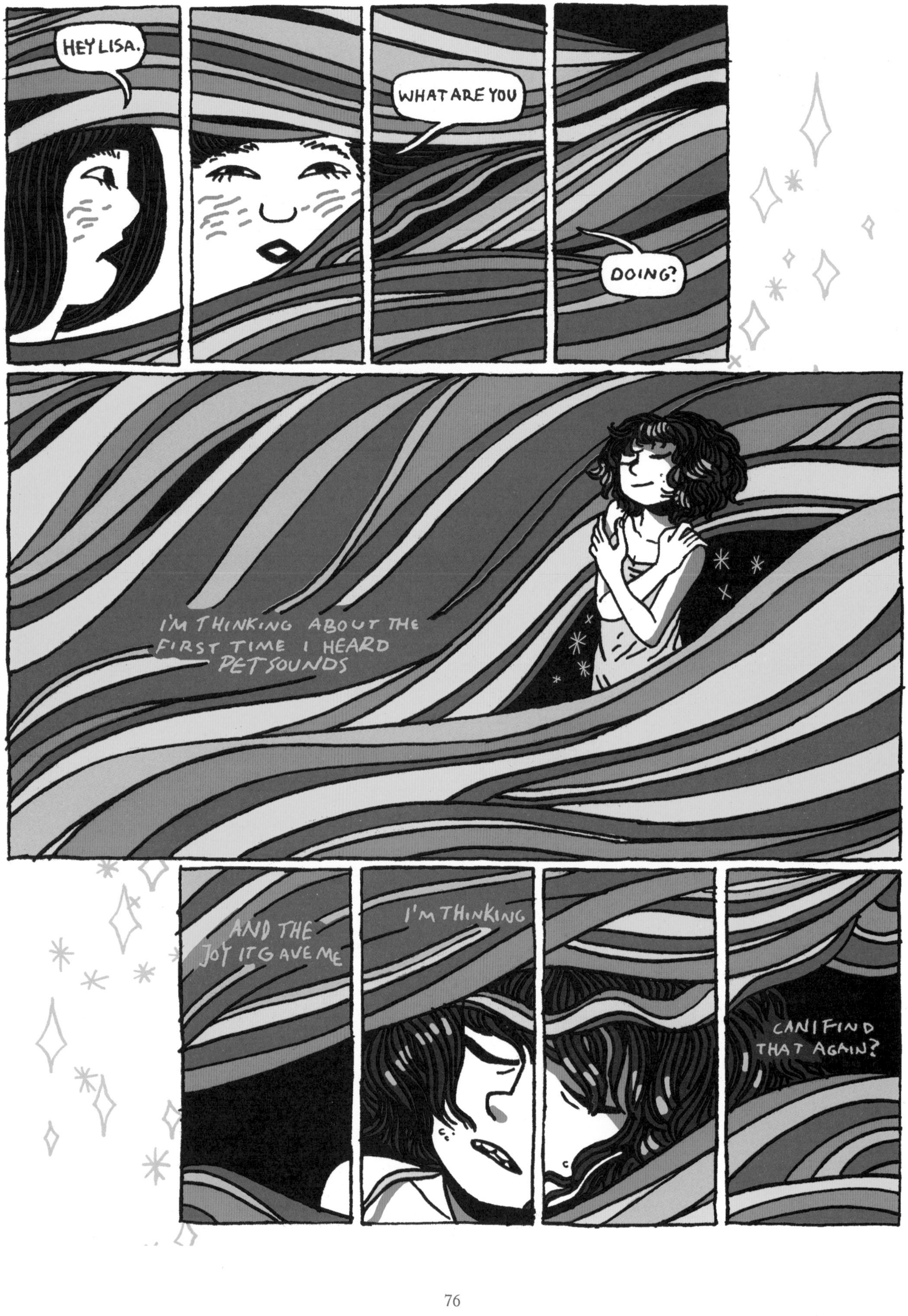

HEY LISA.
WHAT ARE YOU
DOING?
I'M THINKING ABOUT THE FIRST TIME I HEARD PET SOUNDS
AND THE JOY IT GAVE ME
I'M THINKING
CAN I FIND THAT AGAIN?

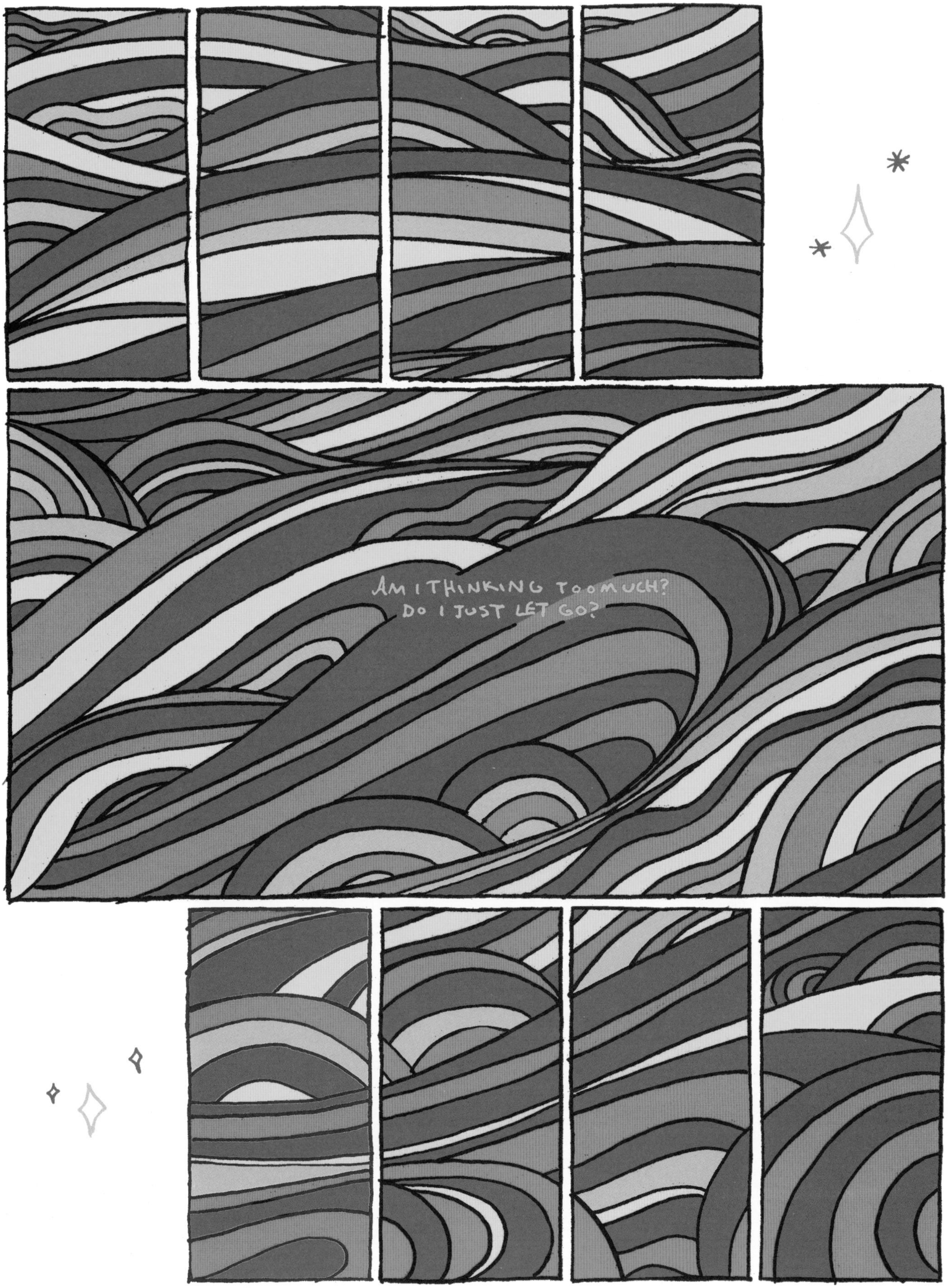
AM I THINKING TOO MUCH?
DO I JUST LET GO?

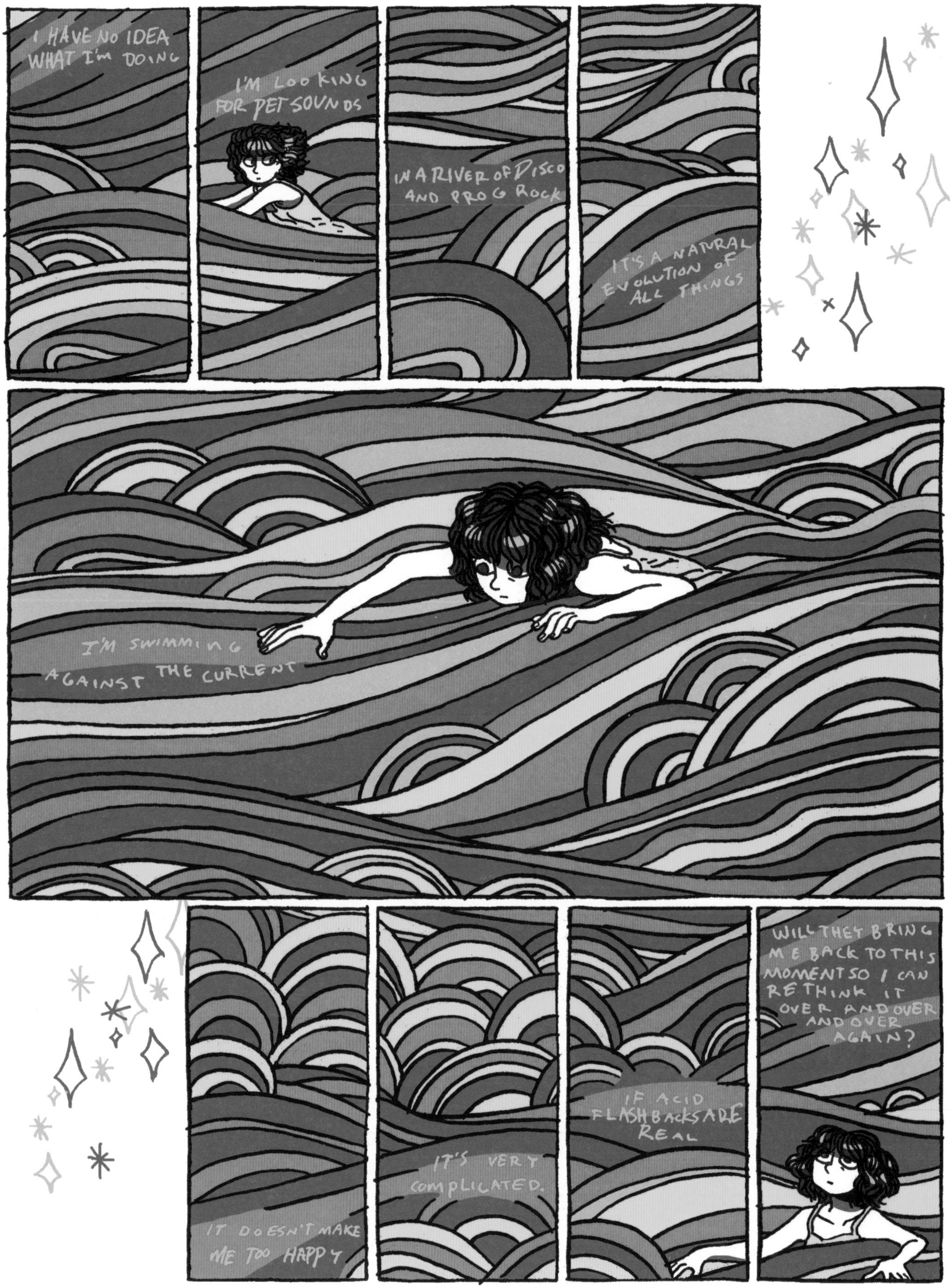
I HAVE NO IDEA WHAT I'M DOING
I'M LOOKING FOR PET SOUNDS
IN A RIVER OF DISCO AND PROG ROCK
IT'S A NATURAL EVOLUTION OF ALL THINGS
I'M SWIMMING AGAINST THE CURRENT
IT DOESN'T MAKE ME TOO HAPPY
IT'S VERY COMPLICATED.
IF ACID FLASHBACKS ARE REAL
WILL THEY BRING ME BACK TO THIS MOMENT SO I CAN RETHINK IT OVER AND OVER AND OVER AGAIN?

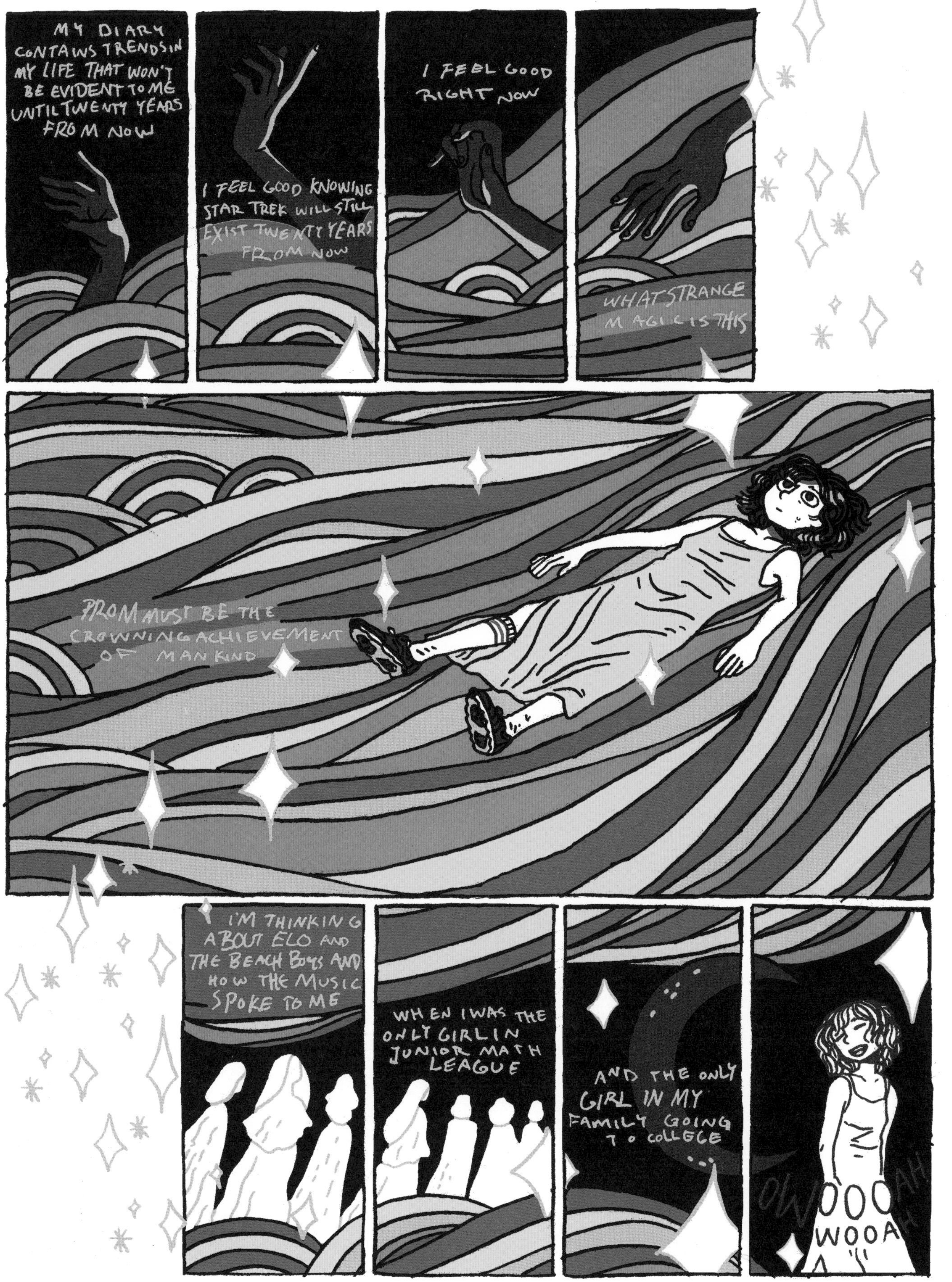
MY DIARY CONTAINS TRENDS IN MY LIFE THAT WON'T BE EVIDENT TO ME UNTIL TWENTY YEARS FROM NOW
I FEEL GOOD KNOWING STAR TREK WILL STILL EXIST TWENTY YEARS FROM NOW
I FEEL GOOD RIGHT NOW
WHAT STRANGE MAGIC IS THIS
PROM MUST BE THE CROWNING ACHIEVEMENT OF MANKIND
I'M THINKING ABOUT ELO AND THE BEACH BOYS AND HOW THE MUSIC SPOKE TO ME
WHEN I WAS THE ONLY GIRL IN JUNIOR MATH LEAGUE
AND THE ONLY GIRL IN MY FAMILY GOING TO COLLEGE
OOOOAH
WOOAH

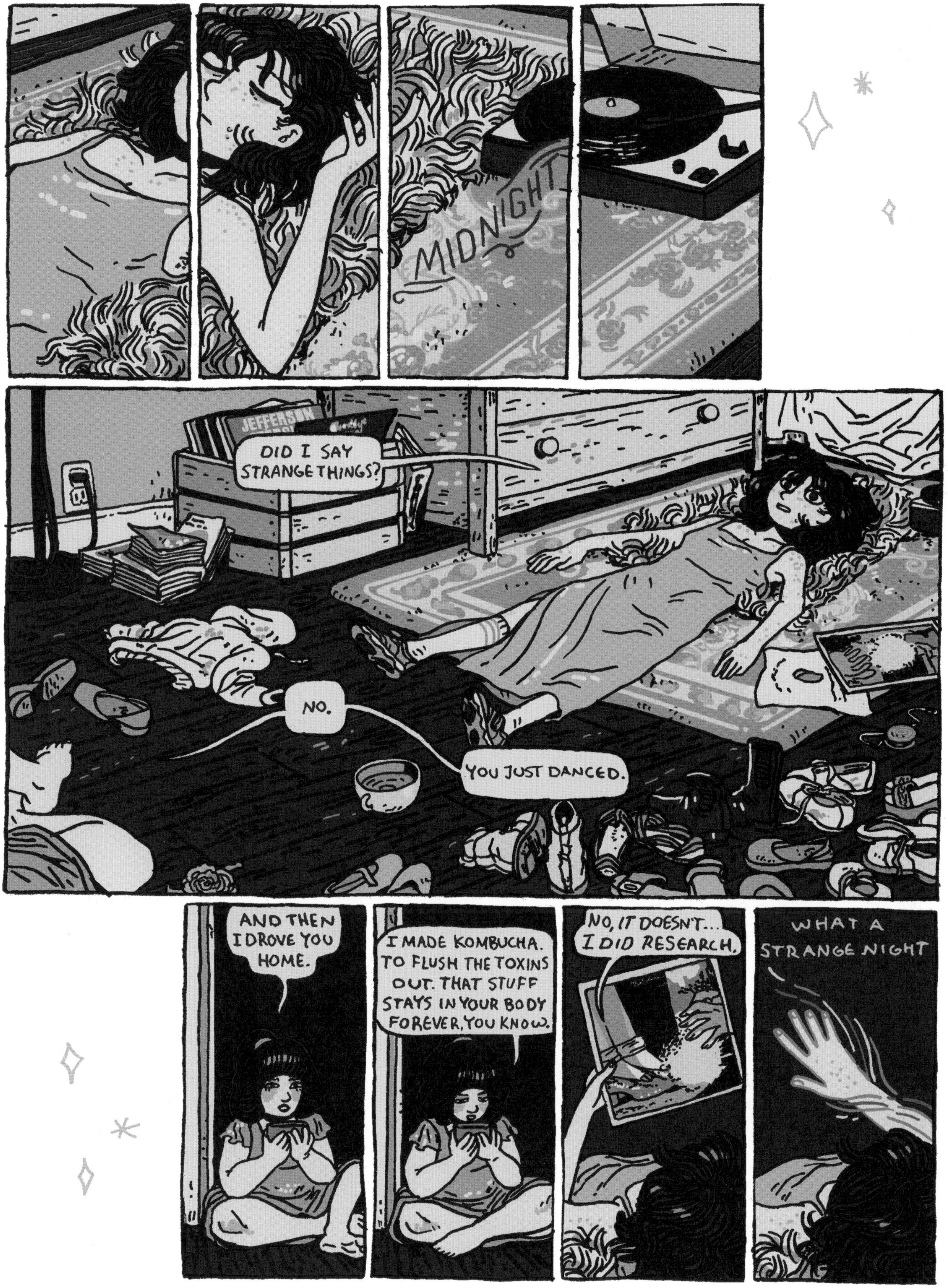
MIDNIGHT
JEFFERSON
DID I SAY STRANGE THINGS?
NO.
YOU JUST DANCED.
AND THEN I DROVE YOU HOME.
I MADE KOMBUCHA. TO FLUSH THE TOXINS OUT. THAT STUFF STAYS IN YOUR BODY FOREVER, YOU KNOW.
NO, IT DOESN'T... I DID RESEARCH.
WHAT A STRANGE NIGHT

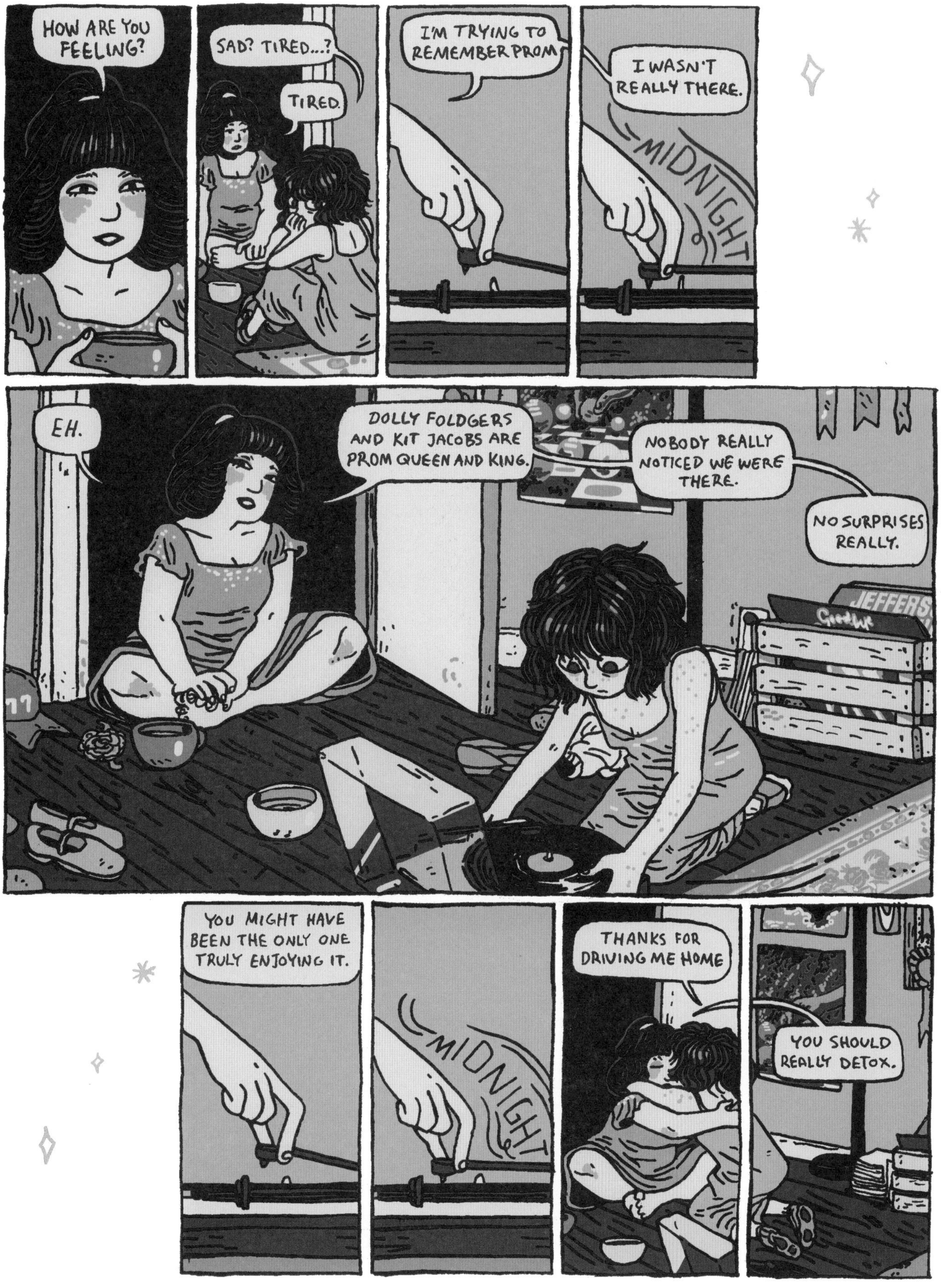
HOW ARE YOU FEELING?
SAD? TIRED...?
TIRED.
I'M TRYING TO REMEMBER PROM
I WASN'T REALLY THERE.
MIDNIGHT
EH.
DOLLY FOLDGERS AND KIT JACOBS ARE PROM QUEEN AND KING.
NOBODY REALLY NOTICED WE WERE THERE.
NO SURPRISES REALLY.
YOU MIGHT HAVE BEEN THE ONLY ONE TRULY ENJOYING IT.
MIDNIGHT
THANKS FOR DRIVING ME HOME
YOU SHOULD REALLY DETOX.

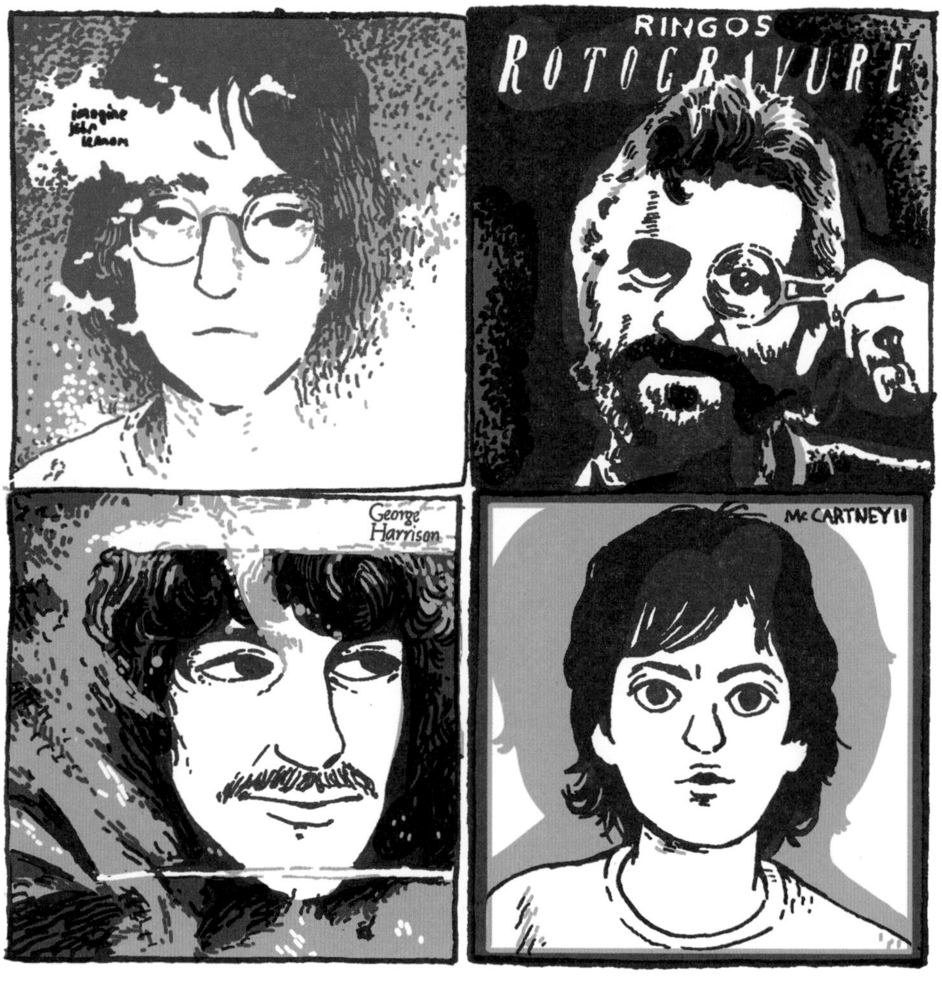
RINGOS
ROTOGRAVURE
George Harrison
McCARTNEY II

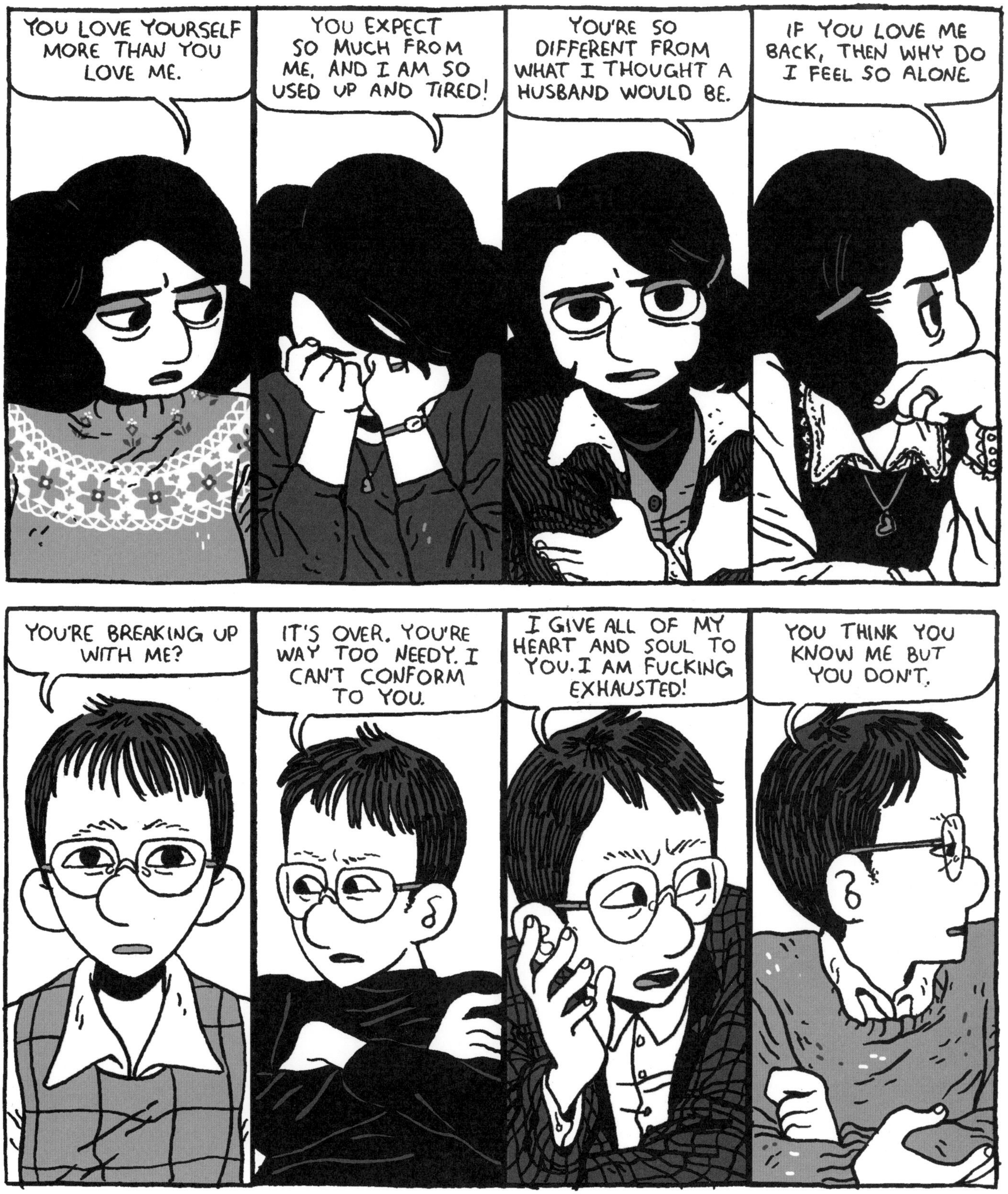
YOU LOVE YOURSELF MORE THAN YOU LOVE ME.
YOU EXPECT SO MUCH FROM ME, AND I AM SO USED UP AND TIRED!
YOU'RE SO DIFFERENT FROM WHAT I THOUGHT A HUSBAND WOULD BE.
IF YOU LOVE ME BACK, THEN WHY DO I FEEL SO ALONE
YOU'RE BREAKING UP WITH ME?
IT'S OVER. YOU'RE WAY TOO NEEDY. I CAN'T CONFORM TO YOU.
I GIVE ALL OF MY HEART AND SOUL TO YOU. I AM FUCKING EXHAUSTED!
YOU THINK YOU KNOW ME BUT YOU DON'T.

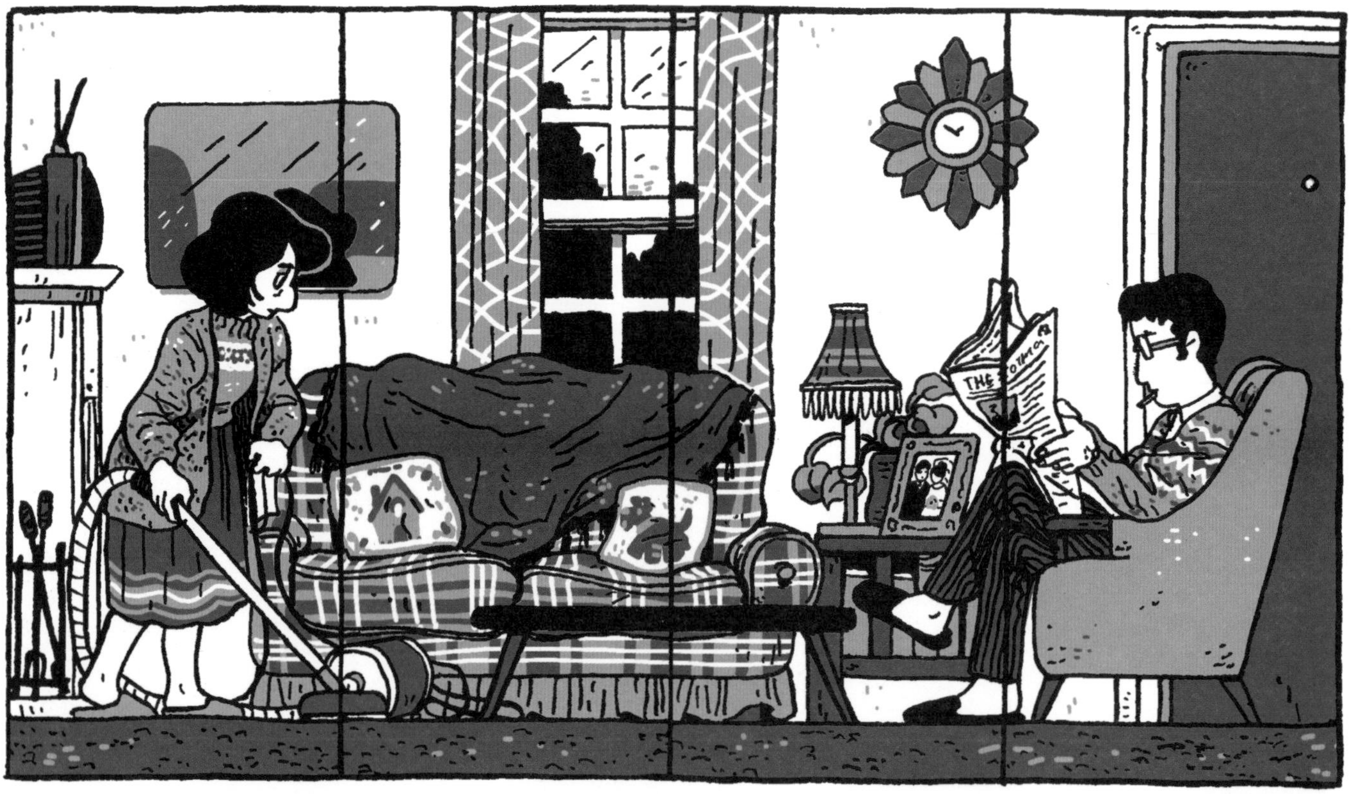

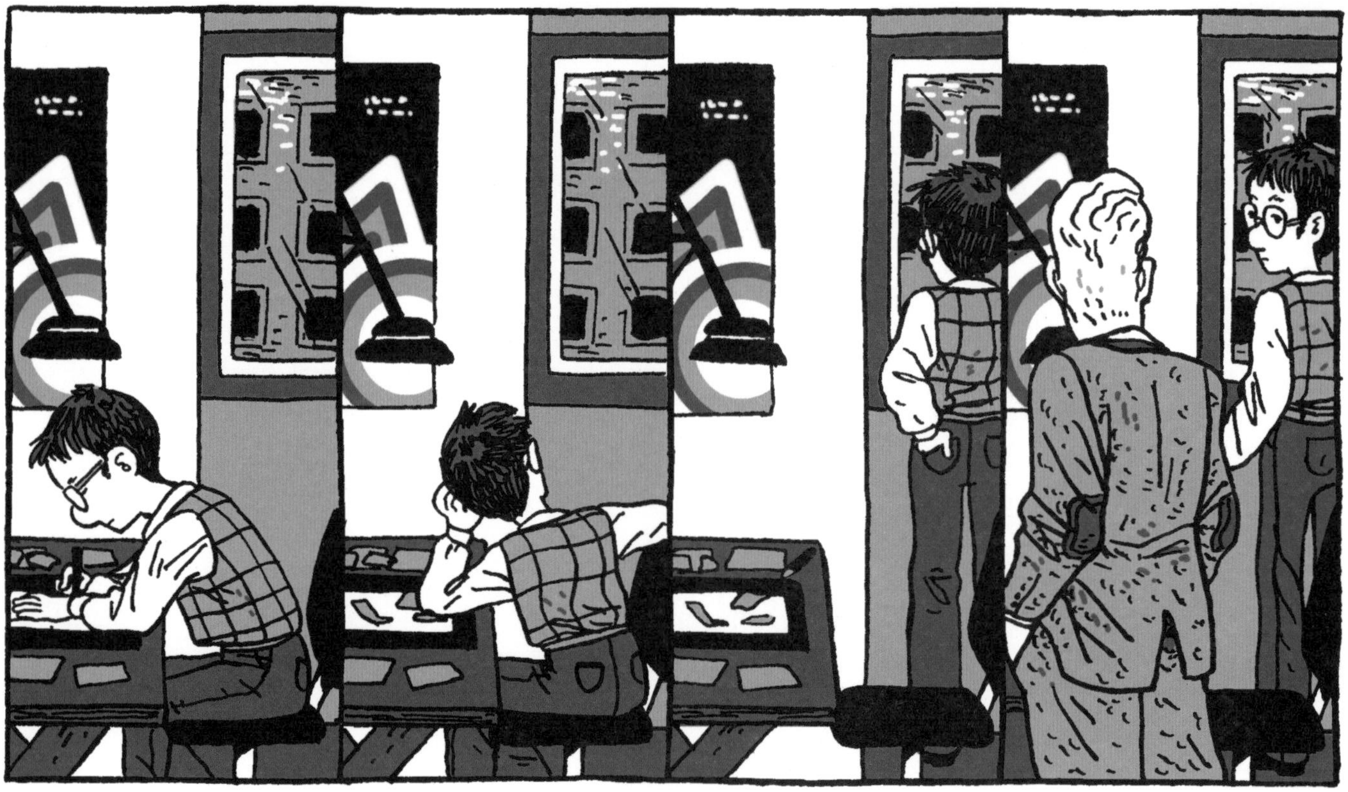

Dear George,

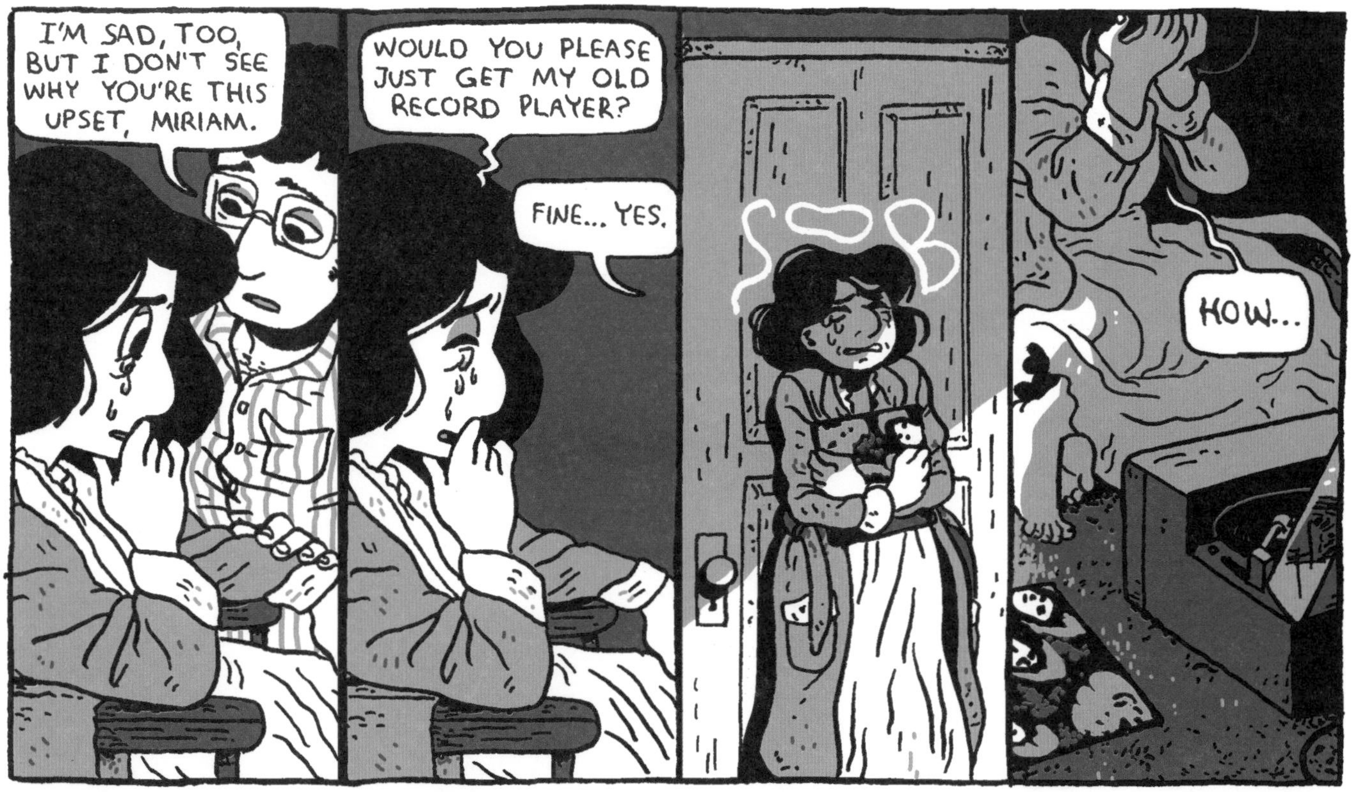
I'M SAD, TOO, BUT I DON'T SEE WHY YOU'RE THIS UPSET, MIRIAM.
WOULD YOU PLEASE JUST GET MY OLD RECORD PLAYER?
FINE... YES.
SOB
HOW...

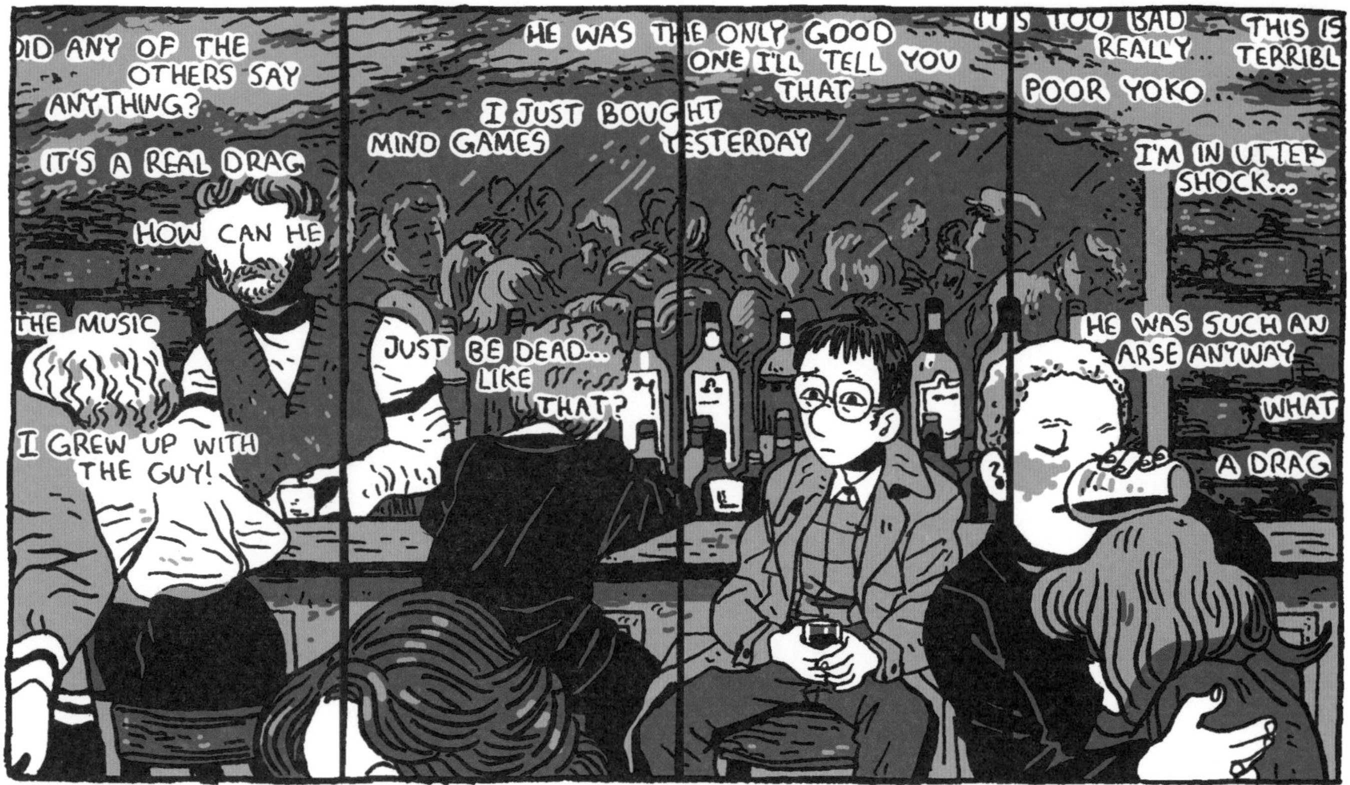
DID ANY OF THE OTHERS SAY ANYTHING?
IT'S A REAL DRAG
HOW CAN HE
THE MUSIC
I GREW UP WITH THE GUY!
HE WAS THE ONLY GOOD ONE I'LL TELL YOU THAT
I JUST BOUGHT MIND GAMES YESTERDAY
JUST BE DEAD... LIKE THAT?
IT'S TOO BAD REALLY
THIS IS TERRIBL
POOR YOKO
I'M IN UTTER SHOCK...
HE WAS SUCH AN ARSE ANYWAY
WHAT A DRAG

Dear Mir,

It's been so long since we
last saw each other... should
we meet for the vigil...?

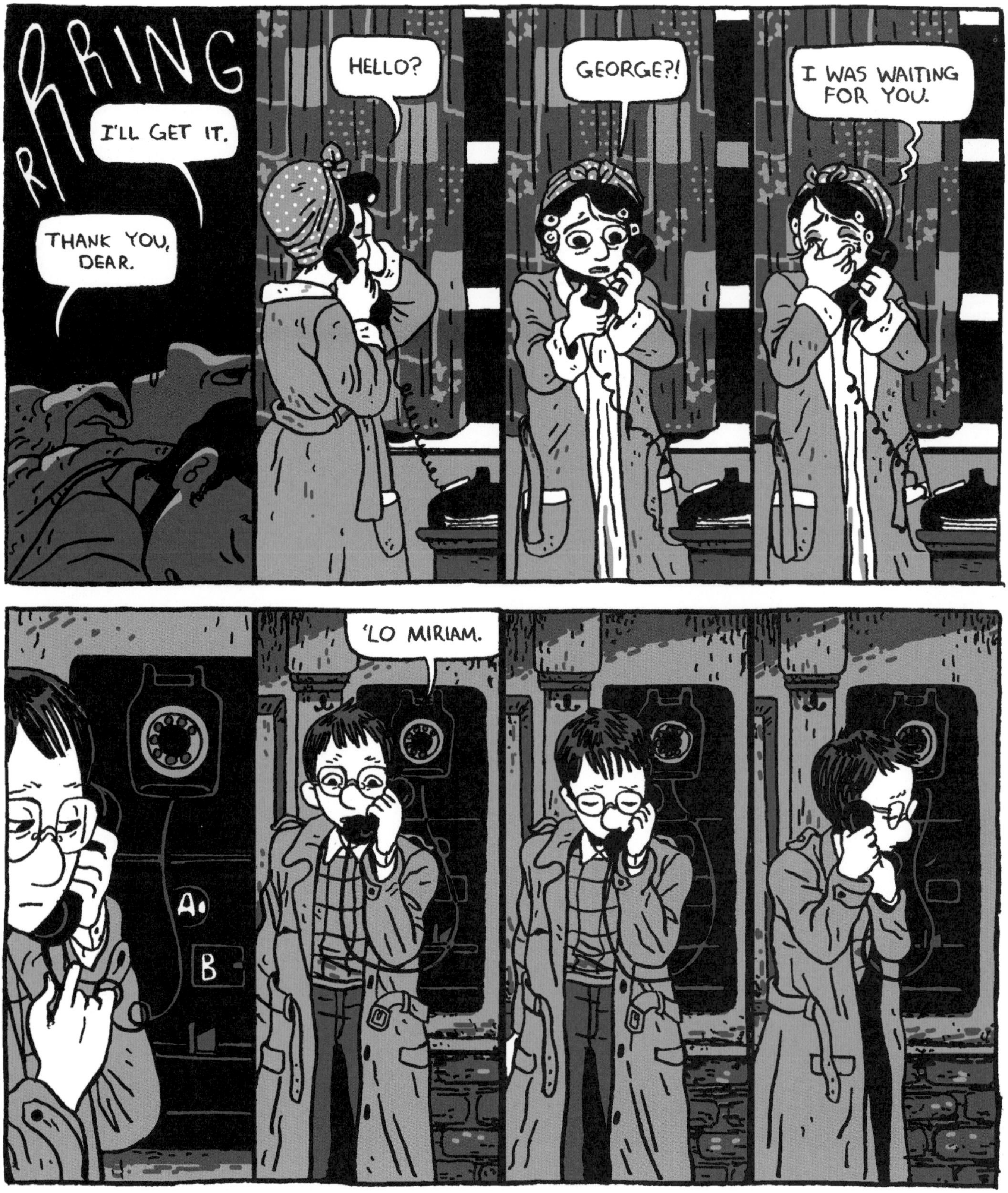

RRING
I'LL GET IT.
THANK YOU, DEAR.
HELLO?
GEORGE?!
I WAS WAITING FOR YOU.
'LO MIRIAM.

I can't believe I wasn't drunk when
I called you... your voice...

It's... a sad reunion. But I need something familiar to hold onto these days...

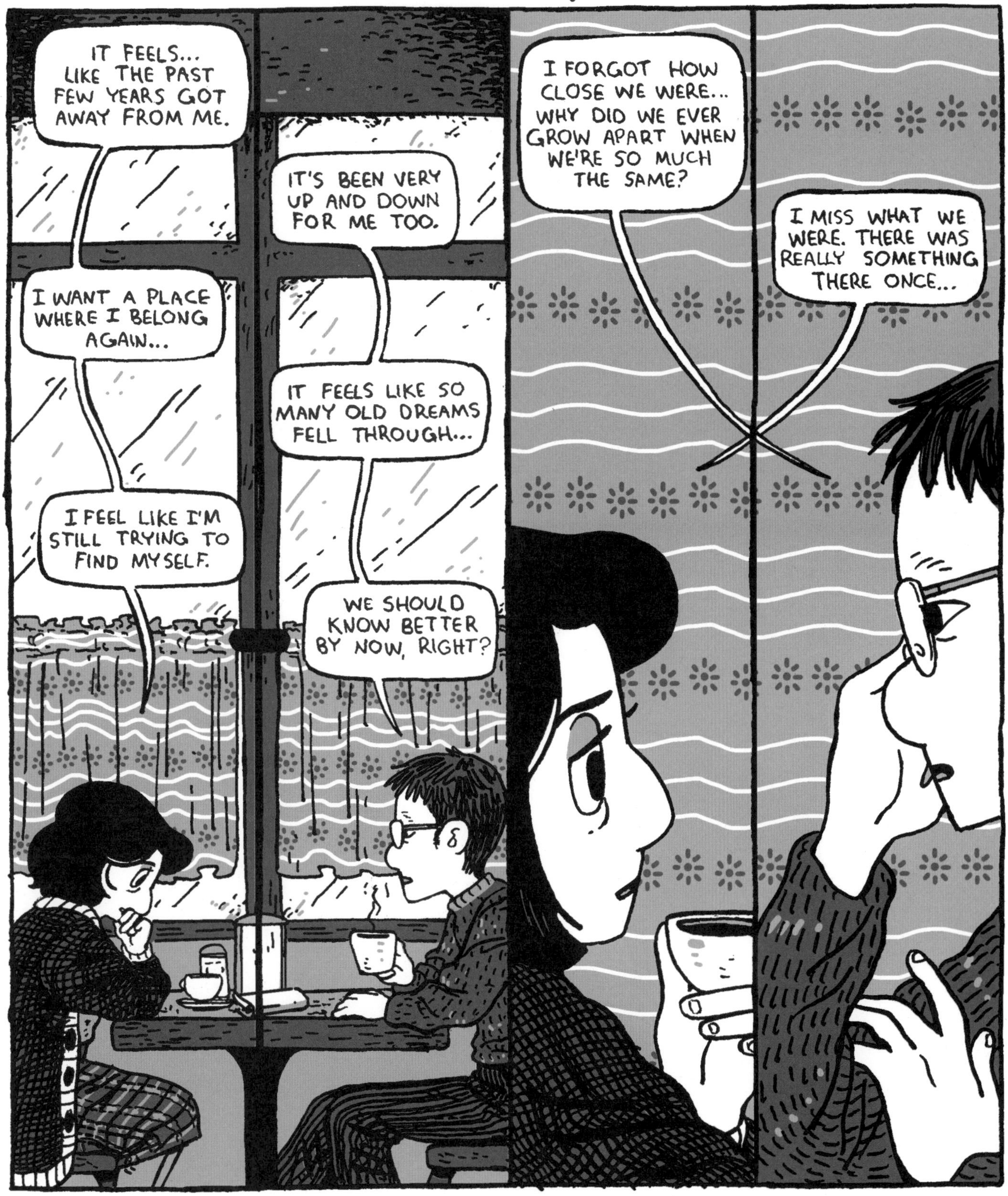
IT FEELS... LIKE THE PAST FEW YEARS GOT AWAY FROM ME.
IT'S BEEN VERY UP AND DOWN FOR ME TOO.
I WANT A PLACE WHERE I BELONG AGAIN...
IT FEELS LIKE SO MANY OLD DREAMS FELL THROUGH...
I FEEL LIKE I'M STILL TRYING TO FIND MYSELF.
WE SHOULD KNOW BETTER BY NOW, RIGHT?
I FORGOT HOW CLOSE WE WERE... WHY DID WE EVER GROW APART WHEN WE'RE SO MUCH THE SAME?
I MISS WHAT WE WERE. THERE WAS REALLY SOMETHING THERE ONCE...

I can't describe how I'm feeling. I want to see you again.

You gave me so much
happiness for so long.

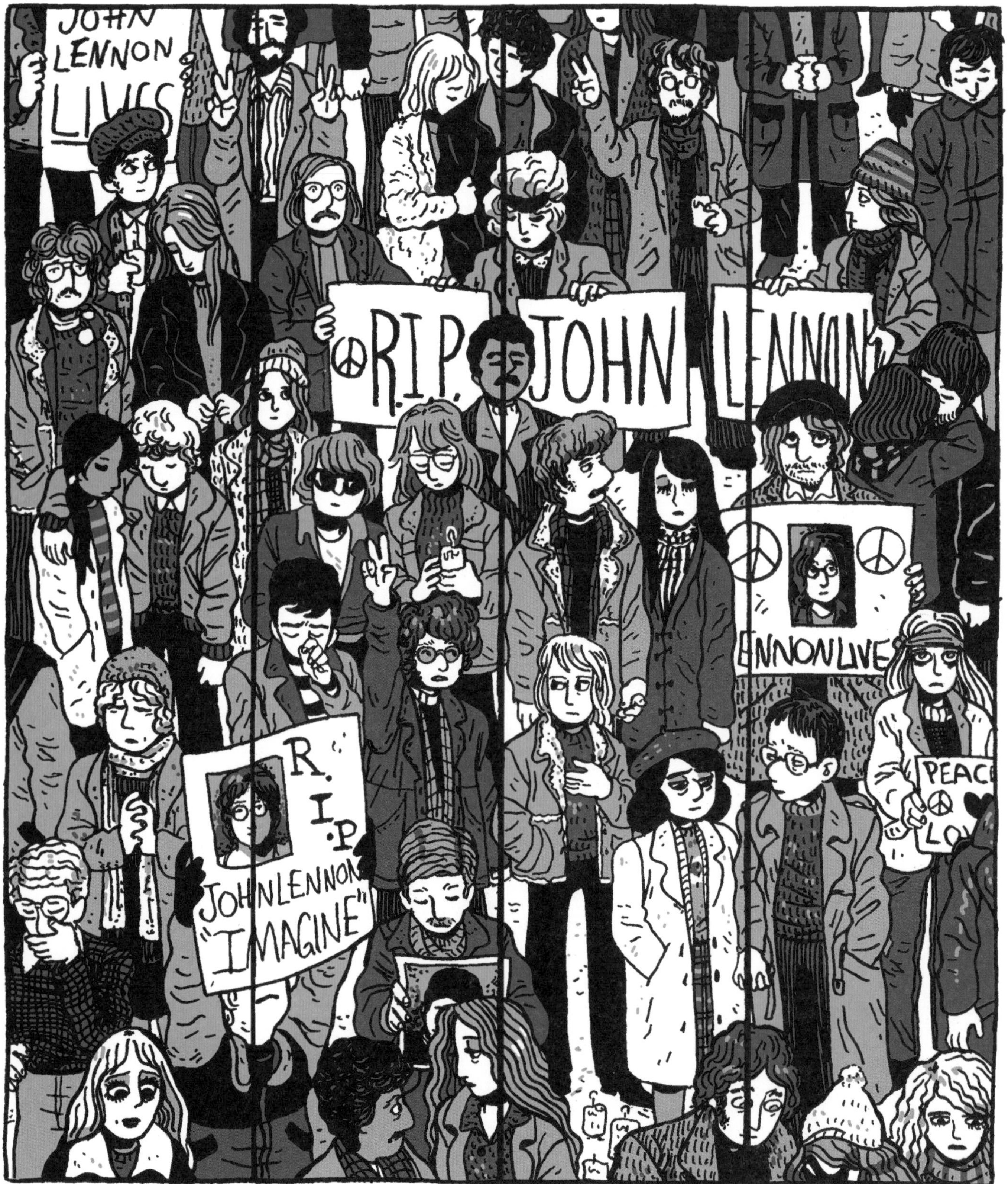

JOHN LENNON LIVES
R.I.P. JOHN LENNON
ENNON LIVE
R.I.P JOHN LENNON "IMAGINE"
PEAC
LO

We both know I've wandered a lot...
But something always brings me
back to you.

I still have all the old photos
and records and letters.
They're in the closet now.

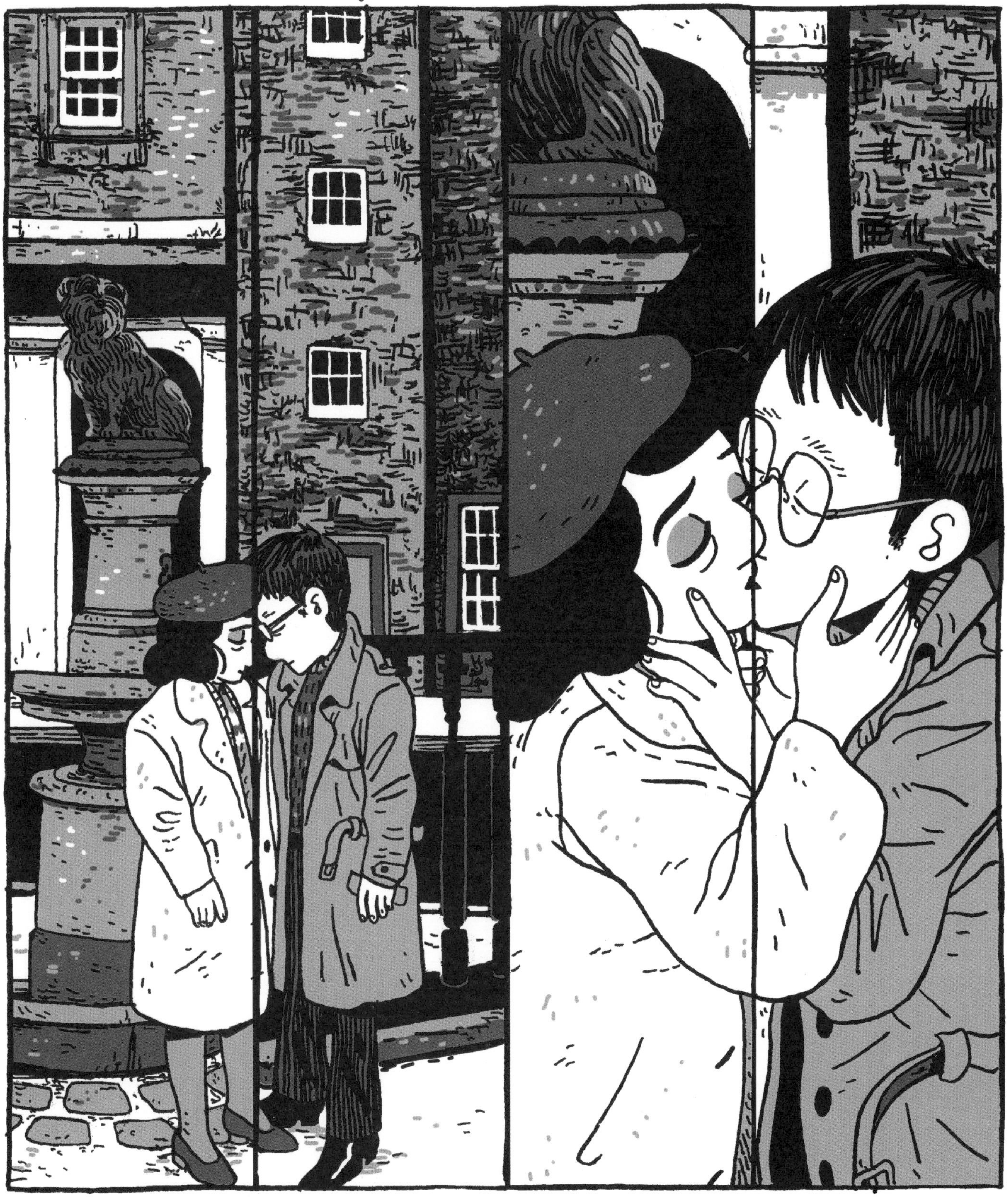

I can't seem to escape this
pit in my stomach...

When I look at them, we're always stupid, happy kids. But...

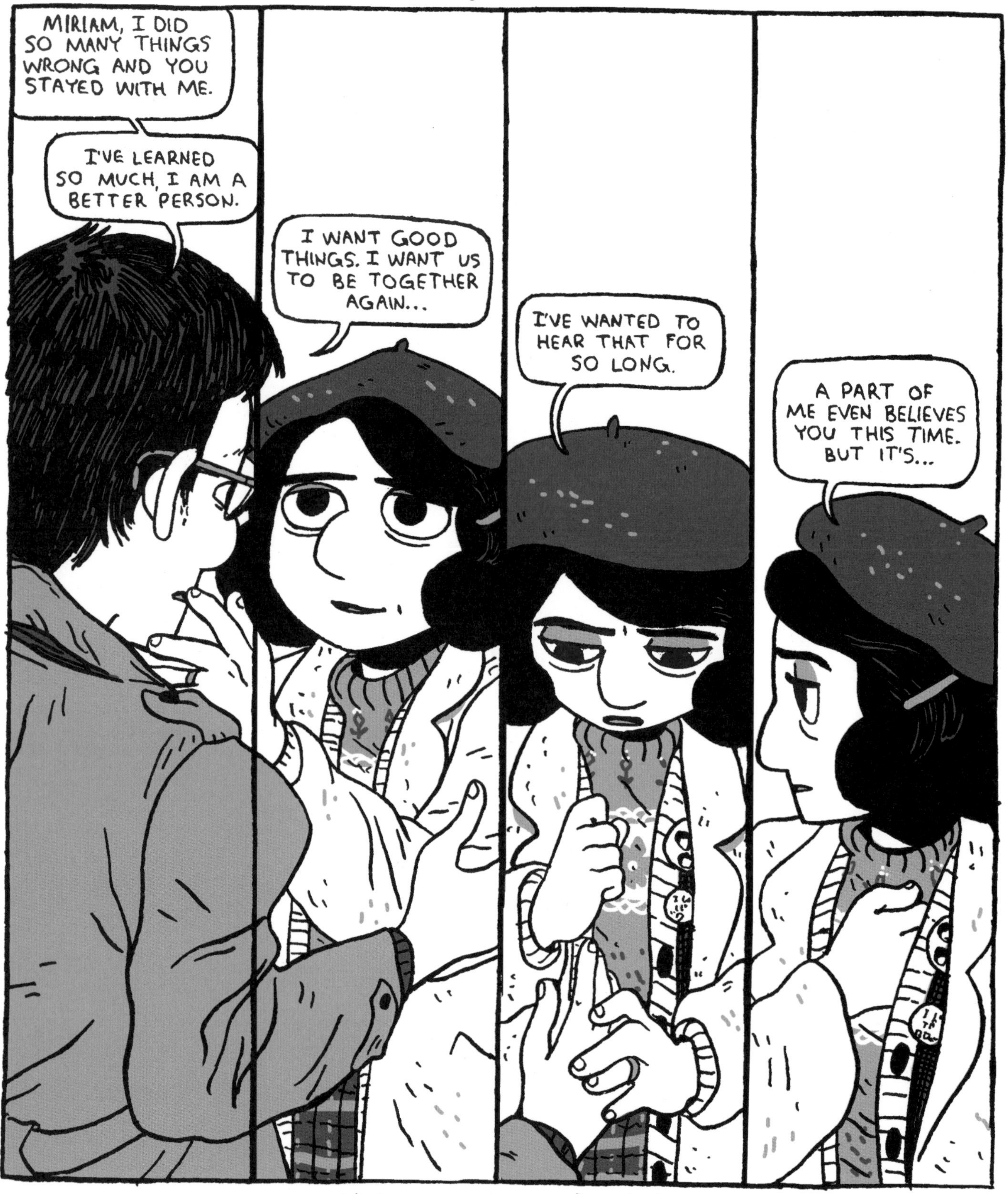
MIRIAM, I DID SO MANY THINGS WRONG AND YOU STAYED WITH ME.
I'VE LEARNED SO MUCH, I AM A BETTER PERSON.
I WANT GOOD THINGS. I WANT US TO BE TOGETHER AGAIN...
I'VE WANTED TO HEAR THAT FOR SO LONG.
A PART OF ME EVEN BELIEVES YOU THIS TIME. BUT IT'S...

...that no matter what I do, nothing will be as good as when we were together.

We're not.
It stings sometimes...
It can be sweet too.

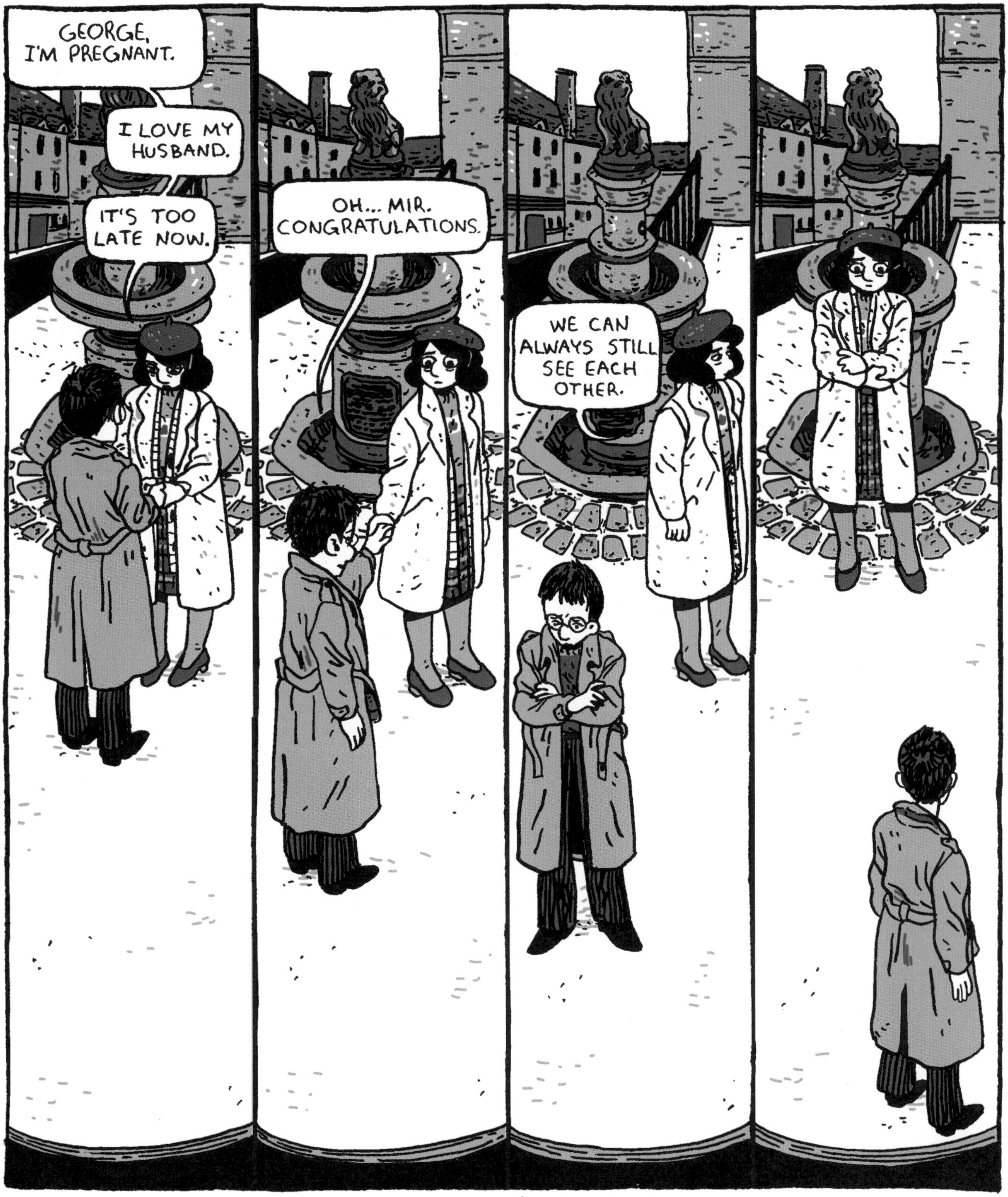
GEORGE, I'M PREGNANT.
I LOVE MY HUSBAND.
IT'S TOO LATE NOW.
OH... MIR. CONGRATULATIONS.
WE CAN ALWAYS STILL SEE EACH OTHER.

We can't go back, but when I think about you, I can think about the future again.

anyway. I hope you're well
and happy forever, always.

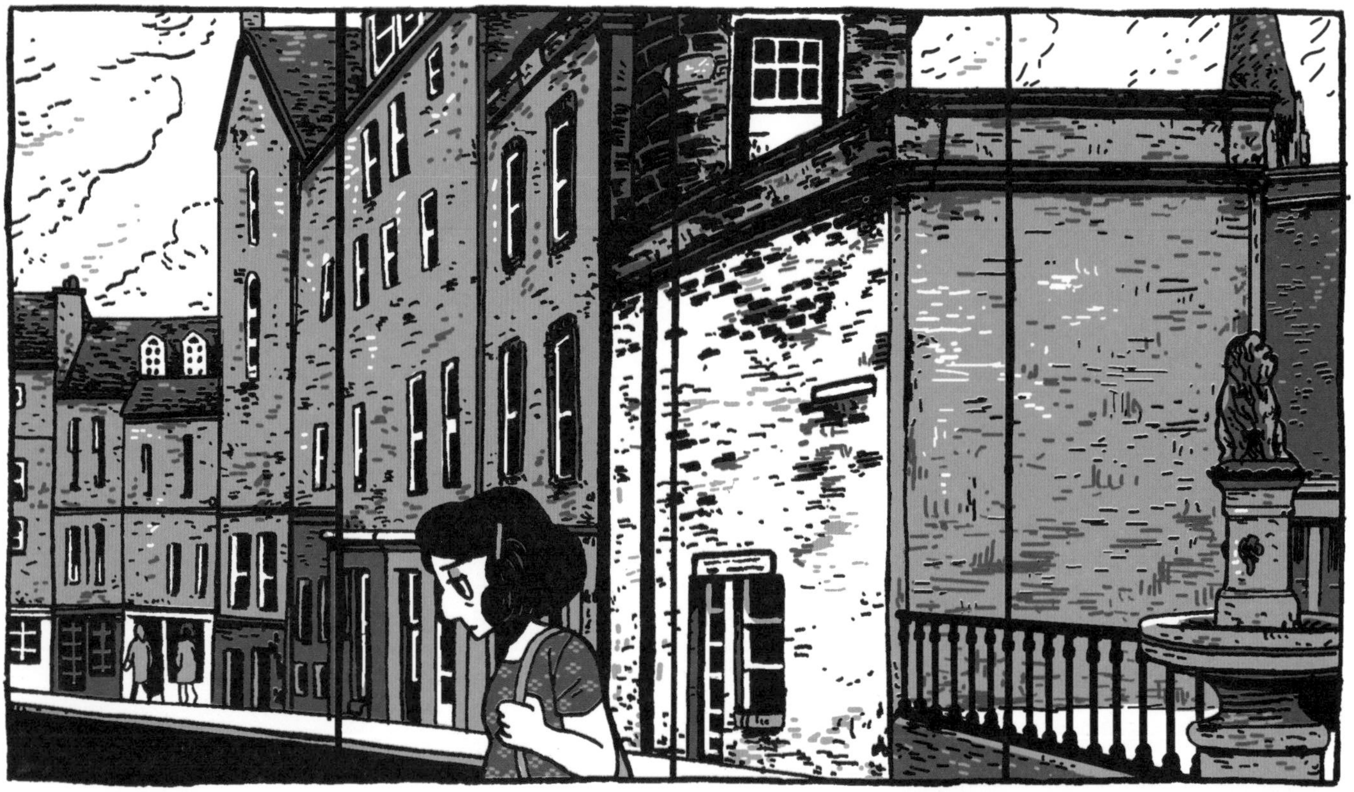

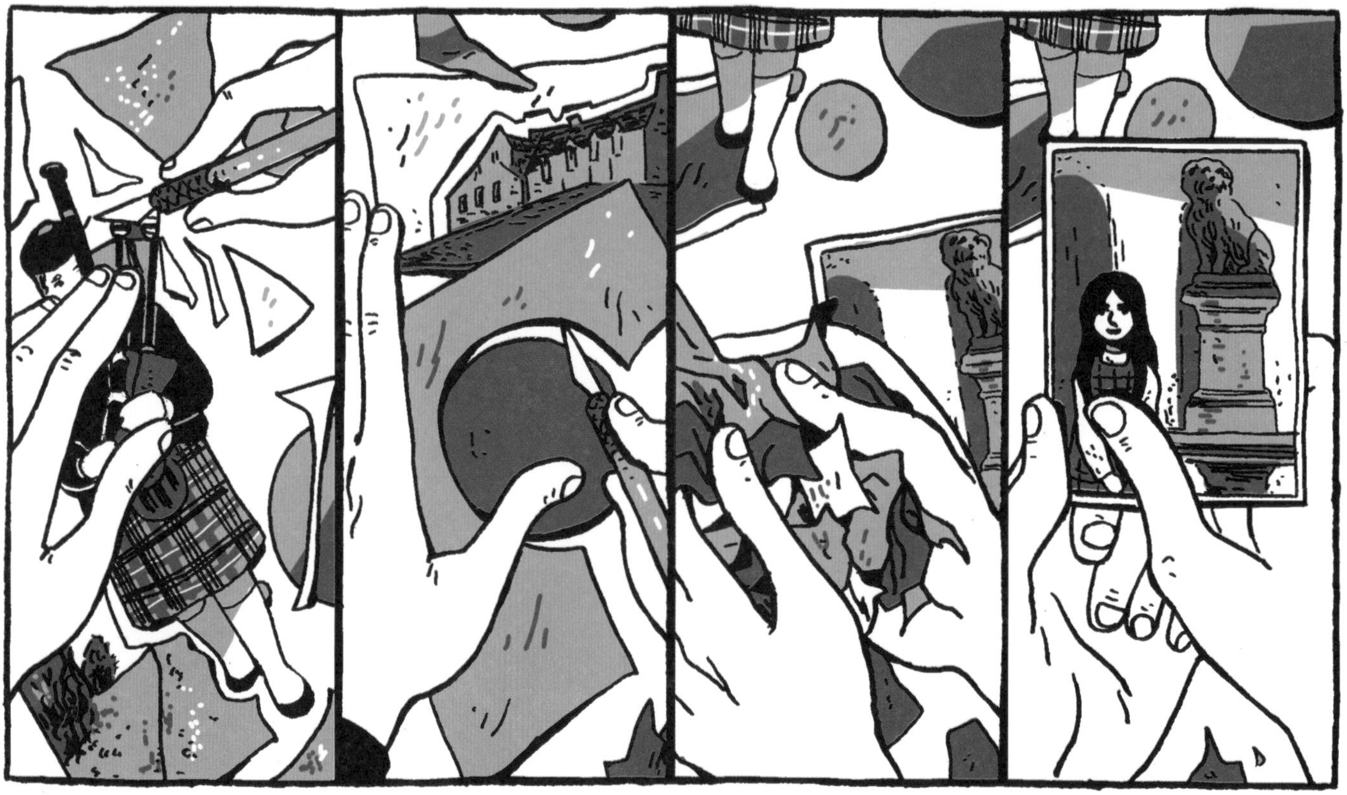

Will you make some new
wonderful memories with me?

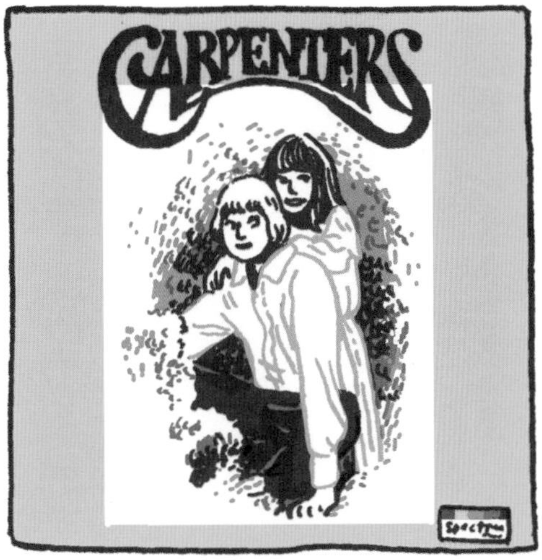
CARPENTERS

"Nana"

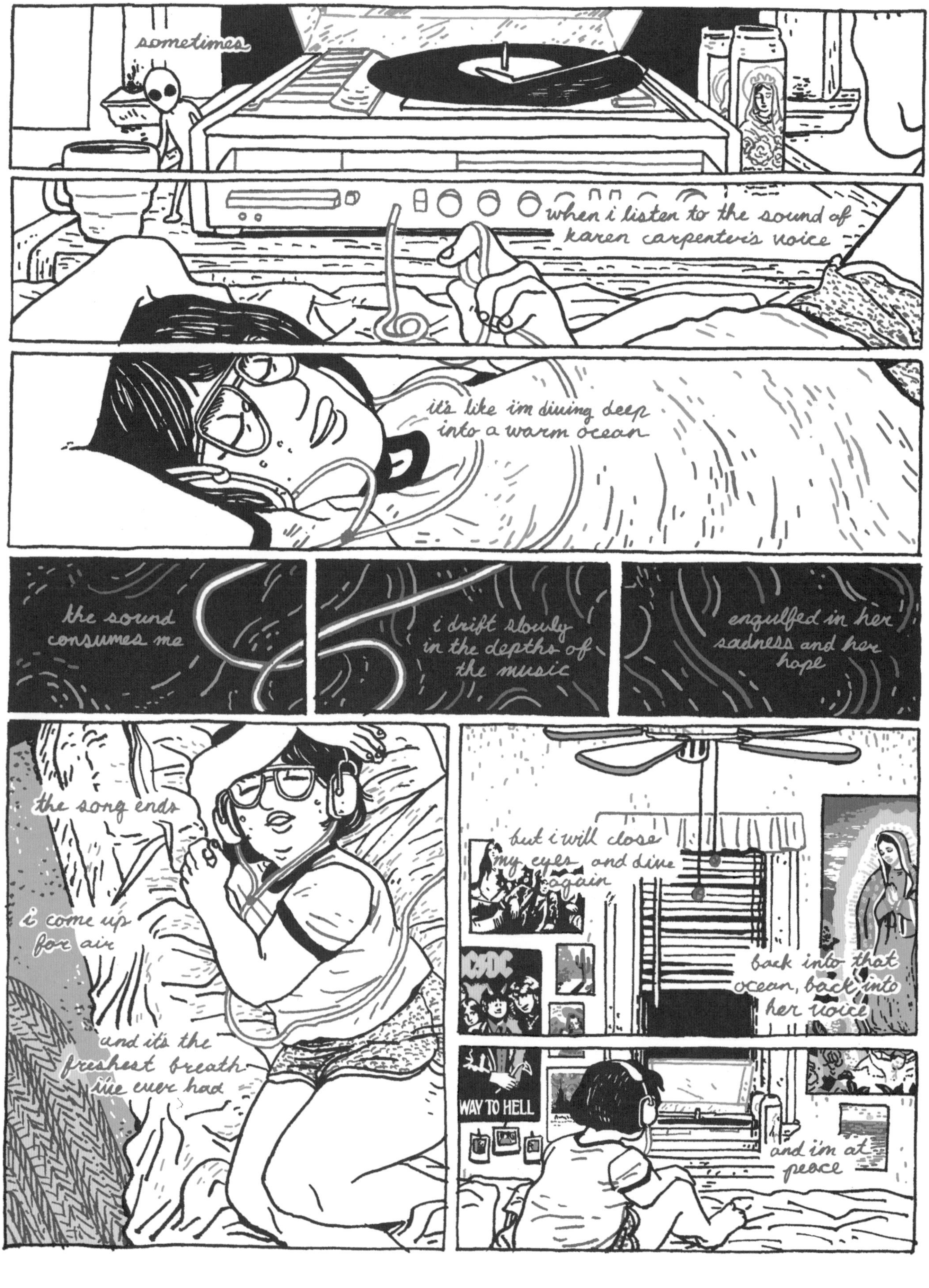
sometimes
when i listen to the sound of karen carpenter's voice
it's like im diving deep into a warm ocean
the sound consumes me
i drift slowly in the depths of the music
engulfed in her sadness and her hope
the song ends
i come up for air
and it's the freshest breath i've ever had
but i will close my eyes and dive again
AC/DC
back into that ocean, back into her voice
WAY TO HELL
and i'm at peace

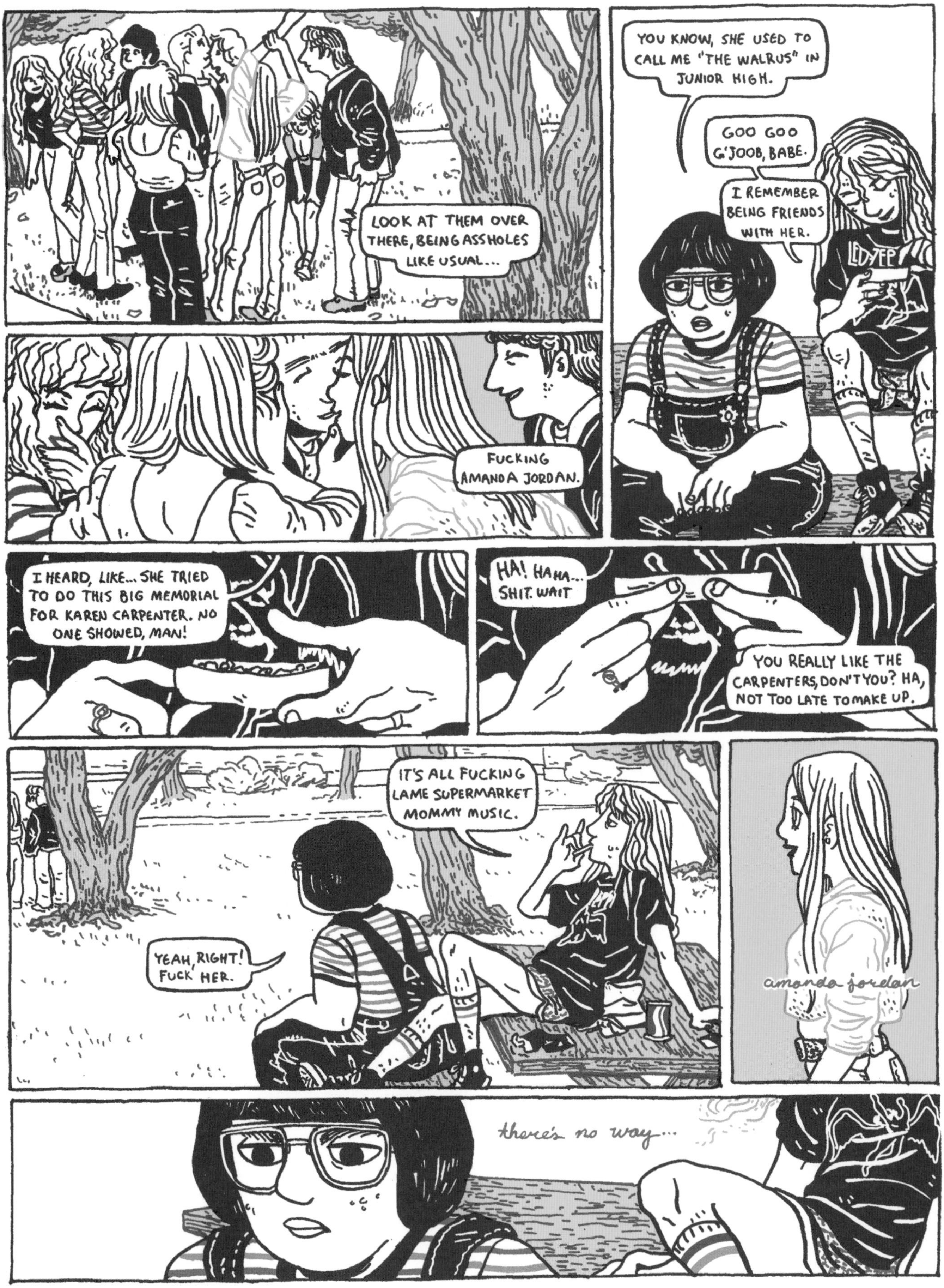
LOOK AT THEM OVER THERE, BEING ASSHOLES LIKE USUAL...
YOU KNOW, SHE USED TO CALL ME "THE WALRUS" IN JUNIOR HIGH.
GOO GOO G'JOOB, BABE.
I REMEMBER BEING FRIENDS WITH HER.
FUCKING AMANDA JORDAN.
I HEARD, LIKE... SHE TRIED TO DO THIS BIG MEMORIAL FOR KAREN CARPENTER. NO ONE SHOWED, MAN!
HA! HAHA... SHIT. WAIT
YOU REALLY LIKE THE CARPENTERS, DON'T YOU? HA, NOT TOO LATE TO MAKE UP.
IT'S ALL FUCKING LAME SUPERMARKET MOMMY MUSIC.
YEAH, RIGHT! FUCK HER.
amanda jordan
there's no way...

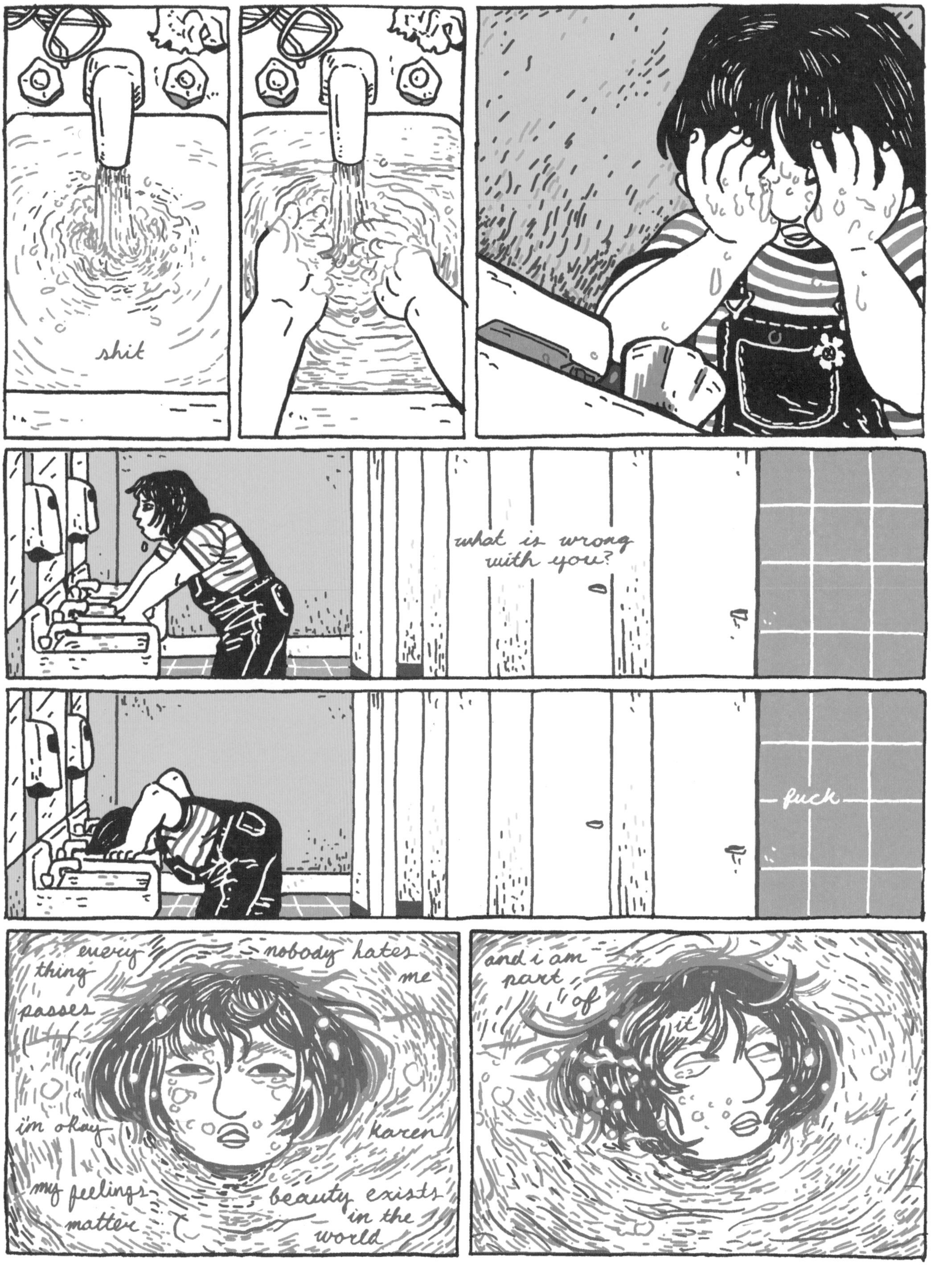
shit
what is wrong with you?
fuck
every thing passes
nobody hates me
im okay
karen
my feelings matter
beauty exists in the world
and i am part of it

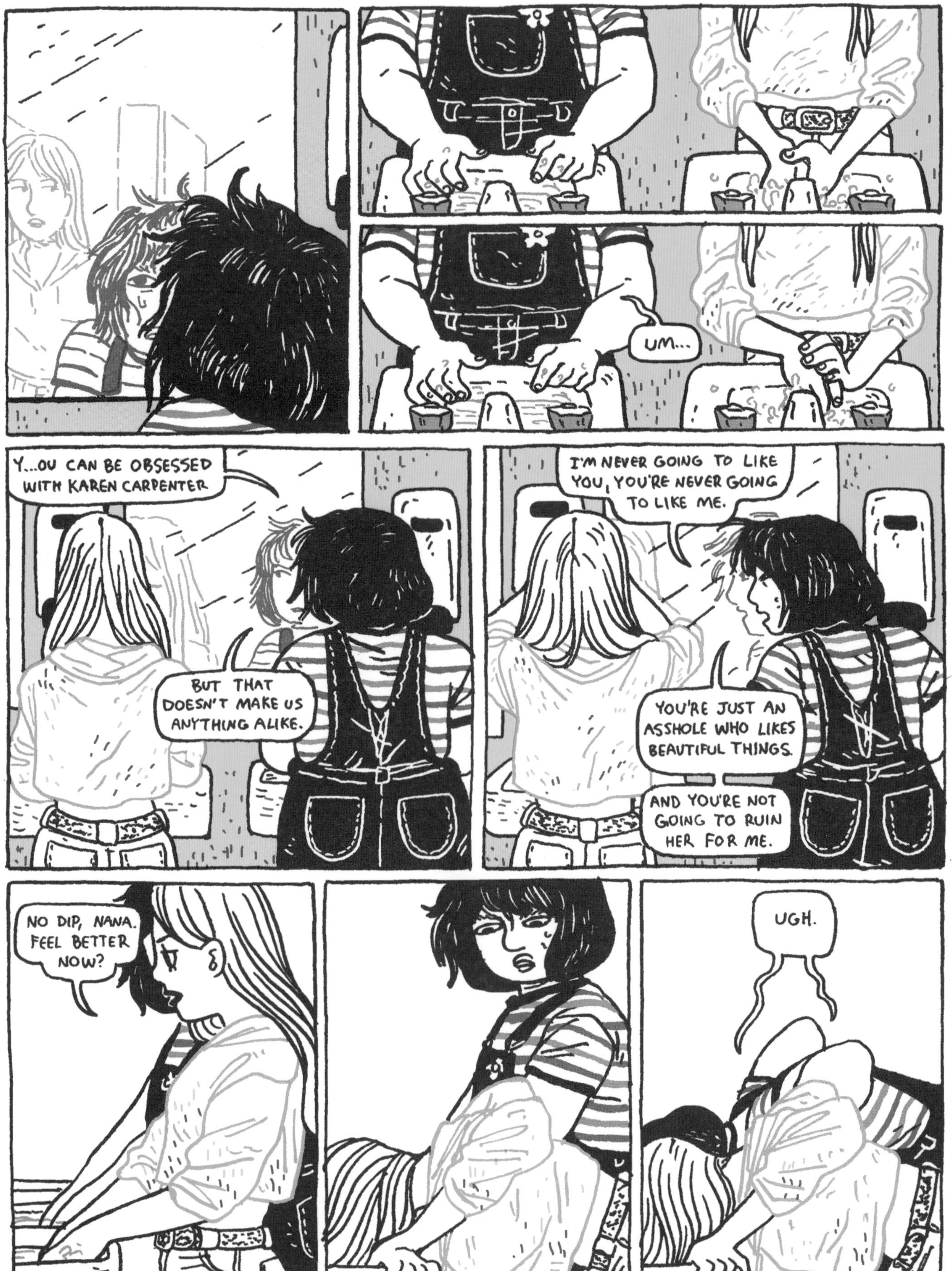
UM...
Y...OU CAN BE OBSESSED WITH KAREN CARPENTER
BUT THAT DOESN'T MAKE US ANYTHING ALIKE.
I'M NEVER GOING TO LIKE YOU, YOU'RE NEVER GOING TO LIKE ME.
YOU'RE JUST AN ASSHOLE WHO LIKES BEAUTIFUL THINGS.
AND YOU'RE NOT GOING TO RUIN HER FOR ME.
NO DIP, NANA. FEEL BETTER NOW?
UGH.

the Great
Twenty-Eight
CHUCK
BERRY

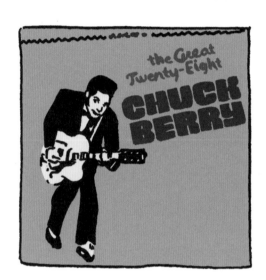

"Alvin"

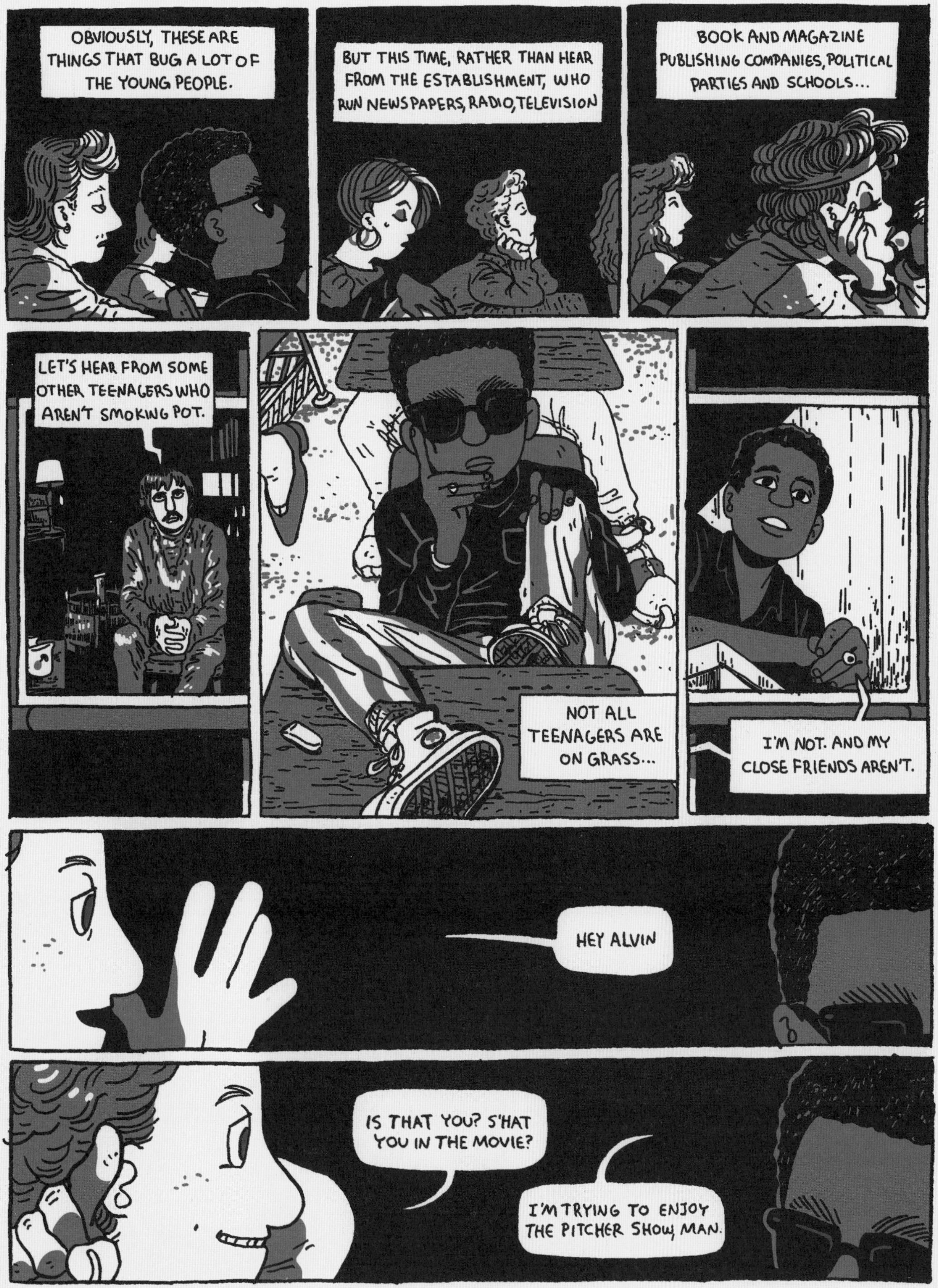
OBVIOUSLY, THESE ARE THINGS THAT BUG A LOT OF THE YOUNG PEOPLE.
BUT THIS TIME, RATHER THAN HEAR FROM THE ESTABLISHMENT, WHO RUN NEWSPAPERS, RADIO, TELEVISION
BOOK AND MAGAZINE PUBLISHING COMPANIES, POLITICAL PARTIES AND SCHOOLS...
LET'S HEAR FROM SOME OTHER TEENAGERS WHO AREN'T SMOKING POT.
NOT ALL TEENAGERS ARE ON GRASS...
I'M NOT. AND MY CLOSE FRIENDS AREN'T.
HEY ALVIN
IS THAT YOU? S'HAT YOU IN THE MOVIE?
I'M TRYING TO ENJOY THE PITCHER SHOW, MAN.

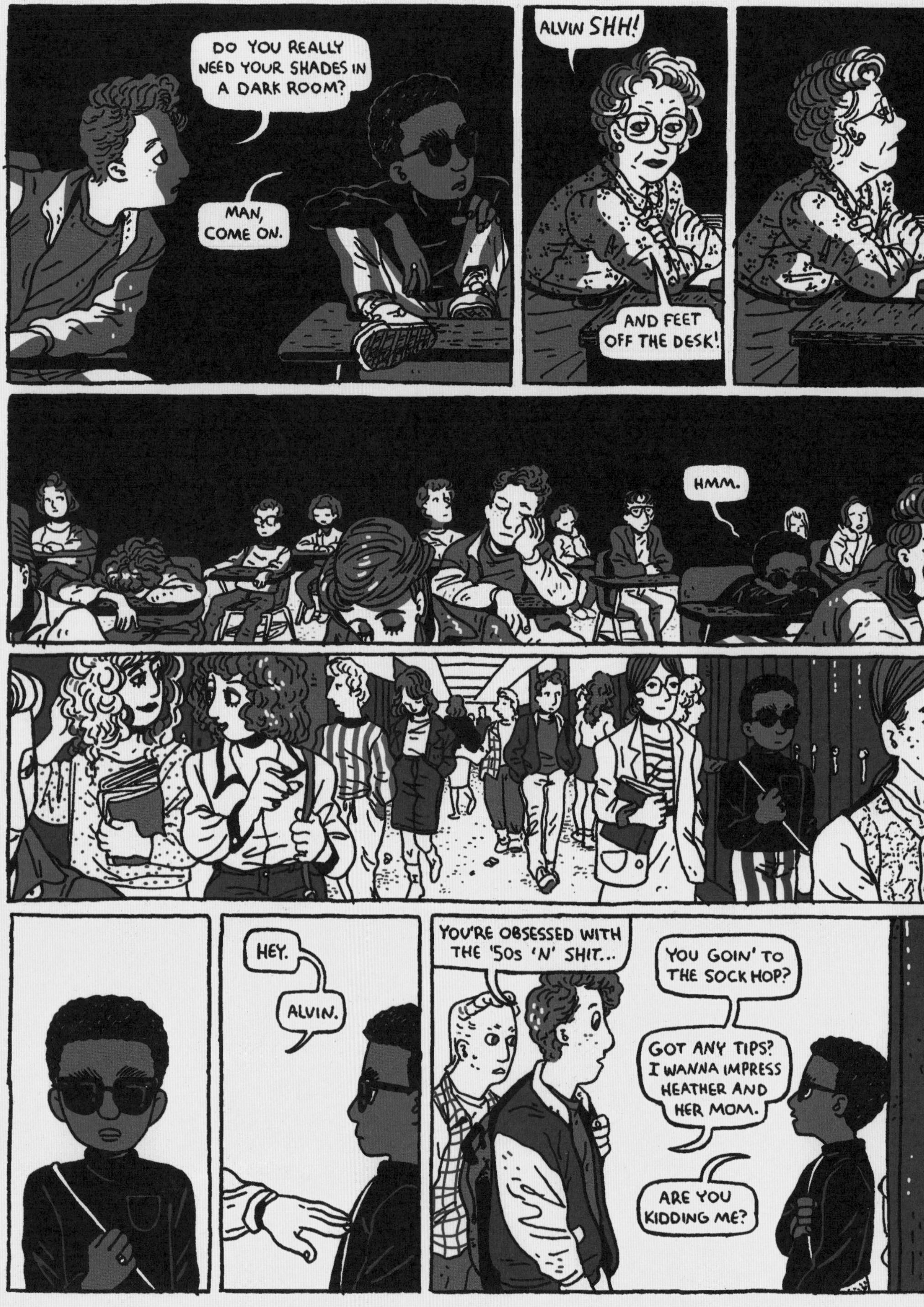
DO YOU REALLY NEED YOUR SHADES IN A DARK ROOM?
MAN, COME ON.
ALVIN SHH!
AND FEET OFF THE DESK!
HMM.
HEY.
ALVIN.
YOU'RE OBSESSED WITH THE '50s 'N' SHIT...
YOU GOIN' TO THE SOCK HOP?
GOT ANY TIPS? I WANNA IMPRESS HEATHER AND HER MOM.
ARE YOU KIDDING ME?

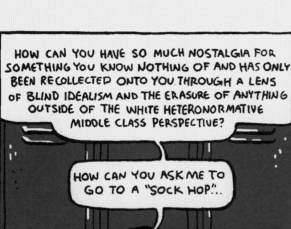

HOW CAN YOU HAVE SO MUCH NOSTALGIA FOR SOMETHING YOU KNOW NOTHING OF AND HAS ONLY BEEN RECOLLECTED ONTO YOU THROUGH A LENS OF BLIND IDEALISM AND THE ERASURE OF ANYTHING OUTSIDE OF THE WHITE HETERONORMATIVE MIDDLE CLASS PERSPECTIVE?

HOW CAN YOU ASK ME TO GO TO A "SOCK HOP"...

...AND IGNORE THE IMPACT BLACK COMMUNITIES HAVE ON AMERICAN CULTURE, WHILE SIMULTANEOUSLY BEING SYSTEMATICALLY BARRED FROM ITS SOCIETY.

WITH OUR IDENTITIES SEIZED AND MANIPULATED FOR THE SAKE OF COMMERCIAL AND POLITICAL GAIN.

WHATEVER, MAN. CALM DOWN.

I WAS JUST TRYING TO BE COOL WITCHU.

AND THE...

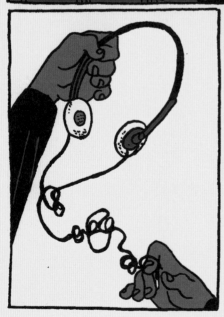

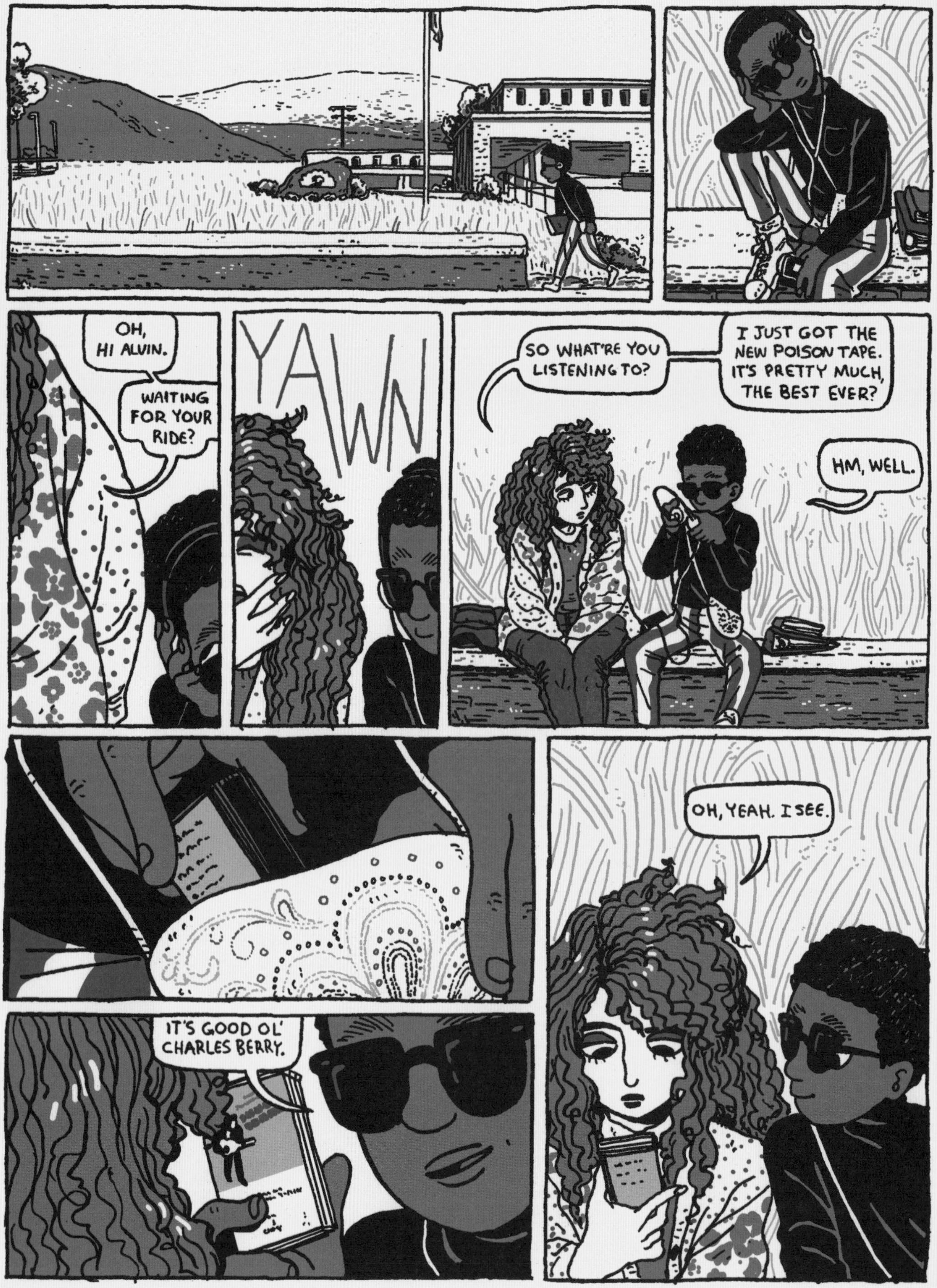
OH, HI ALVIN.
WAITING FOR YOUR RIDE?
YAWN
SO WHAT'RE YOU LISTENING TO?
I JUST GOT THE NEW POISON TAPE. IT'S PRETTY MUCH, THE BEST EVER?
HM, WELL.
IT'S GOOD OL' CHARLES BERRY.
OH, YEAH. I SEE.

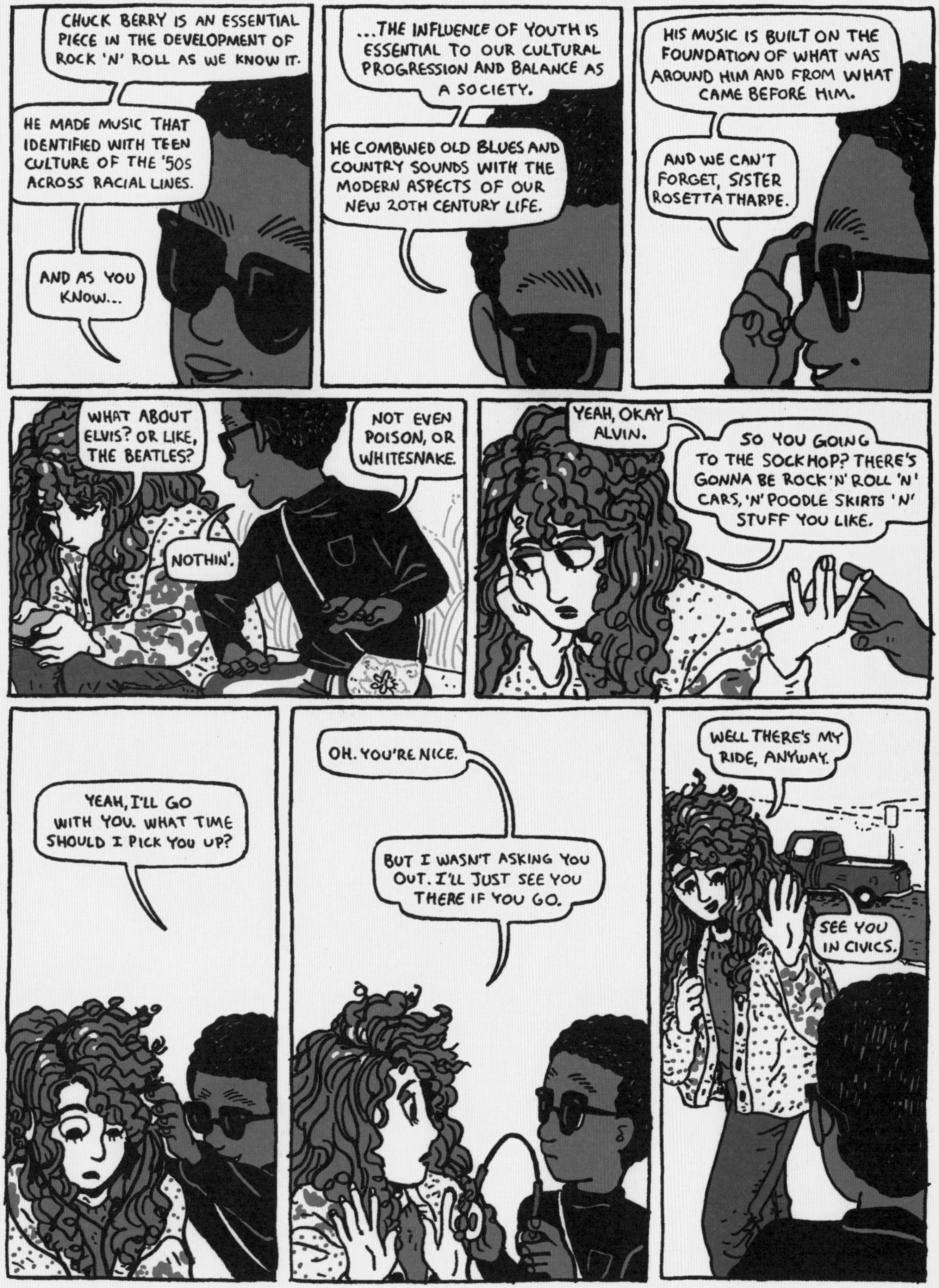
CHUCK BERRY IS AN ESSENTIAL PIECE IN THE DEVELOPMENT OF ROCK 'N' ROLL AS WE KNOW IT.
HE MADE MUSIC THAT IDENTIFIED WITH TEEN CULTURE OF THE '50S ACROSS RACIAL LINES.
AND AS YOU KNOW...
...THE INFLUENCE OF YOUTH IS ESSENTIAL TO OUR CULTURAL PROGRESSION AND BALANCE AS A SOCIETY.
HE COMBINED OLD BLUES AND COUNTRY SOUNDS WITH THE MODERN ASPECTS OF OUR NEW 20TH CENTURY LIFE.
HIS MUSIC IS BUILT ON THE FOUNDATION OF WHAT WAS AROUND HIM AND FROM WHAT CAME BEFORE HIM.
AND WE CAN'T FORGET, SISTER ROSETTA THARPE.
WHAT ABOUT ELVIS? OR LIKE, THE BEATLES?
NOTHIN'.
NOT EVEN POISON, OR WHITESNAKE.
YEAH, OKAY ALVIN.
SO YOU GOING TO THE SOCKHOP? THERE'S GONNA BE ROCK'N' ROLL 'N' CARS, 'N' POODLE SKIRTS 'N' STUFF YOU LIKE.
YEAH, I'LL GO WITH YOU. WHAT TIME SHOULD I PICK YOU UP?
OH. YOU'RE NICE.
BUT I WASN'T ASKING YOU OUT. I'LL JUST SEE YOU THERE IF YOU GO.
WELL THERE'S MY RIDE, ANYWAY.
SEE YOU IN CIVICS.

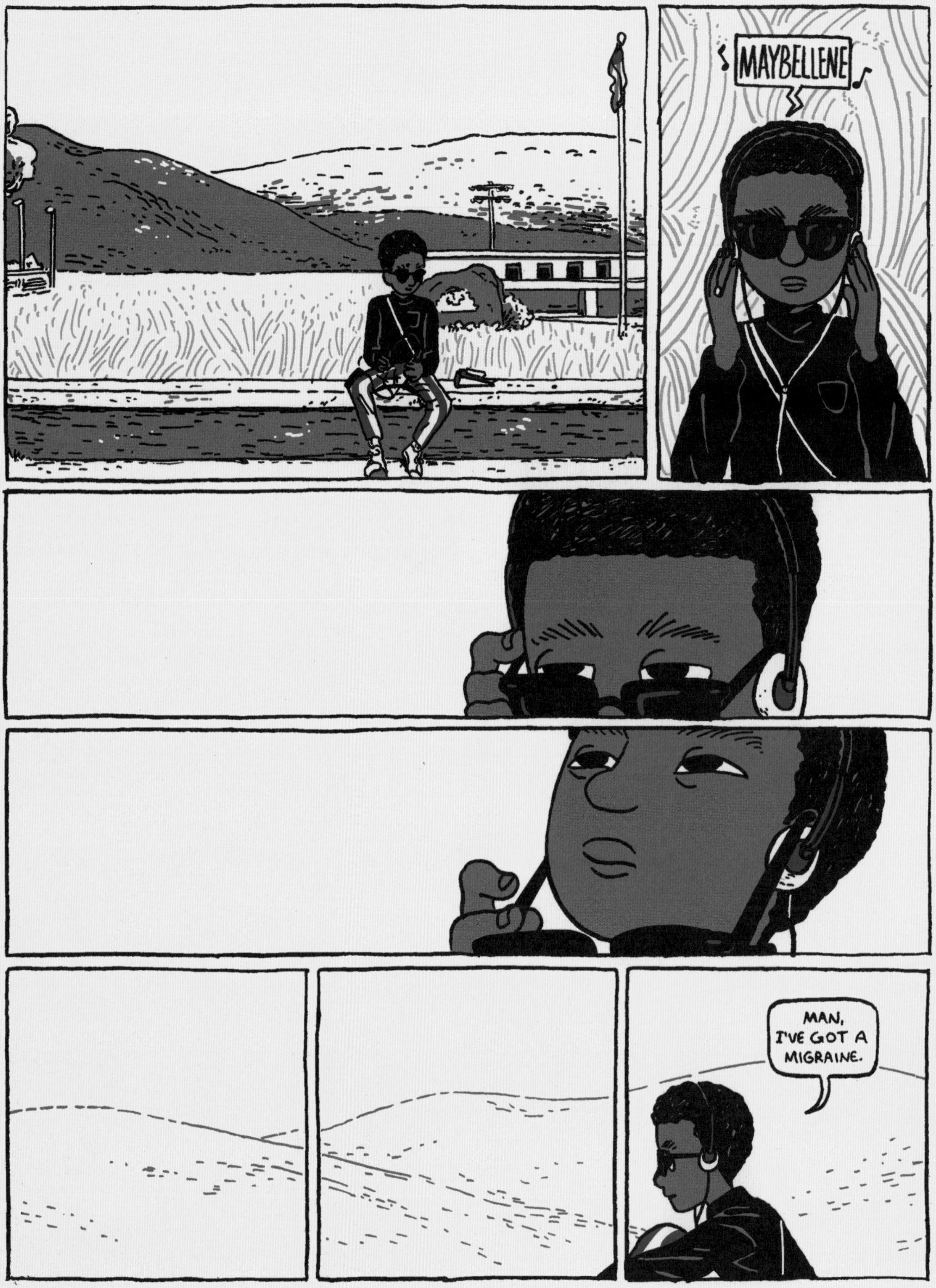
MAYBELLENE
MAN, I'VE GOT A MIGRAINE.

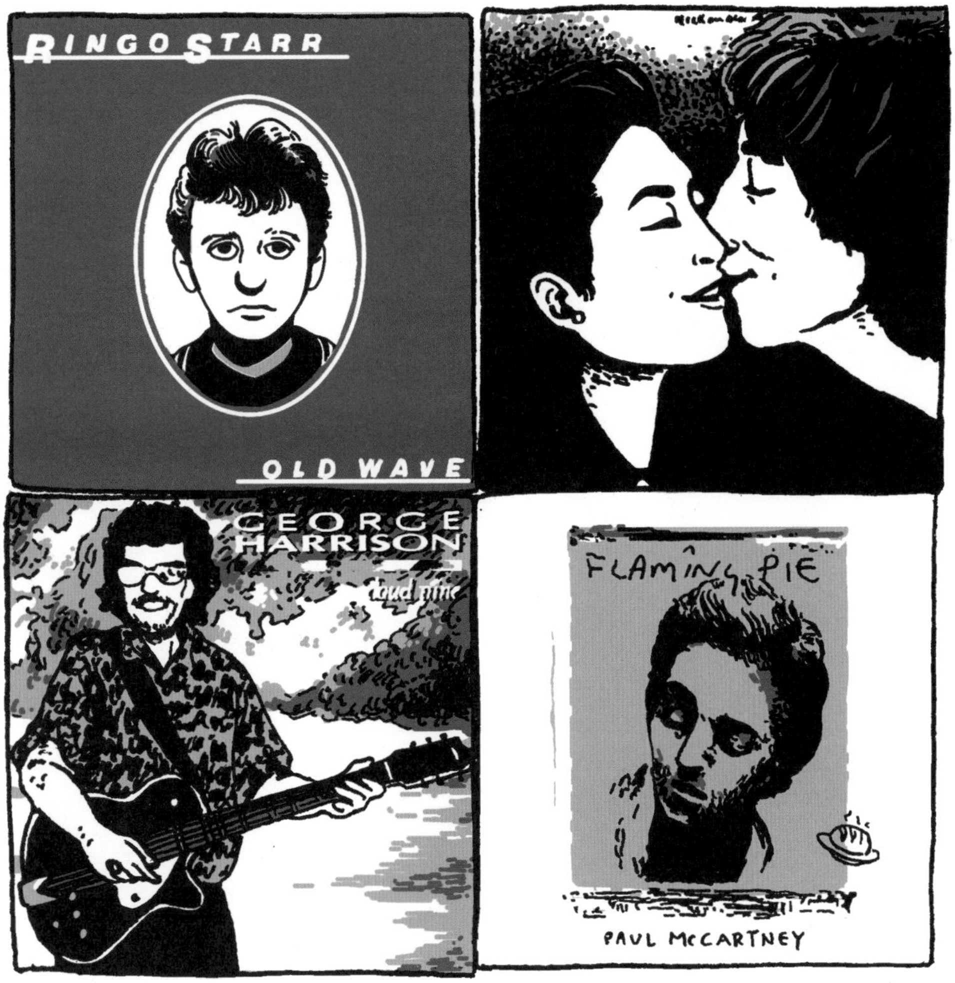
RINGO STARR
OLD WAVE
GEORGE
HARRISON
cloud nine
FLAMING PIE
PAUL McCARTNEY

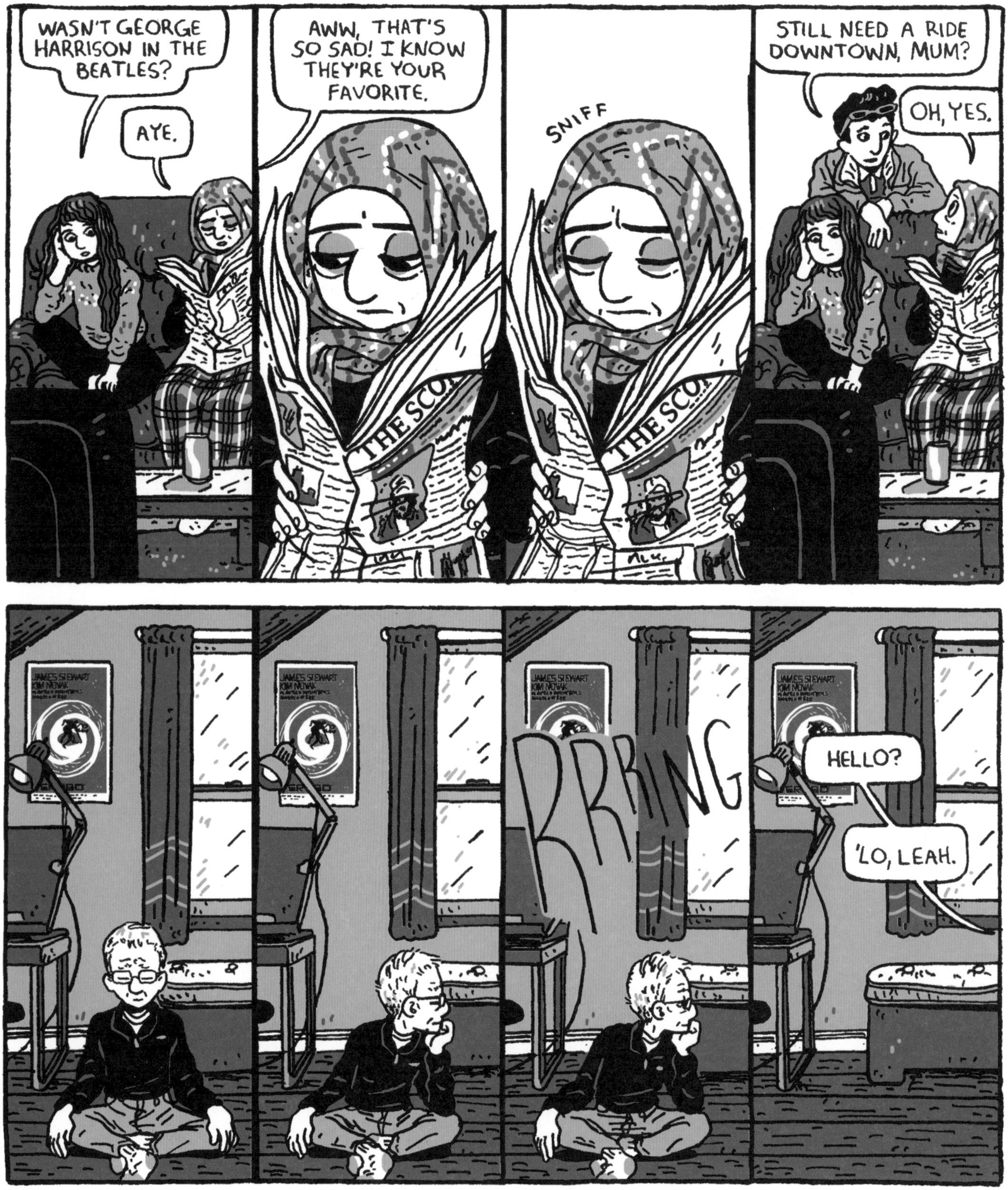
WASN'T GEORGE HARRISON IN THE BEATLES?
AYE.
AWW, THAT'S SO SAD! I KNOW THEY'RE YOUR FAVORITE.
SNIFF
STILL NEED A RIDE DOWNTOWN, MUM?
OH, YES.
JAMES STEWART
KIM NOVAK
RRRING
HELLO?
'LO, LEAH.

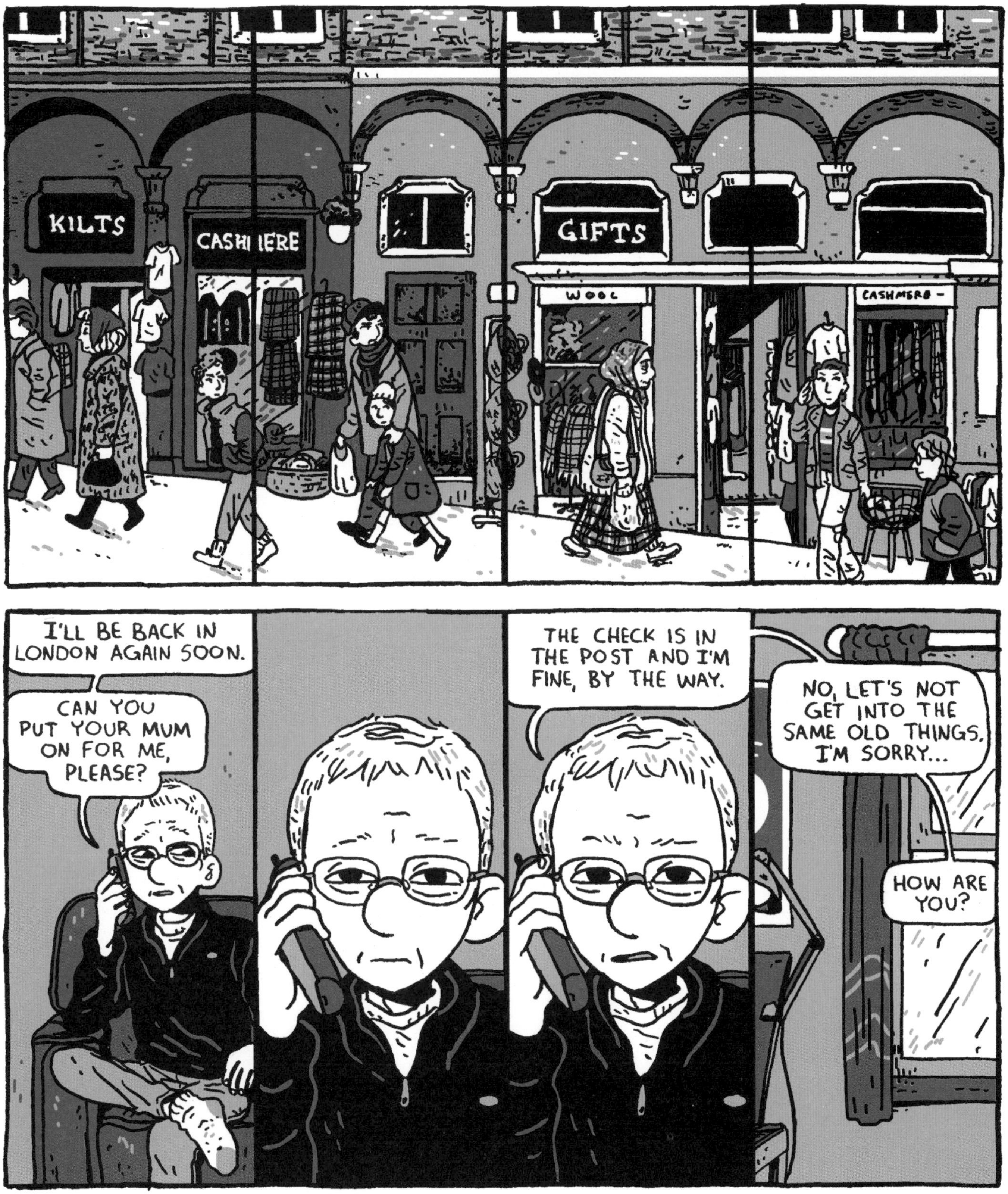
KILTS
CASHMERE
GIFTS
WOOL
CASHMERE
I'LL BE BACK IN LONDON AGAIN SOON.
CAN YOU PUT YOUR MUM ON FOR ME, PLEASE?
THE CHECK IS IN THE POST AND I'M FINE, BY THE WAY.
NO, LET'S NOT GET INTO THE SAME OLD THINGS. I'M SORRY...
HOW ARE YOU?

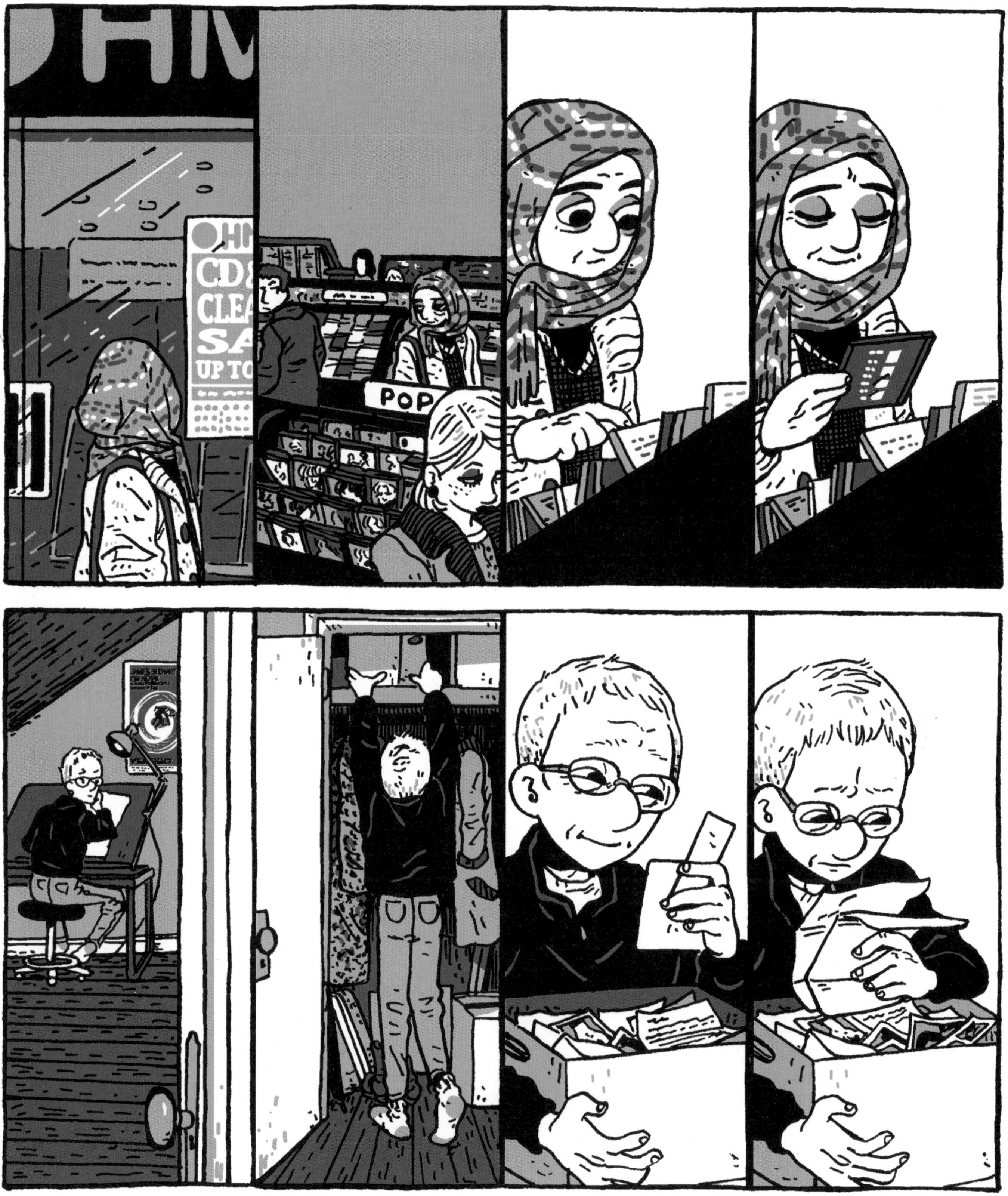

HM
CD&
CLEA
SA
UP TO
POP

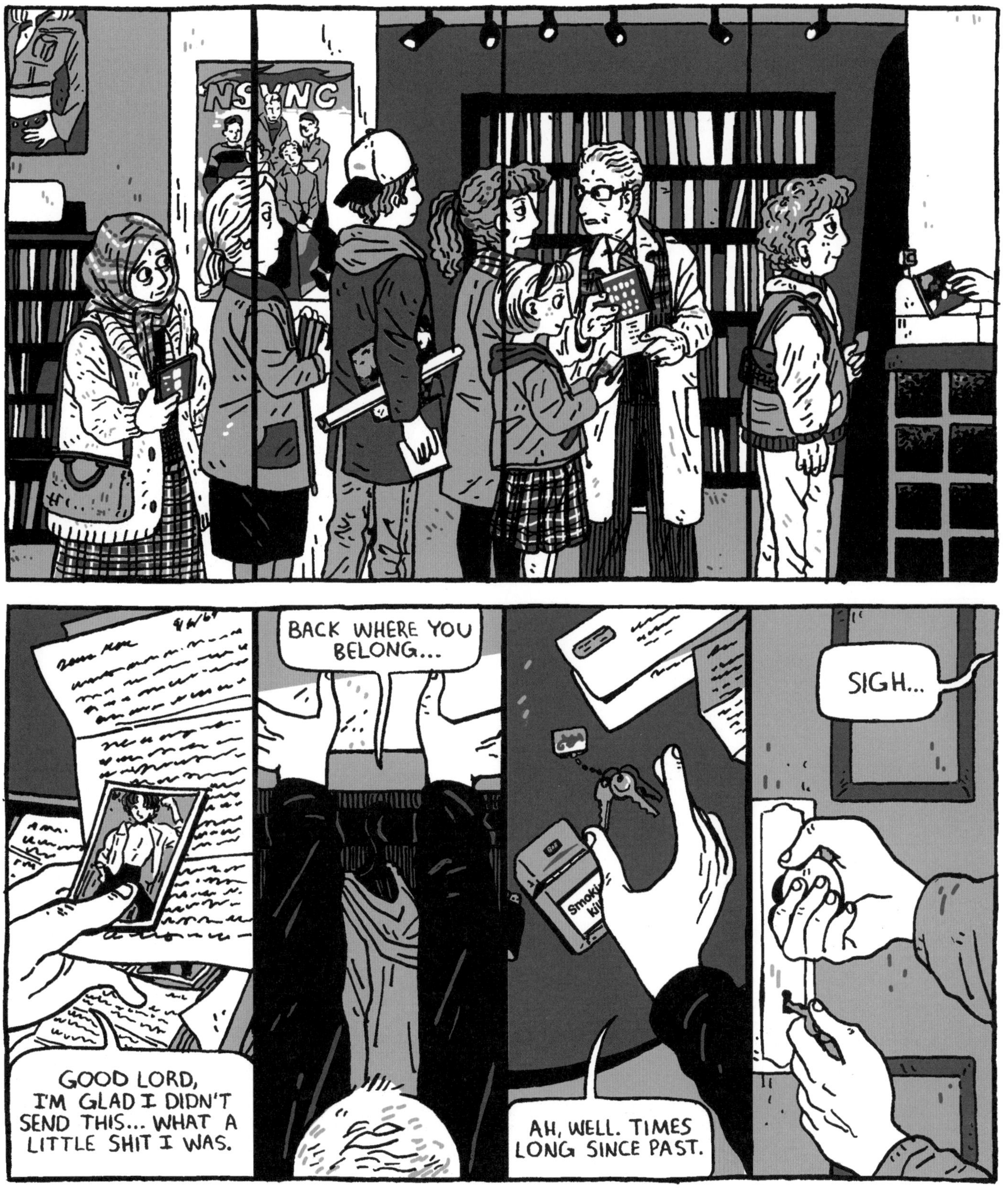

NSYNC
GOOD LORD, I'M GLAD I DIDN'T SEND THIS... WHAT A LITTLE SHIT I WAS.
BACK WHERE YOU BELONG...
AH, WELL. TIMES LONG SINCE PAST.
SIGH...

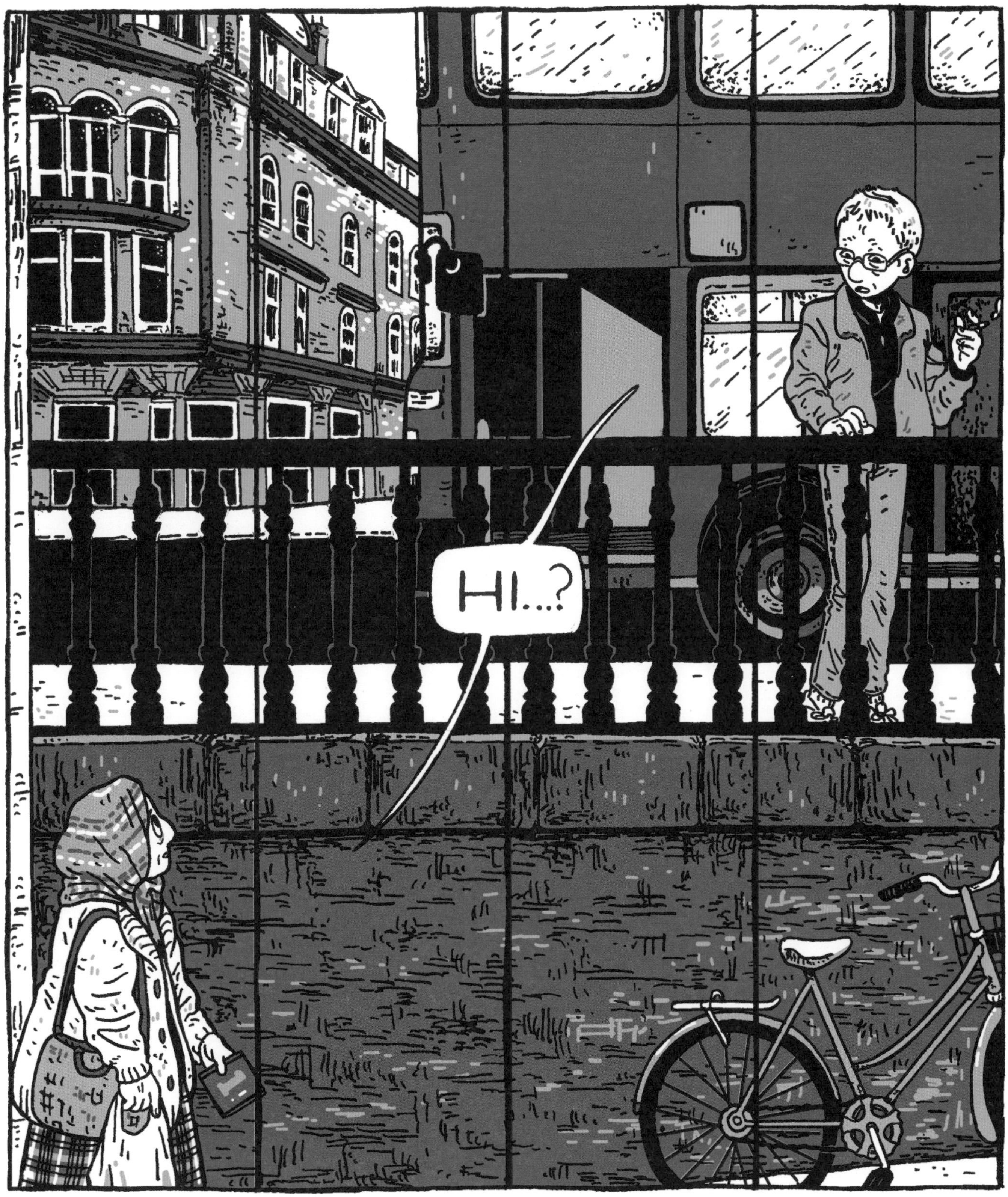
HI...?

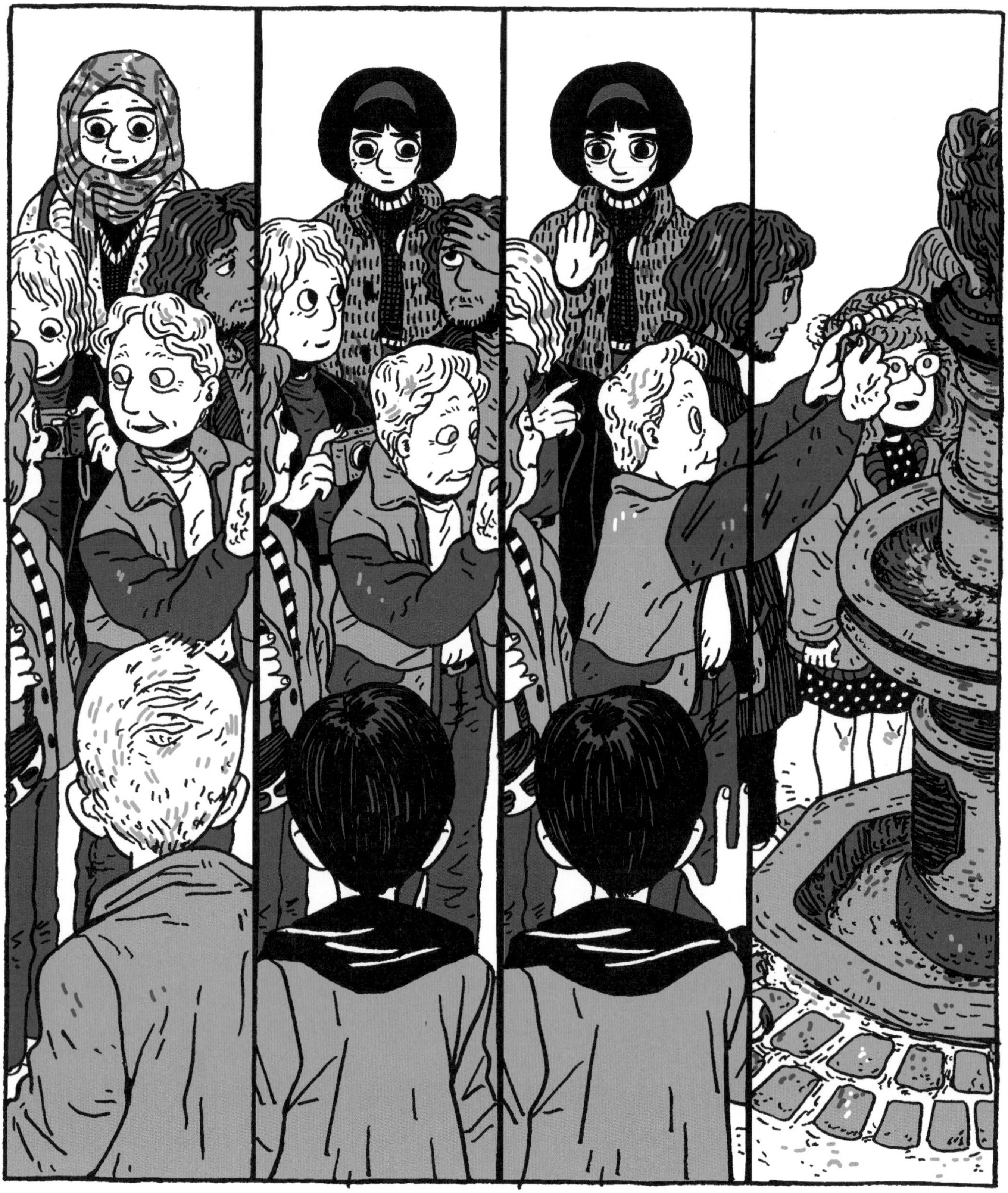

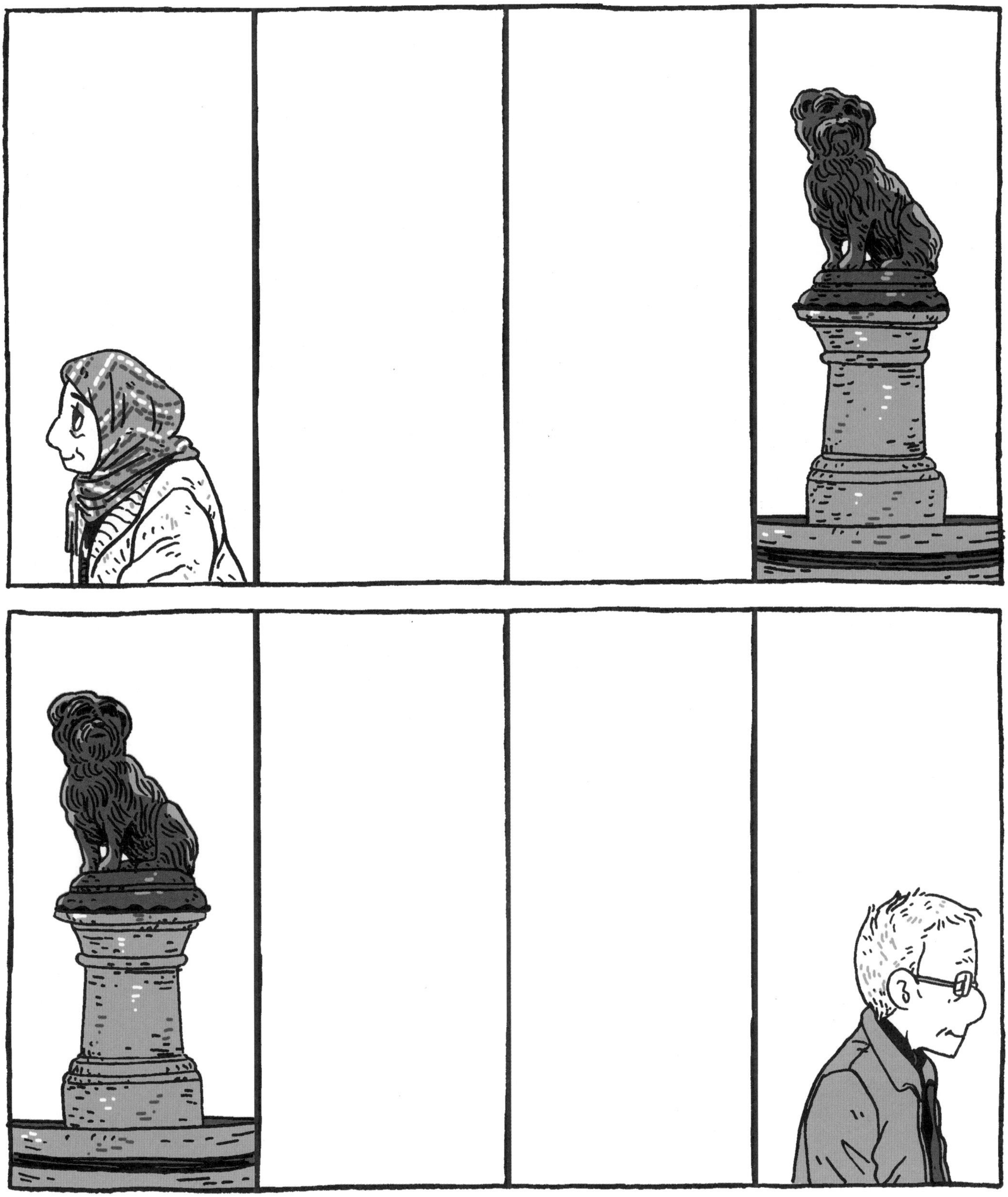

JAMES STEWART
KIM NOVAK

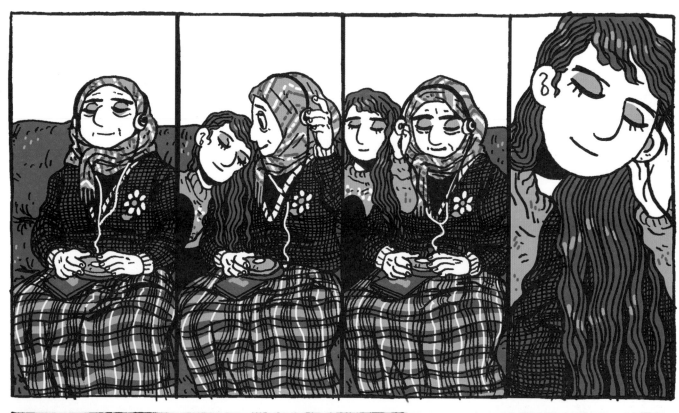

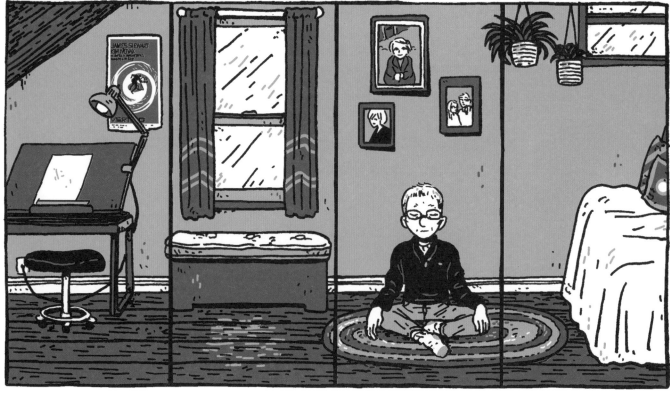

Dear George,

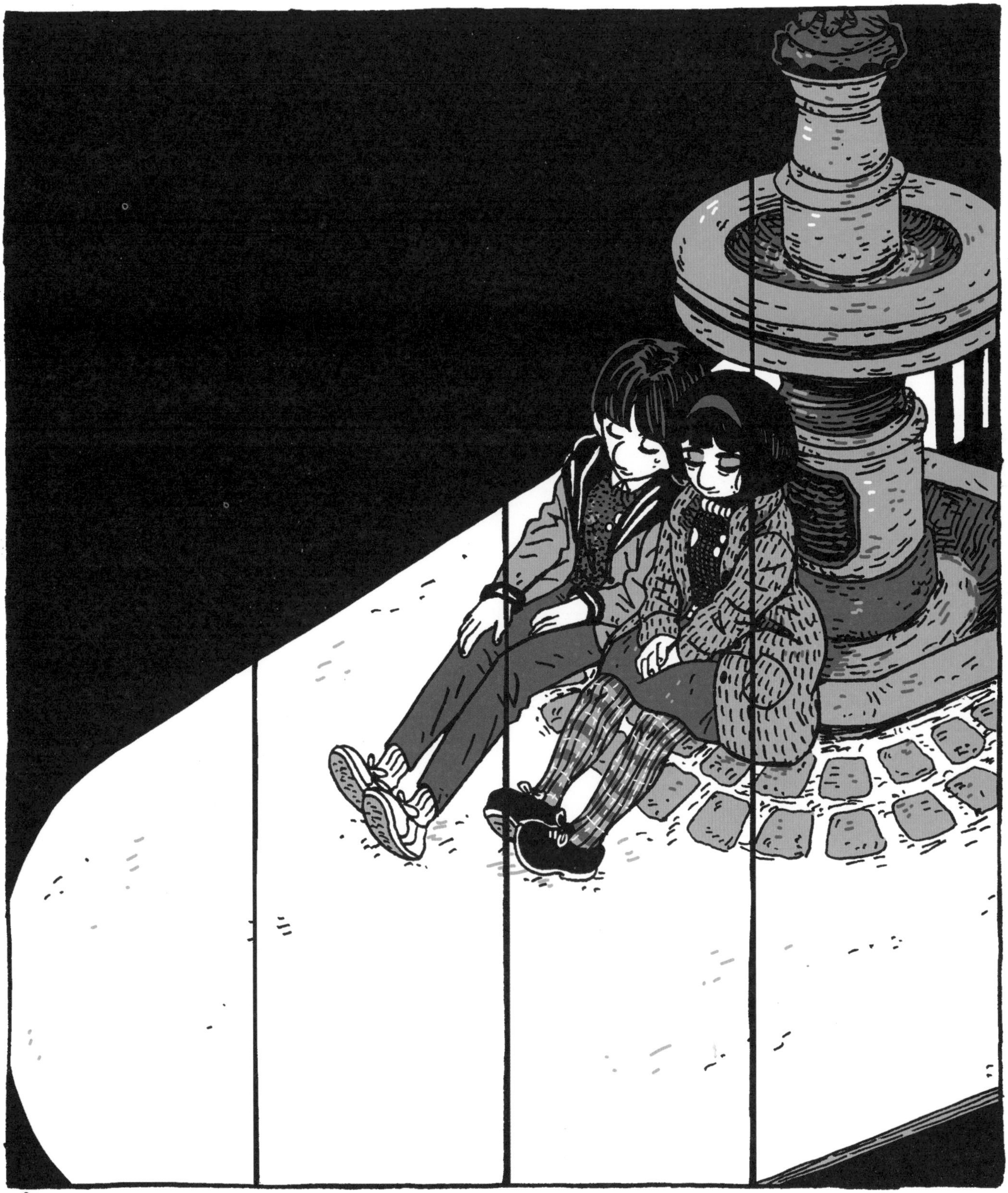

Dear Mir,

M. Dean is a cartoonist and illustrator originally from the west coast of Florida, where she attended Ringling College of Art and Design. She is the inaugural recipient of the Creators for Creators grant, creator and co-creator respectively of the webcomics *The Girl Who Flew Away* and *Coming Soon: Regents Walk*. She currently lives in Brooklyn with her partner, a dog, and a big black cat.